MW00778504

A NOVEL BASED ON THE LIFE OF

ADMIRAL ANDREA DORIA

THE
PIRATE PRINCE
OF
GENOA

Maurizio Marmorstein

THE
M
MENTORIS
PROJECT

The Mentoris Project
745 Sierra Madre Boulevard
San Marino, CA 91108

Cover design: Jim Villaflores

More information at www.mentorisproject.org

ISBN: 978-1-947431-38-6

Library of Congress Control Number: 2022936025

All net proceeds from the sale of this book will be donated to The Mentoris Project whose mission is to support educational initiatives that foster an appreciation of history and culture to encourage and inspire young people to create a stronger future.

Publisher's Cataloging-In-Publication Data
(Prepared by The Donohue Group, Inc.)

Names: Marmorstein, Maurizio, author.
Title: The pirate prince of Genoa : a novel based on the life of Admiral Andrea Doria / Maurizio Marmorstein.
Description: San Marino, CA : The Mentoris Project, [2022]
Identifiers: ISBN 9781947431386 (paperback) | ISBN 9798201565763 (ePub)
Subjects: LCSH: Doria, Andrea, 1466-1560--Fiction. | Admirals--Italy--Genoa--History--16th century--Fiction. | Statesmen--Italy--Genoa--History--16th century--Fiction. | Genoa (Italy)--History--16th century--Fiction. | LCGFT: Biographical fiction. | Historical fiction.
Classification: LCC PS3613.A76665 P57 2022 | DDC 813/.6--dc23

The Mentoris Project is a series of novels and biographies about the lives of great men and women who have changed history through their contributions as scientists, inventors, explorers, thinkers, and creators. The Barbera Foundation sponsors this series in the hope that, like a mentor, each book will inspire the reader to discover how she or he can make a positive contribution to society.

Contents

Foreword

First and foremost, Mentor was a person. We tend to think of the word *mentor* as a noun (a mentor) or a verb (to mentor), but there is a very human dimension embedded in the term. Mentor appears in Homer's *Odyssey* as the old friend entrusted to care for Odysseus's household and his son Telemachus during the Trojan War. When years pass and Telemachus sets out to search for his missing father, the goddess Athena assumes the form of Mentor to accompany him. The human being welcomes a human form for counsel. From its very origins, becoming a mentor is a transcendent act; it carries with it something of the holy.

The Mentoris Project sets out on an Athena-like mission: We hope the books that form this series will be an inspiration to all those who are seekers, to those of the twenty-first century who are on their own odysseys, trying to find enduring principles that will guide them to a spiritual home. The stories that comprise the series are all deeply human. These books dramatize the lives of great men and women whose stories bridge the ancient and the modern, taking many forms, just as Athena did, but always holding up a light for those living today.

Whether in novel form or traditional biography, these books

plumb the individual characters of our heroes' journeys. The power of storytelling has always been to envelop the reader in a vivid and continuous dream, and to forge a link with the subject. Our goal is for that link to guide the reader home with a new inspiration.

What is a mentor? A guide, a moral compass, an inspiration. A friend who points you toward true north. We hope that the Mentoris Project will become that friend, and it will help us all transcend our daily lives with something that can only be called holy.

—Robert J. Barbera, Founder, The Mentoris Project
—Ken LaZebnik, Founding Editor, The Mentoris Project

Introduction

The nightmares came in droves, always with the same consistency and unsettling cruelty. After nearly twenty years as a soldier, and another forty at the helm of the Republic of Genoa's naval fleet, Admiral Andrea Doria endured each horrid dream as if it were just another military adventure, seeing it to its ungodly end, never stirring, never bolting up from a dead sleep to shake off the myriad sea monsters, tempests, and evil spirits invading his subconscious. Serving as a *condottiero*, or mercenary captain, to emperors, kings, and popes for most of his eighty-one years of life had inured him to the images of brutality that attacked him in his sleep. They rarely frightened him, incessant as they were, and the torrents of blood inhabiting nearly every frame of these nightly episodes of terror had long ago lost their shock value. He'd seen so much blood seeping into the floorboards of ships, or spurting from the severed limbs of his men in battle, that shadowy visions of barbarity, horrific as they were, failed to have any effect on him. The demons that haunted him in the dead of night couldn't hold a candle to the brutality he witnessed and personally suffered during combat in the name of independence for his beloved homeland.

One particular dream, however, never failed to send shivers down Andrea's spine: the faded image of an endless blue sky looming over a tranquil sea of blood. No movement stirred within it. No sound permeated its murky boundaries. Nothing of consequence ever happened. What stood out, and terrified the admiral to his core, was its boundless expanse of emptiness. Time stood still. Nothing but emotions existed in this world: sorrow, fear, and regret. Nothing within the contents of this vision could distract him from experiencing those emotions completely and facing the truths they would ultimately reveal. They were his true enemies and eternal nemeses. He'd spent a lifetime trying to keep them in check in order to maintain appearances in society, or to affect a stoic demeanor for the soldiers and sailors under his command. *Such emotions should be stifled at all costs,* he always told himself, *for reasons of decorum, or simple peace of mind.* They required introspection, or rather they imposed it, which bothered him. He certainly wasn't averse to long periods of contemplation or self-reflection; they were essential tools for leaders wishing to hatch new political schemes or deliberate battle strategies. But in sixteenth-century Italy, the age of *homo faber*, where men were meant to craft their own destinies, such indulgences were reserved for the intelligentsia and holy men of the Catholic Church.

The mere sight of placid skies and blood-drenched waters was somehow able to do what nightmarish visions of brutal warfare never could: They roused a seasoned warrior from the gaping depths of unconsciousness. No level of fatigue, exhaustion, or inebriation could quell the pain triggered by these simple but utterly relentless images. Try as he might, Andrea couldn't possibly sleep through such dreams.

He woke up the moment those very images reared their mighty heads, and as the world racked into focus, all emotional discomfort gave way to the physical pain he felt in his eighty-one-year-old body. Andrea had always maintained an exceptionally strong, athletic constitution; he was lean and muscular in aspect, unusually agile for a man six feet two inches tall, and rarely given to fatigue. But the long days, weeks, and even months he'd survived at sea steeped in the heavy salt air of the Mediterranean had eaten away at his bones and rusted his joints to the point of no return. The pangs of arthritis and his debilitating gout blocked nearly all forward movement. He tried shuffling a bit, propping his head on the goose-feather pillows stacked against his bed's massive headboard, but it gave him precious little comfort. It wasn't until an electrical charge of misery shot down his spinal cord to the tips of his toes that a wry smile finally managed to crease his lips.

"I'm still alive," he mumbled.

Chapter One

THE AFTERNOON OF JANUARY 2, 1547

Only when Andrea wiped the sleep from his eyes did he notice a woman standing at the foot of his elaborately draped canopy. She seemed a million miles away at first, hidden by some distant impenetrable fog, but her sharp topaz eyes called to him like a beacon in the night. That same pair of eyes had melted his young heart nearly sixty years ago after he'd caught a glimpse of her in the family chapel of San Matteo during Sunday mass. The woman rounded the bed and pulled in closer. Andrea said nothing. She, too, remained silent as she leaned in to feel his forehead with the back of her hand.

"Are you in any mood to entertain guests?" Peretta asked.

Andrea grunted. He always woke up a bit groggy after his afternoon nap. She waited a few seconds longer, knowing he'd respond to her question sooner or later.

He sighed. "My God, Peretta, must I really? I can barely bend a finger without wanting to scream bloody hell."

He and Peretta were coevals, both distinguished members of Genoa's noble class. Despite having been struck by love's thunderbolt all those many years ago, Andrea didn't get around to asking for her hand in marriage until an entire generation later; he was sixty-one at the time. She was slightly younger, but still spry and a force to be reckoned with. Marriage had never quite appealed to Andrea. His thirst for independence and adventure was legendary, and his early maritime career kept him busy and far from Genoese shores for months at a time. It would be no exaggeration to say that the deck of his private galley, the *Capitana*, felt more like home than anywhere else. And, of course, his natural aversion to domestication continually kept him from the altar as well. Yet the underlying reason behind the protracted delay of their marriage was quite simple: Peretta was already married. In fact, she was betrothed by the age of ten to a respected nobleman. She tied the knot several years later, and subsequently gave birth to four children before her husband died suddenly in 1516. She remained a widow for eleven years after that, finally joining Andrea in holy matrimony in 1527.

"Your fever has passed," she said as she gathered the thick linens of Dutch cotton neatly around him to stave off the chill in the room.

"Whom have you invited this time?" he asked flatly.

Peretta's frown was quite familiar to Andrea. He may have been the most revered military man on the European continent, not to mention an astute political strategist of some repute, but Peretta had set the record straight long ago that she was neither a member of his ship's crew nor a low-level government official under his authority, and was to be treated with the deference her family name demanded.

"I've invited no one," she retorted. "If you can think back to as far as yesterday, you will recall that it was you who issued invitations to half of Genoa to visit us this afternoon. Heaven forbid anyone should think our mighty *pater patriae* was losing his legendary vigor," she added.

Andrea could not argue with that last statement, despite her sarcasm. He always did all he could to live up to the title of "father of the homeland," an honor bestowed on him twenty years earlier after leading Genoese forces against the French to give rise to the independent Republic of Genoa.

"We've brought in the new year with friends and family as far back as I can remember," Andrea shot back.

"Ambassadors, cardinals, diplomats, and spies are not friends," she calmly stated. "Now please answer me—do you feel you are in any condition to face the world?"

"Have you ever known me to drop my guard?" he countered without missing a beat.

Peretta burst out laughing. This couldn't be more true. Over the years, Andrea had become quite the master of dissimulation. Just yesterday, at the Doria family's annual New Year's Day banquet, he masterfully put all his charm, exuberance, and conviviality on full display despite the debilitating pangs of gout continually gnawing at him, and the inflammation of his joints rendering movement nearly impossible. Under no circumstances would he dare exhibit signs of weakness and thus jeopardize his position of respect and authority in the community or on the political stage. He knew all too well the consequences of exposing frailty of any kind. Genoa was no different than any other city-state inhabiting the Italian peninsula during those tumultuous years. Political intrigue, revolt, conspiracy, usurpation of power, and assassination awaited the unprepared and inattentive.

"You've made self-control your life's work," she quipped. "That is common knowledge."

"You say that as if it were a defect," he snapped back. "How can a leader possibly claim dominion over his men, and I daresay over world events, if he exacts no control over his own mind and body?"

"You hold your cards close to your chest, this is true, but I remember quite well that in your youth—oh so many, many years ago, before all this self-restraint and sanity—you were terribly insolent and even reckless," she uttered with a smile.

"I believe you meant to say 'insistent and fearless,'" he countered, hardly bothering to conceal a grin. "And, may I add, that was to ensure absolute obedience from my men as well as deference from my enemies."

Peretta matched Andrea's grin with one of her own. "It was precisely your fearlessness that drew me to you back then," she whispered, "and your levelheadedness that draws me to you now." She pulled in closer to give him a tender kiss on the forehead.

Andrea found it impossible to do anything but smile in such situations. Peretta's talent for disarming him with a few choice words both frustrated and completely beguiled him. His unruffled composure while in the heat of battle or during tense negotiations with pirates, popes, and kings had become almost mythical over the years, but with Peretta, and quite frankly with all women, he simply lacked the wherewithal to compete. Truth be told, Peretta's character differed little from her husband's, which more than likely threw him for a loop. He surrendered to her every time. She was a classic Ligurian noblewoman, austere with just enough elegance to lend an air of congeniality and warmth to her overall bearing. The Prince's Palace, as their sumptuous residence was called, fell into good hands each time Andrea sailed off to police the high seas in defense of Spain, Genoa's protector, and his wife's parsimonious distribution of finances proved exemplary. Peretta hailed, after all, from one of the oldest and most esteemed families in Genoa, the Usodimare. She was granddaughter to Pope Innocent VIII of the Cybo dynasty, also from Genoa, who occupied the Vatican during Andrea's early military career. It was there, in fact, that Andrea and Peretta formally met.

Andrea's eyes shifted to the immense fireplace that covered a good portion of the far wall. Its black limestone facade, mined from the Promontorio quarry—an area just above Genoa's Lanterna, the world's tallest and most imposing lighthouse at the time—cast a solemn aura over what would have otherwise been a rather accommodating and hospitable chamber. The embers from the previous evening's fire still sparkled within its massive belly, but did little to fend off the draft that whisked through the room and stiffened Andrea's aching joints. Intuiting her husband's thoughts, Peretta tucked the lambswool blanket under his perpetually long, ruffled beard, and secured it firmly around the contours of his neck and shoulders.

Andrea's eyes eased shut as he savored the tenderness of the moment, so distant from the rigors he weathered at sea. He'd been so superhumanly resilient his whole life that everyone began to think he'd live forever. But the last few years had taken their toll. Bedridden days like these came more often and with greater ferocity. Although Andrea never put it into words, Peretta could glean from the gentle smile that creased his lips that he treasured the succor she so liberally offered in times like these.

Andrea finally opened his eyes, then breathed deeply as if trying to summon the willpower to face the onslaught of scheduled guests. Before he could even raise his head from the pillow, Peretta pressed him back down with the full force of her outstretched hands.

"You're not going anywhere," she said. "I've taken the liberty to cut the number of visitors to an intimate few. They'll come directly into your chamber here."

"Include Governor Gonzaga and Ambassador Figueroa in that list," Andrea was quick to add. "With the election of the new doge planned for the day after tomorrow, I'm dying to hear what rumors are being bandied about."

Keeping a finger on the pulse of Spain's agents and delegates on the peninsula helped Andrea stay continually ahead of the game, especially when it came to choosing future government officials. Ferrante Gonzaga's allegiance to Spain dated back to his youth in Mantua, first as a page in the service of Charles V, future Holy Roman Emperor, then as an officer participating in the devastating Sack of Rome, and finally as Viceroy of Sicily before assuming his current position as the governor of the

Duchy of Milan, Genoa's immediate neighbor to the north. As was the case for the duchy under previous rulers, Gonzaga had a friendship with the Republic of Genoa that ran hot and cold. Immediately upon meeting Gonzaga for the first time, Andrea assessed him as being sly and ambitious enough to keep as a confidant, but not enough to trust completely.

Don Gómez Suárez de Figueroa y Córdoba, on the other hand, enjoyed Andrea's absolute confidence. As Charles V's ambassador, Figueroa resided in Genoa on a permanent basis. His penchant for social interaction, whether it was cavorting with spies or the city's numerous noble families, provided him with an inside track on any and all happenings of political import.

Both men visited Andrea regularly and shared their intelligence without reserve. Although Andrea chose not to occupy any formal position within the government other than city magistrate, he held uncontested sway over the city's affairs. Heads of state and diplomats from all over Europe, as well as Ottoman emperors and Barbary pirates, channeled their negotiations with the Republic through one single individual, Admiral Andrea Doria, and officials of the Genoese government would have it no other way.

"Both men have promised a short visit," said Peretta as she hurried over to attend to a knock at the chamber door.

The admiral sat up in his bed. "Let us pray that is not them already!" he cried out as he propped the pillows higher against the headboard to support his aching back.

It took every ounce of strength he could muster to withstand the pain shooting through each one of the twenty-eight swollen joints in his aging hands. It didn't take long, however, for the pangs to subside when he saw who came running in.

"*Buongiorno*, Mesiavo!" cried little Giovannandrea in his nasal Genoese dialect.

For a boy of eight, Giovannandrea already commanded the respect of someone three times his age. His charm was contagious, his intelligence peerless, and his wit razor-sharp. Andrea simply adored him. Rather than use the more accurate and appropriate term *barba*, the Genoese word for "uncle," the boy always referred to Andrea as his *mesiavo*, "grandfather," which endeared him to Andrea even more.

When Giovannandrea's father, Giannettino Doria, pranced in right behind him, Andrea's face lit up even brighter. Since Andrea had gone a lifetime without producing heirs of his own, he came to view Giannettino as a son. Seeing two generations of Dorias poised to carry on his legacy filled him with unspeakable joy. Neither a blindly religious man nor an overtly secular one, Andrea was a product of his times. He put limited stock in the idea of an afterlife and held firmly to the notion that immortality could best be savored in this world. Therefore, finding a proper and sustainable line of succession had become a near fixation. *What is the sense of working your entire life in the pursuit of fortune*, he told himself, *struggling endlessly for a modicum of influence and status, or risking your life for the sake of freedom and the privilege of living another day, if everything dies with you?*

"Come here, little one!" Andrea shouted, his arms

outstretched, ready to catch young Giovannandrea as he leaped onto the bed. Andrea then smothered the boy with kisses.

Giannettino approached Peretta first. "He couldn't wait to see his favorite uncle and aunt," he whispered as he pecked her on the cheek.

Despite his sweet words, Peretta struggled to offer a smile. The tension between them had been brewing ever since Giannettino had risen to the level of lieutenant and captain of his own squadron of galleys in Genoa's fleet, placing him first in line as Andrea's heir apparent and, by extension, the most powerful man in the Genoese Republic. These were honors Peretta felt should have gone to her own son, Marc'Antonio del Carretto. Both men were offshoots of the same generation, and at their mental and physical prime: Giannettino, born in 1510, would soon turn thirty-seven, while Marc'Antonio was just a few years younger. It was long established that Marc'Antonio would inherit the title of Prince of Melfi, an honor bestowed on Andrea after his marriage to Peretta, but he had since fallen into disfavor with the Doria family, and with Andrea in particular. Giannettino's bold leadership qualities and stunning military victories, on the other hand, spoke directly to the type of future Andrea had envisioned for himself and the city of Genoa.

"Welcome, Giannettino, my dear," Peretta replied in a voice free of emotion. "Have a seat, won't you?"

"Not before greeting our dear Prince," he said as he crossed the room.

On a personal level, Giannettino lacked Andrea's

graciousness. He was simultaneously admired and reviled by the general populace. His arrogance, penchant for cruelty, and aggressiveness might have had their advantages on the battlefield, but in the back rooms of government where the muted violence of intrigue replaced the sheer honesty of cold steel, he had much to learn. The tufts of auburn curls that framed the soft, boyish features of his face gave him an almost angelic mien, which, combined with his bad-boy persona, rendered him hopelessly alluring to the opposite sex, and only added to his notorious reputation as a womanizer.

Andrea, of course, knew all this about him and more; he'd undoubtedly assessed all of Giannettino's pros and cons a thousand times before dubbing him Genoa's next Prince. Sure, he was presumptuous, authoritarian, and opinionated, all traits that tended to draw more detractors than admirers, but his instincts as a naval officer were uncanny. As far as Andrea was concerned, Giannettino had every right to project pride and self-confidence, as overbearing as it may have been at times, because as a leader of men and a military strategist, he'd earned it tenfold. In a mercantile society like Genoa where pragmatism, productivity, and meritocracy often transcended the loftier Christian virtues of faith, hope, and love, Andrea had little doubt that Giannettino would gain the acceptance of the Genoese people for the simple reason that he was the best man for the job.

By now Andrea had thrown the blankets aside and was sitting up in bed.

"Have you eaten a *merenda*?" he asked little Giovannandrea, referring to Genoa's traditional midafternoon snack. Before the child could respond, Andrea signaled to Peretta. "Have Tonino bring the *canestrelli*!" he cried out. "Can't you see he's a growing boy?"

"Which boy are you speaking of?" Peretta quipped, knowing full well her husband couldn't resist a dessert or two himself.

Andrea concealed a smile and pretended not to hear her, turning his attention instead to Giovannandrea, who had already hopped onto his knee. As a rule, Andrea's dietary needs were simple. He'd always shied away from elaborate foods, fatty cuisines of any sort, and desserts in particular. But it seemed that the older he got, the more he enjoyed a treat now and then, especially canestrelli, the sweet shortbread cookies that graced the dinner table of every tried-and-true Genoese family during the Christmas season. Peretta liked to joke that he preferred canestrelli over other holiday sweets because their classic six-cornered shape was featured prominently on the *genovino d'oro*, a local currency of the Middle Ages, and Andrea found it hard to disagree.

"Come, Giovannandrea, shall we?" Peretta said, taking the boy by the hand. "Let us fetch the canestrelli ourselves and leave the men to their business."

She didn't need to say another word. Giovannandrea leaped off Andrea's knee and hurried out the door, dragging Peretta behind him.

Andrea gestured toward a finely upholstered X-shaped chair that stood to one side of the canopy. Giannettino picked it up and slid it in his direction. He was careful not to crease his stylish brocade doublet or ruffle his pleated breeches as he sat down.

"You are looking more and more like your father," said Andrea, clearly happy to be alone with him.

Andrea and Giannettino's father were first cousins, and bound by an unusually strong family connection. While at sea, or in the company of officers, politicians, and clergymen, Giannettino would refer to Andrea as his Admiral or Prince, but in the sanctuary of the Doria palace, outside the western walls of the city, Andrea was simply his *caro barba*, dear uncle.

"You look better today," said Giannettino.

"If you mean well rested, you speak the truth," said Andrea, shaking his head in dismay. "I've done nothing but sleep."

He stood up slowly, stretching his legs and straightening his back oh-so gingerly to avoid the shooting pains that would inevitably follow. As he reached for his blue velvet house coat hanging on a nearby rack, Giannettino jumped to his feet to lend a hand. Eager to prove he still possessed a spark of his old athletic self, Andrea sprang forward to grab it first.

"So, tell me, what has Genoa dared to do in my absence?" Andrea growled as he handed the coat to Giannettino to help him put it on. "And before you answer, don't think I don't know you held back and let me get this silly coat before you did. I appreciate the gesture, but I would prefer you didn't patronize your old, decrepit uncle. It makes me soft, and besides, I'd like to think I've got a few years left in me."

"I suggest you let Ambassador Figueroa and that snake Gonzaga know just how healthy you are," Giannettino was quick to add. "They're in the garden below waiting to see you."

"No doubt wondering if I'm still breathing," Andrea snarled.

"*Hoping* you're still breathing is more like it," Giannettino said, doing little to hide a smirk. "Nothing would trouble them more than having to defer to me on future matters of importance."

"Figueroa is your grappling hook to Emperor Charles," Andrea shot back. "Keep him close. And as for Gonzaga, he is no different from any other ruler on this godforsaken peninsula. His eyes are bigger than his stomach, but he is a friend of the family and, for now, a cherished ally of the Republic."

Exchanges of this tone and direction took place between these two men on a continual basis. No aspect of Giannettino's personality or maritime skills would go unaddressed. As far as Andrea was concerned, molding a successful heir and future leader capable of juggling all the duties, powers, and responsibilities needed to keep Genoa free and independent required constant vigilance. The trick, he thought, lay in finding a diamond in the rough early in the process, and polishing it day in and day out until it sparkled for all to see. He usually limited his candidates to young members of the Doria family, venturing outside the clan every so often as he did with his stepson, Marc'Antonio, who unfortunately failed to meet his standards. Even close cousins who led their own squadrons of galleys and rose to prominence under Andrea's tutelage were denied, for one reason or another, the distinction of rising to the level of Andrea's direct successor. Therefore, since no one else matched Giannettino's natural flair for the role, and time was of the essence, Andrea pounded him hard like a swordsmith honing a high carbon blade for battle. But as Andrea soon found out, Giannettino was too much like him to take it lying down; the two men sparred incessantly.

"The minute he sees his chance, Gonzaga will make his move on us," warned Giannettino. "He would like nothing more than to return to the days when Genoa answered to Milan's whims."

The abrupt entrance of Tonino, Andrea's personal waiter, stifled Andrea's response.

"Please welcome Ambassador Gómez Suárez de Figueroa y Córdoba of Spain and Ferrante Gonzaga, governor of the Duchy of Milan," Tonino announced with some gravity.

Before either of the two visitors could set foot in the room, little Giovannandrea came running in, hauling a salver of canestrelli covered with finely granulated sugar and setting it on a short marble-top table by the bed. Andrea wasted no time reaching for one and sneaking a bite. He was careful to wipe the powdery white sugar from his lips as he and Giannettino stood up to greet their guests.

"Do come in," Andrea said, waving them over to the bed.

Gonzaga and Figueroa took a moment to stop at the threshold and nod respectfully before entering. In that instant, Tonino grabbed two straight-backed chairs by the fireplace and slid them over to the bed. Then, with a mild flourish of the hand and a reverential bow, he invited them to take a seat, which they promptly did. Little Giovannandrea assumed his usual spot on Andrea's knee.

"Bring the Madeira Malvasia for our visitors, Tonino," said

Andrea. "I can think of no finer wine to complement the lovely biscuits our dear Giovannandrea has brought us."

"Immediately, my Prince," replied Tonino.

"And do prepare a fire upon your return," Andrea added, indicating the meager embers smoldering in the fireplace.

Tonino nodded in the affirmative as he backed out of the room.

"So wonderful to see you," said Figueroa, turning to address Giannettino as well.

Ferrante Gonzaga's greeting was equally gracious. Andrea's eyes never left their gaze, which served to help them feel welcome at first, but also produced the unfortunate result of having the four men sit, just staring at each other, for entirely too long. The awkwardness of the moment didn't seem to affect little Giovannandrea, however, who continued to munch on the canestrelli unimpeded.

"What can you tell me about our next doge?" Andrea finally asked, cutting right to the heart of the matter. "If there are any obstacles to install the man I want, I must know now."

"The name Benedetto Gentile Pevere is not sitting well with everyone," Gonzaga replied after a moment's hesitation.

"And why is that?" Andrea inquired, a bit surprised.

"For one, he has held no prior position with the Republic," Figueroa chimed in.

"And his name appears quite late on the *Libro d'oro della nobiltà italiana*," added Gonzaga, referring to the city's register of noble families, and clearly meant to cast aspersions on the newer class of nobles, mostly merchants and artisans, known as *popolari*, of which Pevere was a member. The popolari had gained access to the registry through reforms Andrea had put in place twenty years earlier, elevating them to the same rank and status as the older feudal families such as the Grimaldi, Spinola, Fieschi, and, of course, the Doria themselves.

"I can only share your predilection for Genoa's well-established nobility up to a certain point, gentlemen," Andrea said sharply. "Is he a man with whom I can reason on matters of import? This is what I ask myself, and my answer is a resounding *yes*."

"His perceived partiality for the French should give you pause," said Gonzaga, knowing full well that Andrea's loyalty to the Spanish was unwavering.

Giannettino shifted impatiently in his seat. "He has proven to be a good servant of His Majesty in Spain, has he not?" he said in a tone sufficiently masking his mounting anger.

"This is true," said Figueroa, "but his affinity for the Fieschi raises some concerns."

"This notion that certain members of the Fieschi family side with France is an exaggeration," Andrea added, his eyes boring right through his two guests. "The Fieschi are loyal friends and patriots."

Figueroa and Gonzaga exchanged looks, each reluctant to utter the next word. Andrea decided to simply wait for a reply rather than pound his message home. He was a tolerant man, though being lectured by two outsiders, one a Spanish nobleman of twenty-seven and the other a haughty Mantuan, tested his patience. But as always, he maintained his composure, which, of course, yielded the intended effect of increasing the pressure on his visitors. The two men continued to steal sideward glances and squirm in their chairs just enough to telegraph their growing anxiety. *What the devil is going on?* thought Andrea. Even little Giovannandrea picked up on the mood and stopped chomping on his cookies. Giannettino leaned forward as if to say something, but Andrea halted him with a glare. Andrea had lured many an enemy into his traps utilizing the same maneuver. The waiting game had officially begun.

Ambassador Figueroa spoke first. "I am always grateful for your warmth and hospitality, dear Prince, and it pleases me greatly to speak with you on issues of political import, but I am afraid this is not the matter that compels us here today."

The ambassador stopped there, deferring to the governor of Milan to elaborate. Gonzaga cleared his throat and adjusted the starched lace ruff around his neck to buy some time.

Now it was Andrea's turn to trade glances with his dear nephew. Once again, he gestured to Giannettino to hold his tongue. Andrea's attention then shifted to Gonzaga, while keeping Figueroa neatly within his sights. Andrea's ability to orchestrate events with a slight tilt of the head, or a routine hand motion, was on full display. Gonzaga's time in the spotlight had come whether he liked it or not.

"Galleys bringing armed soldiers have been entering the harbor of late," Gonzaga began, "many of whom have been spotted in the palace at Via Lata."

Andrea remained unfazed. Giannettino, however, was quick to jump in.

"And why do you suppose Gian Luigi Fieschi would welcome these men into his residence at Via Lata?" he asked.

All eyes focused back on Gonzaga, who by now was eager to lay it all on the line. He took a deep breath, and then, careful not draw little Giovannandrea's attention, leaned in to whisper in Andrea's ear: "We believe your life is in peril, dear Prince, as well as the very future of the Genoese Republic."

Chapter Two

BOYHOOD DREAMS

Hearing Gonzaga's threatening words had little effect on Andrea's frame of mind. As long as he could remember, the notion of death failed to intimidate him. People had been trying to kill him since he joined the ranks of the papal guard nearly sixty-five years ago, and as far back as when he was a ten-year-old boy he'd suffered a traumatic emotional setback that went a long way toward desensitizing him. From that day forward, he walked fearlessly through life, pushing the anguish of that experience aside and meeting each challenge head-on. His obsession with fortune and adventure took seed that day. The commonplace fears and anxieties associated with carrying on an ordinary, peaceful life abandoned him, and the need for excitement and daring filled the void.

It may have been the grogginess of sleep or that awful recurring nightmare that still muddied Andrea's consciousness and distracted him from the warnings of his two visitors—or perhaps it was the simple pleasure of bouncing his nephew, Giovannandrea, on his knee that triggered memories of that fateful day as a young boy—but in that moment, everything began to fade: Gonzaga's and Figueroa's expressions of concern, Giannettino's impulsive response to their menacing words, and the animated discussion that ensued. It all fell into the background, devoid of sound or consequence, and gave way to clear, crisp images of an unusually warm November day in his boyhood home of Oneglia, a small port town on the Italian Riviera seventy miles west of Genoa, where the Doria family had ruled as *signori* for nearly two centuries.

The year was 1476, a few days before Andrea's tenth birthday. He had just woken up to the sight of his mother, Caracosa, staring idly out the window. His older brother, Davide, was getting dressed in front of their tall walnut armoire. As little Andrea wiped the sleep from his eyes, he could see that his mother was weeping. Davide glanced over at her every so often, but dared not say a word. Caracosa was considerably fragile for a woman of thirty. Upon first glance she appeared much older, her slender frame bent forward at the shoulders as if lacking the will to face the world. As a rule, noble Ligurian tradition infused all women of the region with a substantial dose of determination and perseverance, and Caracosa was no different, but she'd been burdened with one ailment after another her entire life, and now after birthing four strong, healthy children, her energy had given way to fatigue. But today's tears betrayed a deeper pain, and little Andrea could see it.

"What is it, Moæ?" Andrea asked, using the affectionate regional vernacular to refer to his mother. He slipped out of bed and hurried over to her. "Have I done something wrong?"

Without turning away from the view of the sea out the window, Caracosa wrapped her arms around her two sons, and in one warm, comforting motion, she drew them closer to her. Although life had eaten away at her strength and eroded her health, her spirited Ligurian stoicism remained intact. She jerked back her shoulders, stood upright and proud, and fought back the wellspring of tears she wanted so desperately to shed. Davide held tightly to his mother's gown, burying his head in her puffed upper sleeves, but still too shy or simply reluctant to speak up. Andrea's curiosity was piqued, however; he'd never seen his mother like this, but he knew better than to persist. He waited for her to say the first word.

Caracosa tilted her head down to meet Davide's sad gaze. "Go wake up Antonio and your little sister," she murmured, her voice barely audible. "It's time for us to go."

Davide ran off without hesitation, leaving Andrea and his mother alone at the window.

Andrea and his little brother, Antonio Raffaele, were separated by only two years, but it might as well have been decades. Antonio shared a bedroom across the corridor with his sister, Violante, who at four years old still preferred to crawl into bed with her mother and father most nights. The truth of the matter was that Andrea had little in common with any of his siblings. He'd matured physically, mentally, and emotionally well beyond his mere ten years. In fact, his mother usually deferred to him over his older brother, Davide, on delicate matters, or when she needed a specific task carried out to perfection.

The stately Palazzo Doria, which towered over Oneglia's

busy port, had a bird's-eye view of all the vessels that came into and out of the harbor. Andrea's third-story window stood like a crow's nest propped atop the mainmast of a ship, looking out onto an endless horizon. Where most children would occupy their time playing, unconcerned or merely unaware of the outside world, Andrea spent countless hours staring out over the cobalt waters of the Tyrrhenian, dreaming of pirates, far-off lands, and a life of adventure. Whenever he got the chance he would sneak off to watch the fishermen as they mended their nets, readied their boats to cast off, or shared kegs of Vermentino wine with their shipmates after dropping anchor. Galleys that pulled into port in preparation for exotic journeys to the Barbary coast, the Greek isles, or the shores of the Holy Land merited his full attention as well. The colorful jargon used by the sailors on these ships, brimming with newfangled and often crude language, never failed to capture the attention of his innocent young ears. What could they possibly mean by *spankers, hawsers, lazy jacks, foresails,* and *leeches*? And, of course, *clew lines, toe rails, spinnakers, scuttlebutts,* and *nippers* didn't make much sense either, but he was determined not only to decipher their significance, but to someday utter each word or phrase with absolute authority.

As little Andrea stared out his bedroom window, past the rooftop of the loggia whose portside arcade housed a bustling marketplace rife with fishmongers, greengrocers, spice sellers, and vendors of all sorts, he noticed an imposing three-masted galley moored on the western pier. Its sails stood tall and mighty, flapping in the soft sirocco wind. Topsails had never reached so high into the sky. He couldn't take his eyes off it, and for that one isolated moment, his mother's emotional state felt a million miles away. Caracosa, too, found herself distracted by her son's unbroken focus out the window. She had noticed little Andrea's growing fixation with the port lately, especially when he would accompany her and their housemaid, Angelina, to the market. He would often slip away when they weren't looking, wandering off to the far end of the dock to take in all the activity.

Over the past few months, she, too, would stroll to the water's edge hoping to catch sight of her dear husband, Ceva, who months earlier had joined a crusade to liberate the city of Otranto from Ottoman occupation. She would fantasize seeing his galley in the distance returning home to a hero's welcome. On more than one occasion she found Andrea at the end of the pier, all alone, peacefully gazing out to sea. Rather than berate the boy for straying off, she would sidle up next to him and raise her eyes to the heavens to pray for her husband's speedy return, while little Andrea would no doubt stand there dreaming of someday following in his father's footsteps.

"Get dressed, Andrea," Caracosa said, turning away from the window to face her young son. "A promenade along the port will do you all good."

Andrea didn't move. Instead, he took his mother's hand in his. "Will you come with us, Moæ?" he asked.

Something in Andrea's manner, or perhaps the sweet tone of his voice, brought a steady stream of tears to her eyes as if a dam had been breached. Her knees buckled, and as she stumbled backward, she clamped onto a nearby chair to break her fall. Andrea was quick to catch her and help her into her seat.

"Don't pay any attention to your foolish mother," she uttered between sobs.

Andrea delved deep into his mother's eyes to divine the source of her misery. The poise and degree of self-assurance he demonstrated restored Caracosa's strength almost immediately, and allayed the burden she had been carrying all these months.

She took Andrea into her arms: "You mustn't speak of this to Violante or dear Antonio," she whispered. "And not even to Davide. They are not strong like you."

"Is it about Poæ?" he inquired without hesitation.

Caracosa lowered her gaze ever so slightly, pausing to reflect before answering.

"Your father is not well," she said, combing Andrea's curls away from his face with her fingers as she spoke.

Ever since Ceva returned home from his journey, Caracosa noticed something had changed in him. Although the campaign against the Ottomans had attracted many would-be warriors in search of fortune, Ceva's experience on the open seas concluded with little glory, and none of the loot he desperately needed to maintain his home and feudal lands. The Doria family had long held positions of authority throughout the Ligurian Riviera, even serving as doge in Genoa on several occasions, but Ceva's immediate relatives had been struggling financially for years, and Caracosa's side of the family—also descendants of the Doria clan, albeit a distant branch from Dolceacqua—could offer no help.

As it stood, Ceva owned only a portion of the palazzo in Oneglia, sharing it with his cousin Domenico. His uncle Giovanni who resided in Genoa could not lend a hand either. Giovanni was of considerable noble stature and held in high regard, but his star had long since faded. And to add insult to injury, a good number of his relatives had simply moved away to take advantage of the opportunities created in Rome by the new pope, Sixtus IV, a Ligurian native.

The pope's desire to reconquer the southern region of Italy from the Turks filled Ceva with renewed hope. He saw the crusade as the occasion of a lifetime, his chance to reshape a destiny that had not been kind to him. However, no sooner had he left the port of Genoa than the pope signed a peace treaty with the Turks, restoring Otranto's sovereignty and freedom. Not only were Ceva's dreams to cash in on the spoils of war dashed right there and then, but his emotional and physical state deteriorated along with it. When Caracosa finally met him on the dock upon his return, just one short week ago, she found a depressed, frail, seriously broken man. She immediately accompanied him to his room in his palazzo chamber and put him to bed, where he remained since then.

"The doctor is due this morning," Caracosa admitted to little Andrea, her voice cracking, "and I do not want to alarm anyone when he arrives."

"I want to visit Poæ before the doctor comes," the boy replied.

Caracosa turned away from her son, unable to look him in the eye. "Your father refuses to let anyone into the room," she said. "I think it is better if you take in some of the warm air God has given us today. A walk to the port, perhaps."

"But I haven't spoken to him since before he left us," little Andrea lamented.

"He is not the man you remember, my son. His illness has done terrible things."

"But the doctor will cure him," Andrea blurted out with an air of confidence that did little to mask his deep-rooted anxiety.

"You must find courage," Caracosa exclaimed, doing all she could to summon in him the strength of character and resolve she knew he possessed. "And you are not to say a word to anyone," she added firmly, her eyes once again welling with tears.

Andrea realized his mother depended on him to calm the waters and placate whatever distress the doctor's visit would arouse in his siblings. The moment he nodded his assent, Caracosa wrapped her arms around him and smothered him in kisses.

Something about that moment triggered a change in him, a gentle awakening. Images of his own destiny took shape within his young, receptive mind. His first reaction was to breathe in deeply, as if wanting to consume her pain, absorb it, and free her of it forever. His outbreath brought further lucidity and filled him with a sense of purpose, eliminating all the confusion and emotional turmoil in the air.

He hugged his mother as hard as he could, and uttered four simple words that were rarely heard in traditional Genoese households where stoicism and restraint rose above all other virtues: "I love you, Moæ." A single tear rolled down his cheek.

As the Doria children cut onto the narrow street behind their palazzo and descended the gradual incline leading to the harbor, Andrea was careful not to divulge the true purpose of their venture. His goal, he told himself, was to deflect the conversation away from their mother's curious behavior, and field all references to their father with equal parts delicacy and evasion. The composure with which he managed to circumvent the truth actually surprised him. Having been trained to be a trustworthy Christian boy, he felt guilty about it at first, but it wasn't long before he saw that his words and actions were having the desired effect of calming the waters, and that his obfuscations, as dishonest and deceptive as they were, were serving a higher purpose. He realized that when his mother gave him the task of preserving the innocence and well-being of his siblings, she was, in effect, asking him to lie to them.

Up to this point, straying from the truth was simply part of every child's repertoire, a much-needed skill to avoid the wrath of parents, schoolmasters, or clergymen. Little white lies were the devilish, acutely instinctual tools learned at an early age to protect oneself from harm or punishment, then easily confessed to the parish priest on Sunday morning to clear the way for receiving the holy sacrament of communion. But the falsehoods he spoke today were of a different nature entirely; they seemingly transcended personal gain, and were told solely for the benefit of others. This thrilled him at first. But, being a thoughtful and principled young man, Andrea quickly recognized how easily he could manipulate others, wield power over them, and even lead them astray if he so wanted. And this terrified him.

At the port, beneath the loggia where fishermen peddled their daily catch, the Doria children spotted Angelina, their household maid, at the fishmonger's stand. She held a slithery pink and gray octopus by its head, allowing its long, sinewy tentacles to stretch like kneaded dough. Then, in one swift, fluid motion, she swung it high into the air and smashed it down onto a slab of cold, wet granite. She repeated this action several times before she caught sight of the children out of the corner of her eye.

"Lord Jesus, Mary, and Joseph, what are you doing here?" she cried out without breaking her rhythm.

The children had seen Angelina utilize this tenderizing technique on squid, cuttlefish, and octopi dozens of times, and weren't the least bit taken aback by its apparent violence. On the contrary, they understood it meant one of Angelina's exquisite *burridas*, a grand stew of freshly netted seafood, herbs, nuts, and tangy vinegar, was in the offing. Knowing the tenacity with which Angelina went about such procedures, Andrea didn't bother to wait for her to finish before answering her.

"Moæ thinks we shouldn't waste such a beautiful day inside the house," he said, having finally found the proper moment between smashes to blurt it out. "She told us you would be here."

Since Caracosa had already informed her that she would share Ceva's condition with the boy, Angelina gave Andrea a knowing look. This surprised Andrea. He acknowledged her glance with a discreet nod, making sure not to tip his hand to Davide, who sensed that something was amiss, but was far too timid, and perhaps even reluctant, to ask any questions for fear of finding out the awful truth.

"The *Tempesta* has moored this morning," said Angelina, slapping the octopus onto the slab for the last time and tossing it into her canvas sack. "Allow me to pay this thief over here his due," she quipped as she handed the fishmonger a gold florin, "and we shall be on our way."

She was referring to the galley Andrea was admiring earlier from his bedroom window. Angelina's crusty, seafaring husband, Gustavo, who had been patrolling the eastern shores of the Mediterranean for the Republic of Genoa for the past few months, was aboard that ship, and she was eager to greet him. As much as her special recipe of burrida pleased everyone in the Doria family, in her heart she was preparing it in celebration of her dear Gustavo's safe return.

Visiting the *Tempesta* was music to Andrea's ears. He made extra sure not to tarry as the five of them strode through the port's busy esplanade. He could see the topsail of the mainmast in the distance, rising above all the rest, and followed it like his north star. Along the way he and Angelina would exchange glances, she wondering how Andrea was handling his newfound responsibilities, and he anxiously waiting for the right moment to confront her about his father.

They arrived at the gangway of the *Tempesta* as most of its crew was disembarking and no doubt heading to the nearest *taverna* for a bit of warm food and cool local wine. Oneglia hosted all ships friendly to the Republic of Genoa as well as to the Duchy of Milan, which ruled over the entire region at the time, and it welcomed all its sailors, the vast majority of whom hailed from other towns along the coast, including the capital city of Genoa. Accommodating this last group inevitably meant providing seaside establishments with all their gastronomical, enological, and carnal desires. In this regard, Oneglia differed little from other port towns along the Italian Riviera. And business was booming.

Andrea stood ogling the galley as if it had descended from heaven. His eyes widened taking in its coarse, weather-beaten grandeur. He estimated the ship's length as roughly seventy or eighty arm lengths, and at least fifteen arm lengths wide. It had a high bridge at its bow that housed a battery of cannons in keeping with the tactical tradition of favoring head-on attacks. At its stern, a multihued canvas covered an even taller bridge brandishing an array of banners as well as the ship's standard of an eagle clutching a serpent tightly in its claws.

Andrea found himself so mesmerized by the ship's majesty that he failed to notice Gustavo plodding down the gangway and meeting Angelina with an impassioned kiss. He was a hulk of a man whose wide, toothless smile melted hearts. He adored the Doria children and gave each one a heartfelt hug, starting with little Violante, then Antonio, Davide, and finally Andrea, with whom he'd always felt a particular affinity.

"Let us go home," Gustavo said, taking his wife by the arm

and corralling the children around him. "I'm so hungry I could eat a horse."

Gustavo spied the disappointment on Andrea's face and immediately asked him what was the matter. Andrea said nothing, but his sidelong glance back at the *Tempesta* spoke volumes. Gustavo knew that look. It was less a twinkle in the eye and more an unreachable itch that needed scratching. He'd seen that same exact expression on scores of aspiring seafarers. A brute in appearance, Gustavo was unusually sensitive for a hardened sailor.

He stopped in his tracks and asked Andrea point-blank: "What would you say to a stroll aboard the *Tempesta*?"

Andrea did nothing to hide his elation. He turned immediately to register Angelina's reaction. He would need her permission, and of course there was the little issue of protecting his siblings from the realities at home, which he knew couldn't be ignored. Could he dare leave them and run off with Gustavo? Would he be abandoning his responsibilities?

Angelina read the conflict in Andrea's eyes. She also knew the boy all too well; she'd practically raised him. Boarding a galley, the preeminent battleship of its day, was the fantasy of every young boy along the Ligurian coast, but with Andrea it was a fever-pitched craving. How could she deny him that dream?

"Take Davide with you as well," Angelina said, turning to Gustavo with a wink and a twisted grin. "I'll take Antonio and Violante for a walk along the pier, then back to the palazzo to start the burrida," she added. "And try not to eat a horse or any other wild animal, or you'll spoil your appetite."

As expected, Davide's face lit up along with Andrea's.

"Thank you, Angelina!" exclaimed the two boys in unison. "Thank you!"

Andrea locked eyes with Angelina, trying his best to signal his heartfelt appreciation.

"Don't thank me," she said, lifting Violante up with one arm and leading Antonio forward with the other. "Thank Gustavo here, and make sure to bring him home in one piece."

And with that, Angelina hurried off into the market with the two younger children in tow, making sure to offer Andrea a warm smile before she left.

At the same time, Gustavo led the boys up the gangway and onto the *Tempesta*. The ship was still a beehive of activity. After gaining the boatswain's approval, they headed straight for the large bronze cannon beneath the forecastle. Andrea's eyes widened in awe. Gustavo rubbed his hand along its hefty barrel as if caressing Angelina's soft skin.

"We call this our warhorse," he said proudly.

"How far can it shoot?" inquired Andrea without hesitation.

"It spits out nearly five hundred arm lengths of pure iron," Gustavo replied. "And it's a front loader," he added.

"That's good, isn't it?" asked Andrea.

"And a great deal safer," Gustavo was quick to point out. "The rear loaders exploded in our faces far too often for my liking."

Andrea studied the cannon intently, inspecting it from all angles like an exigent sea captain.

"How do you aim this thing?" he asked.

"Those are the lateral lynchpins," replied Gustavo, indicating the base of the gun carriage that housed the cannon. "It secures and elevates the cannon to the height you want. When the captain gives the order, the boatswain and helmsman work together to point the ship toward the target, and with a little practice you can split the mainmast and knock an enemy ship out of commission, or even sink it with a broadside to the hold."

Davide jumped in at that point. "What if the enemy boards your ship?"

"You don't want that to happen with pirates," said Gustavo. "They're mighty good fighters and they outnumber you every time."

Andrea was becoming visibly excited. "They say pirate ships are as swift as eagles."

Gustavo pointed portside, then starboard. "We've got as many as thirty-four oars on each side, and hundreds of oarsmen," he said. "That's one way to outmaneuver them."

"What do the oarsmen do when the ship is boarded?" Andrea asked.

"The ones that are paid are usually able warriors and they fight with us, and even share in the booty if we're victorious. But the criminals who have been assigned to the *Tempesta* as punishment for their crimes, and the slaves we captured at war, they remain chained to their oars."

"Chained?" Davide repeated in disbelief. "Do they eat there, too?"

"Eat, sleep, and everything else a man must do," replied Gustavo matter-of-factly. "They would be better off in hell."

The boys stood quiet for a moment, letting the information sink in.

"It would be my fate as well if I were captured in battle," Gustavo added with an ironic grin.

"Have you seen battle?" Andrea inquired.

A darkness crossed the man's face. "In Cembalo, Caffa, and Soldaia, all Genoese strongholds past the Dardanelles," he said flatly. His gaze shifted away from the boys to the vast expanse of sea beyond the harbor. "We fought Gedik Ahmed Pasha, a sly cutthroat of a pirate if there ever was one."

The boys held back their reaction, gleaning from Gustavo's grim expression that there was more to come.

"And we lost everything," he added, his eyes still fixed on the horizon.

Little Andrea's next three words may have seemed rash and perhaps inappropriate, especially coming from the mouth of a ten-year-old, and indeed Gustavo took umbrage at first upon hearing them, but he quickly perceived two things in the young boy: his uncommon ability to remain objective where others would have fallen into sentimentality, and his sincere interest in analyzing the possible reasons for defeat.

"What did you do wrong?" Andrea asked.

Gustavo turned and walked toward midship, speaking to the boys as he went.

"Galleys are like wolves," he said. "There's no escaping them when they travel in packs. But with their shallow draft and low sides, they refuse to perform in bad weather. There's no way around it."

Then, as if wanting to avoid the subject, Gustavo pointed to a cannon on the starboard side and yet another positioned directly opposite it on the portside.

"See them?" he asked. "They're smaller and more limited in range than the big cannon, but they load faster than you can steal a kiss from a young lady, and can do just as much damage."

"As much as the young lady or the big cannon?" quipped Andrea.

Gustavo laughed out loud. "Both," he exclaimed, "both!"

"So galleys can have three cannons?" asked Andrea, continuing to drill for answers.

"Usually," said Gustavo, "but I've seen them with more. They call the extra cannons 'cuckold' guns in the sense that they betray you." When he saw the look of confusion on the boys' faces, he expounded: "After three blasts of cannon fire, the soldiers and crew of the enemy ship expect you to reload and change direction, so they come out of hiding to begin their counterattack. Then—boom! The cuckold guns hit them when they're most exposed."

Gustavo climbed the stairs to the quarterdeck at the ship's rear with Andrea and Davide right behind, then ascended to the poop deck. A sense of raw energy surged through Andrea when he reached that lofty vantage point and peered out over the entire ship, surveying what remained of its crew going about its duties.

It evoked a taste of power he'd never felt before. Even the sound of the banners over the bridge that flapped in the wind and the rustling of the trimmed sails sent shivers down the young boy's spine. It wasn't hard for Andrea to imagine himself the ship's captain, ordering an attack on the enemy, issuing directives that would guide the galley to within striking distance, and then commanding his cannons to let loose. It took a friendly pat on the back from Gustavo to finally jolt Andrea out of his reverie.

"I have no doubt that in those last few moments you managed to conquer the Ottomans, put the King of Spain in his place, and subject France to the will of the Genoese Republic," chortled Gustavo. "Welcome back to the land of the living, my little friend."

Andrea looked around, still a bit dazed, and shaken by a vision that couldn't have appeared more real. On the outside, his face turned beet red, understandably embarrassed, but inside he knew he'd experienced something meaningful and that he'd perhaps glimpsed his future. The realization that he may have come face-to-face with his destiny left him speechless at first. Then, after an awkwardly long pause, he turned to look Gustavo squarely in the eye, and with a combination of determination and sheer audacity, he threw caution to the wind.

"I think it's time we go home," Andrea announced.

On the way back to the palazzo, Andrea informed Davide of the doctor's visit and of the gravity of the situation in an attempt to prepare his brother—and himself—for the worst. Caracosa never revealed the exact nature of Ceva's illness during her early morning chat with Andrea, but her state of mind told him all he needed to know. Andrea was mature enough and certainly wise enough to know that his dear mother would withhold as many of the grim details from her children as possible, and that given how distraught she appeared, and how incapable she was of reigning in her true emotions, the reality of his father's condition must be very serious. Andrea, of course, kept those dire observations to himself. Instead, he decided to use some of his mother's psychology on his older brother to dole out the bitter truth.

"Don't ask too many questions if you see the doctor," he said. "It will upset Moæ."

"He cured your fever when you were young, and mended my broken bones," Davide replied, vigorously flexing his left arm as a show of proof. "He will fix Poæ, too."

"Yes, he will," Andrea was quick to respond. "I'm sure he will."

Andrea's careful, and often circumspect, explanation of why their mother was crying uncontrollably earlier that morning may have helped sidestep any undue stress on Davide for the moment, but Gustavo, walking alongside the boys, was not fooled by Andrea's disclosure. He figured Ceva's condition was serious. Having been at sea for the past six months, the news came as a complete surprise to him. He had watched Ceva's fortunes fade over the years, and knew of his appetite for adventure, especially where expeditions to the northern coast of Africa and the Levant were concerned. He had even discussed with him the pros and cons of taking part in the crusade to Otranto, and eventually advised Ceva against it, warning him of the inherent dangers involved, and beseeching him to stay at home with his family. Gustavo obviously wasn't privy to the actual level of hardship that had befallen the Oneglia branch of the Doria clan and had driven Ceva to such desperation.

Shortly after they reached the palazzo, Gustavo gave the boys a hug, offered up a few words of encouragement, and pealed off to his quarters in the rear of the building. Regardless of the many years Gustavo and Angelina had served the Doria family, and the intimate bond that had developed between them, protocol stipulated that delicate household matters remained solely within the family.

No sooner had Gustavo departed than the two boys spotted a man dressed in black leaving Ceva's bedchamber and stepping lightly down the hallway in their direction. He strode past them and continued on his way. Recognizing him to be a priest and a dear friend of the family, Andrea instantly grasped the tragic meaning of his presence. At that same moment, Andrea saw his mother at the threshold of the bedchamber and broke into a sprint toward her, arriving just as she was about to shut the door. Every emotion ranging from anger to sadness to sheer joy followed Caracosa's look of complete surprise. She let out a faint gasp as she studied the resolve on the young boy's face.

Andrea stood tall. *My father is dying*, he thought to himself, *and I must see him at all costs*. He'd made an executive decision of sorts in that very instant to be at his father's side regardless of the promise he had made earlier that morning to safeguard his siblings. If Davide was being exposed to the harsh realities of life, so be it. On some deep emotional level he realized he was soon to become the dominant male force in the household. The time to wallow in his mother's love and protection had ended.

Caracosa took a step back at the sight of her two oldest sons standing before her. After giving it a moment's thought, she reached down and took them both into her arms, then ushered them into Ceva's bedchamber. The thick velvet drapes, woven from linen and fine silk, that covered all the windows from ceiling to floor kept the sunlight at bay, lending an eeriness to the room's already mournful air. Despite the darkness, Andrea could discern the shadowy image of his father lying in his canopy bed, but couldn't make out whether his eyes were open or shut. With his mother's arms still wrapped securely around him, and as she continued to cry in anguish, Andrea began to pull away from her, inching toward the bed, wanting desperately to join his father. Davide must have been tugging at her just as hard, given the fact that when Caracosa's grip finally loosened, the boys sprang from her arms in near unison and rushed to Ceva's bedside. Only then, after seeing his father lying motionless, eyes closed, hands joined in a position of prayer, and the scent of chrism oil administered during his last rites still hanging in the air, would Andrea fully realize he would never see his father again.

Chapter Three

FAMILY ORIGINS

When Ambassador Figueroa's and Governor Gonzaga's dour expressions eased back into focus, replacing the images of that fateful day in his father's chamber, Andrea hardly knew whether to breathe a sigh of relief or tear out what little hair he had left. He found no solace in reliving such stressful moments from his past, but he far preferred it to the ramblings of two idle gentlemen with nothing better to do than spread their tittle-tattle of conspiracy, armed rebellion, and assassination. Andrea's power was too consolidated, Genoa's merchants too prosperous, and the common people far too contented for this degree of intrigue. Only the presence of little Giovannandrea rocking gently on his knee kept him from shooing the two men out the door. Surely they must have other people to bother with such nonsense. Seeing them sit there seemingly awaiting a response to their warning of revolt only irritated Andrea more, leaving him with nothing to say for fear of losing control of his temper. Fortunately, the appearance of Tonino at the door with a bottle of aged Madeira saved the day.

"Ah, at last you have come, Tonino my friend!" Andrea cried out. "Had another moment passed without providing my friends here with some refreshment, I surely would have been called a boor."

Of course, Andrea's good name resisted such labels. He routinely lavished his guests with feasts and indulged them in luxury, a far cry from the austerity he had to endure when he first set foot in Genoa as a young man. Ceva's death had rendered the Doria house in Oneglia nearly destitute, leaving Caracosa no choice but to surrender her portion of the property to Domenico Doria a few years later in exchange for a paltry sum of cash. This infuriated young Andrea at the time, not only for the dishonor it inflicted upon the family, but also for how the entire episode tormented his mother. One condition of the sale, in particular, that created undo anxiety transferred ownership of the entire feudal estate to Domenico immediately upon Caracosa's death, effectively putting to an end to Ceva's family lineage. Andrea found this nearly impossible to swallow, and swore he would make it his life's mission to reestablish the family name.

He remained true to this pledge over the years, hosting high-born diplomats, kings, and emperors in his palazzo in Genoa, not to mention notorious pirates. His reputation grew, and currently resounded throughout the continent. Therefore, immediately upon seeing Tonino at the door with a bottle of Madeira, he instructed him to serve the guests posthaste.

"Set it down over there," he said, directing Tonino to the fireplace.

"At once, my Prince," replied Tonino, always quick to respond.

Tonino rested the wine and four glasses of Venetian crystal on a stout hexagonal table by the fire, then neatly arranged the black leather chairs that surrounded the table to better accommodate the two guests. Seeing Andrea's intentions, Giannettino stood up and motioned to Gonzaga and Figueroa to join him. Meanwhile, Tonino gathered a bundle of kindling wood piled atop the unusually wide hearth at the base of the fire box and positioned it strategically on the burning embers so as to touch off a burst of flames. He then lifted an armful of beechwood logs from that same stack and loaded them onto the growing fire, nipping the chill in the air almost immediately.

"Do make yourselves at home," Andrea said, urging his guests to follow Giannettino's lead. "I'd like to exchange a word or two with my little nephew here," he added as he snatched another canestrello off the salver and handed it to little Giovannandrea.

"By all means," replied Figueroa.

Just as they joined Giannettino by the fire, the chamber door swung open to reveal an elegantly dressed young woman. Her smile was nothing short of radiant. Alongside her stood a girl slightly older than little Giovannandrea.

"Ginetta, my dear," Andrea called out to the woman, "do come, and bring that little treasure of yours with you."

Ginetta Centurione was the daughter of Genoa's most prosperous banker, Adamo Centurione, and Giannettino's dear wife of ten years. The girl at her side was their daughter, Placidia, who wasted no time running up to Andrea.

"Mesiavo! Mesiavo!" she cried out, using the affectionate term for *grandfather* just as Giovannandrea did.

Andrea's heart melted as Placidia threw her arms around him and kissed him on both cheeks, giggling the whole time. She then promptly hopped on Andrea's other knee, across from her younger brother. By that time, Ginetta had crossed the room, acknowledged her husband with a moment of perfunctory eye contact, and reached Andrea's bedside, where she reenacted the same endearing ritual as her daughter upon greeting him— except, of course, for resting on his knee, although her petite size and delicate manner would not have prohibited her from doing so. Andrea was certainly big enough and sufficiently brawny to sustain it, and, in fact, it wouldn't have been the first time Ginetta and the children cozied up to him at gatherings such as these. Their bond had always been one of tenderness and deep trust. Andrea's love of Giannettino extended to the entire family, and the feeling was quite mutual.

"How are you holding up, my dear Prince?" teased Ginetta.

Andrea's effusive grin showed off an impressive set of teeth for a man his age. "There can be no better remedy for one's ills, my dear princess, than to have your loved ones close," he replied as he wrapped his arms around his little niece and nephew, much like his mother used to do with his brother Davide and him.

"Come, Placidia, you must greet your father," said Ginetta, taking her daughter's hand and guiding her off Andrea's lap. "You know how jealous these men can become."

Placidia obliged without hesitation. She bussed Andrea on the cheek and slid off his knee.

"Wait," said Andrea as he passed off the salver of canestrelli to Placidia. "Bring these to our guests before your brother and I devour them all."

"And Mesiava Peretta will be angry with you again," quipped Placidia as she scooted off.

Now that Andrea found himself alone with his young nephew, he gave him all of his attention.

"Your sister is a jewel," Andrea whispered. "Your mother is a saint and your father is nothing less than a hero," he added with a touch of emotion in his voice. "You are fortunate to have them still with you, my son."

These last words left Giovannandrea a bit confused. He'd never witnessed his mesiavo quite so vulnerable. Andrea's piercing eyes, long silvery beard, and striking presence had always cast him as nearly godlike and invincible to the boy.

"Where is your *poæ*?" Giovannandrea asked innocently.

"He is with my mother," Andrea replied, "in the city where I was born."

"Can we visit them?" inquired the boy.

"I make the voyage to Oneglia each November," said Andrea, "on the Day of the Dead. Perhaps next time I shall take you with me."

"I would like that," said Giovannandrea.

"My mother would have loved you as I do," said Andrea. "She died when I was still young."

"What did you do then?" the boy asked.

For no apparent reason Andrea let out a chuckle. Perhaps because it was the same question he had asked himself at the time—*What do I do now?*—given the fact that the contract his mother had signed with Domenico forced everyone out of the house somewhat unprepared. Davide left to pursue a life at sea; Antonio Raffaele and Violante, being too young to venture out into the world, remained under the protection of relatives; and Andrea traveled to Genoa at the age of eighteen to seek fame and fortune . . . or so he thought, hence the self-deprecating chuckle.

"I walked down to our little harbor and boarded the first ship that would take me," said Andrea.

From the smile that surfaced, he seemed to take pride in that memory. Giovannandrea watched this moment of contemplation with a mix of bemusement and awe, and, as usual, with a healthy dose of curiosity. He was nothing if not the most curious boy on earth, a trait Andrea believed to be the boy's most deserving attribute. He hung on his mesiavo's words like a toddler listening to a bedtime story.

"Where did you go?" Giovannandrea asked, expecting a litany of exotic seaports from the Barbary Coast to the shores of the Black Sea.

"Where else could I go?" exclaimed Andrea. "I came here, of course, to Genoa." Sensing the boy's disappointment, Andrea was quick to continue: "It was the capital of the world for me at the time, but looking back on the period, I now realize I wasn't prepared for it. Genoa turned out to be a stepping stone to much bigger things."

"Like when you met the pirate Barbarossa?" the boy cried out. "My father said the two greatest admirals in the whole wide world met right here in this palazzo. Is that true?"

"Quite true," Andrea said flatly. "As to being great admirals, I can only say that Barbarossa was indeed a formidable adversary. But my victories over pirates, Corsican renegades, and the great kingdoms of this continent were not my most treasured achievements, dear Giovannandrea. Your father, who is also one of our great admirals—just as I am certain you will be someday—can attest to that."

Despite Giovannandrea's prodigious wisdom for a boy of eight, he seemed to ignore Andrea's underlying assertion that violence and war, with all their assumed glory, were not all they were cracked up to be—or perhaps he failed to grasp the true meaning.

In any event, Giovannandrea fell victim to his own youthful impulses: "How can I ever be a great admiral if I've never been out to sea," he groused, "or even known the inside of one of my father's galleys?"

Andrea decided not to respond right away. So much of his nephew's attitude reminded him of himself at that age. Like Giovannandrea, he, too, excelled in all of his studies as a boy. His traditional humanist education had molded him into a cultured and thoughtful adult, well-versed in modern and ancient philosophy, prudent in outlook as well as patient and reflective in demeanor. He didn't perceive his natural, physical prowess as a virtue in and of itself, but as an instrument to be developed in tandem with his formidable intellectual and psychological skills, all of which he would later utilize to become an astute strategist and shrewd political leader. In his youth, however, as a soldier for popes and kings, prior to his experiences at sea, he possessed a keen appetite for heroism and valor, surviving on a calculated recklessness of sorts, driven by the thrill of adventure while judiciously plodding toward greatness.

"When I first traveled from Oneglia to our family's home of origin in Piazza San Matteo, I was but a young man," Andrea proclaimed. "I had much to learn and nothing to offer but a stubborn desire to serve my beloved city," he added. "Genoa is rich in history, and its people noble in nature." Andrea paused to emphasize his next words: "I was much older than your father is now when I commanded my very first ship. The road was long and there was much I had yet to experience."

"Tell me of those experiences, Mesiavo," the boy exclaimed. "Please tell me."

"I've lived too long and there is too much to tell," Andrea quipped. "We'll be here all day and night."

Giovannandrea's face lit up. He could feel one of Andrea's stories coming. The man he called grandfather, the admiral revered by so many, had finally deemed him worthy to share in his exploits. How could Giovannandrea possibly know that Andrea had also been waiting anxiously for this time to come? He'd noticed a considerable spurt in his young nephew's awareness and capacity to absorb information in the last year. *Things grow in their own time*, Andrea always told himself. He drew from his own experience, of course. He was a late bloomer. It took him forty-six years to finally embark on a career as a seaman, and another fifteen to get married! Now, at the tender age of eighty-one, thinking back on his life, he wondered what had taken him so long.

As for why he waited all those many years to tie the knot, the answer slipped off his tongue the second he posed it to himself: ambition. Nothing mattered more to him in his youth than the quest for freedom, which he viewed entirely through the lens of personal power and wealth. It consumed him for his first thirty years of existence. Then something happened. Being a profound and deliberative thinker, he realized that attaining power and influence would give him no satisfaction unless he could put them to good use. His worldly aspirations began to extend outside of himself. Traveling the world had taught him a thing or two about how others lived. He envied Venice's strength and steadiness, and Florence's vision of liberty, while Genoa wallowed in political upheaval. He'd witnessed foreign powers such as France and Spain, the Duchy of Milan, and the Ottomans to the east threaten Genoa's sovereignty, and had vowed to do something about it.

"If you want to hear of my greatest achievement, and my most lasting source of joy, then so be it," he said, assuming a fatherly tone. "It will necessarily involve talk of combat and bloodshed, because unfortunately that is the world in which we now live, but in the end you will learn of our beloved Genoa and how the Republic was formed."

"Wait!" exclaimed Giovannandrea, beside himself with excitement. "I'll be right back."

The boy hopped off Andrea's knee in a flash. He scurried

up to his mother, seated in front of the fire with Giannettino, Gonzaga, and Figueroa, and whispered in her ear. Ginetta promptly leaned over, grabbed a handful of canestrelli, gave one to Placidia seated on her lap, and handed the rest to Giovannandrea, who ran right back to Andrea.

"You can begin your story now, Mesiavo," he said, handing Andrea a cookie. "I'm ready."

"I chose a particularly troubling time to enter our city," Andrea began. "It wouldn't be an exaggeration to say that Genoa in 1484 was in the midst of political and social turmoil."

And for the next hour Andrea chronicled the events of those early days almost entirely uninterrupted. He impressed upon the boy how the petty bickering between families led to increased violence and disruption in the government, a pattern that had persisted on the peninsula for centuries. And, of course, the social and political aspects of the city greatly affected its economic condition as well. Entering into business or into the world of maritime trade for a young neophyte with no capital proved nearly impossible for anyone born outside Genoa's city walls. Andrea was stigmatized as a foreigner and routinely spurned. On the political level, the entire Genoese state, an area encompassing a thin strip of Italy's northwestern coastline, had been governed by the merchant and artisan class, the so-called popolari, since 1339 when the state's first doge took office. From that moment forward, all members of the old noble class, and in particular the Grimaldi, Spinola, Fieschi, and Doria families, were systematically excluded from holding government positions.

Andrea's narration suddenly came to a grinding halt. He

stopped rocking Giovannandrea on his knee, no longer wanting to coddle him as if he were lulling a young child to sleep. What he intended to say next to the boy was serious—more than just a lesson in history or a story meant to entertain or distract, but information of vital import, knowledge to be passed down from generation to generation, and held sacred. He looked Giovannandrea squarely in the eye.

"The Doria are more than a family," he stated firmly. "Like the Romans of old, we are a *gentes*, descendants of one common ancestor, and we have indeed flourished."

Little Giovannandrea couldn't help but interrupt. "Tell me about him, Mesiavo," the boy said. "Tell me about the very first one." After tall tales of war and bloody intrigue, Giovannandrea loved nothing more than hearing stories about the Doria family.

To see Giovannandrea so interested in learning about his family's roots warmed Andrea's heart. *He is surely his father's son*, he thought to himself. As he gazed down at him, then over to Giannettino, engaged in weighty discussions of military strategy and political intrigue with ambassadors and heads of state, he suddenly felt he could see generations into the future, a dynasty of Doria captains, senators, and doges. That gaping hole within his psyche created by the absence of a direct heir was being filled right there and then, and no doubt healed, by an overwhelming sense of calm. Threats of armed revolt and assassination be damned! Imparting the legend of his family's origins was no longer an amusing pastime, something to distract him from his old aching bones, but a sacred ritual to be performed at all costs. Andrea jumped directly into his tale.

"While on his way to the Holy Land to defend our faith in the First Crusade nearly four centuries ago, the French nobleman, Arduino, Count of Narbonne, fell ill outside the gates of our great city and was taken in by the noble house of della Volta, one of Genoa's most respected families. In the days that followed, he met the marquis's young daughter, Orietta, and was impressed by her beauty. The power of love struck him like lightning."

"You mean he didn't go to the Holy Land to fight?" interrupted the boy, obviously a bit disappointed.

Andrea couldn't help but laugh. In a contest between love and war, a young boy's thoughts will always turn to the latter. Andrea knew that well, and of course, he was no different when he was young. Only now, with time as his teacher, did he truly grasp the importance and sheer necessity of love in his life.

He decided to ignore Giovannandrea's question and plow forward, telling him of how the virtuous young Orietta, whom everyone knew as Oria, cared for Arduino night and day, and how she began to return the French nobleman's feelings. After the count regained his health, he asked for Oria's hand in matrimony, which her father happily accepted. Then, driven by his faith and noble sense of duty, Arduino thanked his gracious hosts and resumed his journey east. No sooner did he return from his mission in the Holy Land did he marry the young Oria and settle in our dear city, Andrea explained. Their many sons and daughters were affectionately called *illi d'Auria*, children of Oria, an appellation which eventually gave rise to the family name of d'Oria, or simply Doria.

"And in the centuries that followed, we contributed to the city's vast wealth and culture," Andrea proudly exclaimed.

The names of celebrated forefathers seemed to roll off his tongue. He spoke first of their achievements in the construction of the church of San Matteo, then of their harrowing exploits during the Crusade in the western Mediterranean. In the twelfth century alone, numerous members of the Doria family distinguished themselves in famous sea battles against the Pisans in one instance and the Venetians in another, while a direct forebear to the Oneglia branch of the family, Nicolò di Simone, hosted the emperor of the Holy Roman Empire in his residence in Piazza San Matteo, solidifying the family's fealty to the Ghibelline party as well as to the Empire. It was Nicolò, in fact, who established the Doria coat of arms of an eagle with its wings spread out against a starlit sky. Then, perhaps to add a touch of the legendary to this list of ancestors, Andrea mentioned the infamous Branca Doria, whom Dante Alighieri, the celebrated Florentine poet, had immortalized in his epic poem, *The Divine Comedy*, by tossing him into the frozen depths of hell for treachery and murder, a detail that brought a satisfied grin to little Giovannandrea's face.

"There were thirty-four branches of the Doria family stemming from our noble tree when our first doge drove us all out of the city," Andrea exclaimed. "And we were forbidden all access to the reins of power when we eventually returned." Then, after a moment's reflection, with a bit of irony in his voice, he added: "I, indeed, chose a troubling time to enter our great city."

Chapter Four

CONDOTTIERO DORIA

By the age of thirty, Andrea had established himself as a strong and capable soldier throughout the Italian peninsula and beyond. Years of hard work, bravery in battle, and his natural ability as a leader had eventually won him his first command post in Roccaguglielma, a patch of feudal land 140 kilometers south of Rome. It had been a long and steady road, starting back to when he first entered his Uncle Giovanni's home in Piazza San Matteo, Genoa, after his mother's death. The whiff of animosity and outright hatred that existed between families, political factions, and nobles of older and more recent stock was evident from the moment he set foot in the city. The stench hung in the air like rotting fish. It soon became apparent that he had two distinct paths from which to choose his future: remain in Genoa and enter the fray, or seek his fortunes elsewhere. In the first case he could count only on his good name, but lacked the financial means to secure allies or corrupt his enemies—clear necessities in Genoa's cutthroat environment. As to the second option, the eighteen-year-old could rely on his personal qualities of intelligence, ambition, and strength, which were, quite frankly, the only currencies he could truly depend on at the time. The choice was obvious.

In autumn of that same year, Pope Sixtus IV passed away, giving rise to a papal conclave that brought a Genoese cardinal to the forefront thanks to the combined efforts of his powerful compatriot, Cardinal Giuliano della Rovere, and enough gold to secure a winning number of votes. The new pope, Giovanni Battista Cybo, assumed the title of Innocent VIII, but also bore the informal moniker of "Father" among the people of Rome—a name less laudatory than ironic due to his having sired at least eight illegitimate children. It must be said, however, that he was a proud, albeit shameless, parent since he promptly carted his entire family into the Vatican upon his election and spent much of his time as pope in their company. He therefore left many of his responsibilities to Cardinal della Rovere, who, among other things, was in charge of the papal guard, a military force formed by the cardinal himself under the auspices of the previous pope.

In an age of rampant nepotism, Innocent VIII and Cardinal della Rovere had absolutely no compunctions surrounding themselves with relatives and fellow Genoese citizens such as Nicolò Doria, who was promptly appointed captain general of the papal guard. Upon hearing of his uncle's good fortune, Andrea left Genoa and made his way to Rome in search of employment. After an initial meeting with Nicolò, who took note of the young man's singular intellect and imposing physical stature, Andrea was proffered the rank of officer of the guard.

Not a bad start, Andrea thought to himself. Despite the impressive job title, he had no experience as a soldier, and therefore had to be trained in the martial arts, a discipline he enthusiastically assumed under the guidance of Nicolò himself.

Andrea learned many skills in the eight years that followed, some of which were quite helpful—diplomacy and military strategy, to name a few—but others, unfortunately, less edifying and affirmative in nature, such as cunning and deceit. He saw a world in which having a family or caring for loved ones was viewed as a weakness, and therefore readily exploited by vengeful enemies; a world where arrogance infected all those who called themselves men of the Church, and corruption existed as a normal state of affairs. For better or for worse, Andrea matured under Rome's influence, and it molded him into a man of his times. It honed his natural intelligence. His notion of service to one's city or state grew substantially more personal and even self-serving to an extent, and his sense of heroism and bravery went hand in hand with his natural instinct for self-preservation.

With Pope Innocent VIII's death in 1492, and the election of the notorious Rodrigo Borgia, who assumed the title of Alexander VI, Andrea became persona non grata in Rome. As fortune would have it, he quickly found a position in the service of Guidobaldo da Montefeltro, Duke of Urbino. He was recommended by the prefect of Rome at the time, Giovanni della Rovere, brother to Cardinal Giuliano della Rovere and husband to the duke's sister, Giovanna da Montefeltro. While serving as a palace guard in Urbino, the most refined and cultured realm in

Italy, Andrea no doubt assimilated the courtly arts of gallantry, grace, and decorum to counterbalance the dubious skills he'd picked up in Rome.

But after two years his hunger for adventure eventually got the best of him. He left Urbino to fight alongside King Ferdinand d'Aragon of Naples against the encroaching armies of the French king, Charles VIII, who had recently descended onto the Italian peninsula with twenty-five thousand men, a powerful state-of-the-art artillery, and a burning desire to reclaim the Kingdom of Naples from the Spanish. Andrea's involvement in the war was limited to commanding a small infantry unit, and unfortunately entailed little more than executing a series of retreats from French troops that plowed southward, seemingly at will, through Ferdinand's defenses in Faenza, Rome, and Capua, where the Aragonese king eventually suffered an ignominious defeat and was killed. Andrea then joined forces with Ferdinand's son, Alfonso, who fought valorously against the French, but to no avail. Alfonso, too, had to abandon the cause and flee for his life to Sicily with a select band of confidants. Despite never having the opportunity to effectively showcase his military skills, Andrea possessed bravery and military acumen that must have greatly impressed Alfonso, since the young prince insisted that Andrea accompany his party to Sicily.

Andrea's exploits with the Aragonese were not a total loss, however. He'd earned enough money to bankroll a pilgrimage from Sicily to the Holy Land, and to facilitate his entry into the Order of Solomon's Temple, also known as the Knights Templar. His sojourn in Palestine lasted nearly a year, after which he returned to Italy, where he was able to use the funds he'd accumulated in Rome, Urbino, and Naples to his ultimate advantage. Once back on the peninsula, he saw that the situation had changed substantially since his last experience in Naples. Pope Alexander VI had formed a Holy League that included Spain, the Republic of Venice, the Duchy of Milan, and the Kingdom of Naples in an all-out effort to rid Italy of French occupation. The famous Spanish general Consalvo di Cordova was hired to lead the charge. Andrea could have easily cashed in on his past loyalty to the Neapolitan sovereign, who now seemed to be the winning horse in this conflict, but his intuition pointed him elsewhere. If the last ten years had taught him anything, it was that no amount of magnanimity or good will could buy power and influence, and without them, nothing of greatness could ever be achieved. One needed money for that.

Immediately upon reentering the peninsula, Andrea hired twenty-five expert cavalrymen armed with crossbows, then sold his services to the highest bidder. From his point of view at the time, purging Italy of the French and replacing them with the Spanish changed precious little in the grand scheme of things. In reality, each Italian city-state cared little for its neighbor's welfare or for that of the entire peninsula; each was motivated by its own personal interests and ready to go to war with any number of its confederates once the French had been expelled.

Andrea had made his calculations and figured that throwing his weight behind his old allies, the Spanish, could promise him, at most, a job as a mercenary once the war was over, stamping out skirmishes between local land barons. Siding with the French, on the other hand, despite the likelihood of their defeat, offered him greater financial rewards at the very least, as well as a certain amount of recognition. What further convinced Andrea to team up with the French was Giovanni della Rovere's alliance with them, and the growing probability that Giuliano, his brother and fellow Ligurian, would succeed the current pope. Giovanni had lost portions of his estates to the Spanish and desperately needed to hire someone to make sure his land in Roccaguglielma, a possession a bit south of Rome, didn't suffer a similar fate. But, perhaps most importantly in terms of his long-range goals, Andrea concluded that serving the prefect of Rome would elevate him to the status of *condottiero*—a considerable step up from his present military standing.

It took two days for Andrea and his cavalry to navigate the narrow limestone paths of the Aurunci Mountains from the western coast to the outskirts of Roccaguglielma. There, towering one hundred and fifty meters above a modest hamlet, stood an imposing fortress built by the Normans four centuries earlier. The entire complex was further protected by a massive wall reinforced by twelve bastions of considerable height and density. The fortress's strategic importance became self-evident the moment Andrea laid eyes on it. It controlled the whole area from the ports on the Mediterranean to the territories ruled by the Church to the north. After pausing a moment to take it all in, Andrea proceeded toward the main gate, where he was greeted by Giovanni della Rovere atop a tall, white Andalusian stallion. He was flanked by a squad of four French soldiers who ushered them through the twisted streets of the hamlet and up to the fortress. That evening, after a frugal meal of aged Marzolina goat cheese, dried pork liver sausage seasoned with garlic and orange rinds, local Olivello wine, and generous portions of naturally leavened *criscito* bread, Andrea excused himself and withdrew immediately to his quarters, hoping to get an early start in the morning.

Andrea arose shortly before daybreak to inspect the four corners of the fortress as well as each street, alleyway, and piazza of the hamlet below. Besides wanting to check for breaches and weak spots in the wall, he thought it would be wise and militarily expedient to introduce himself to the shop owners, artisans, and peasants to promote a sense of trust and goodwill among its inhabitants should he be forced to depend on their cooperation. Anxious to get started, he made his way down to the stables. Just as he and two of his soldiers were mounting their horses to begin their reconnaissance, Giovanni della Rovere appeared outside the stable door atop his trusty stallion.

"May I join you?" asked Giovanni with a wide grin that suggested he had no intention of being left behind.

This quickly brought a smile to Andrea's face as well; after all, this was not only Giovanni's land, but the man was also Andrea's commanding officer and a celebrated condottiero in his own right. A special friendship had formed between the two men ever since they had met in Rome, and that bond extended to Giovanni's young son, Francesco, as well as to his wife, Giovanna, whom Andrea had gotten to know quite well during his stay in Urbino.

"By all means come along," Andrea replied as he dug his

stirrups into his horse's underbelly, coaxing it to canter into the bailey.

The two French soldiers accompanying Andrea waited for Giovanni to follow suit before picking up the rear. Within a few minutes they had exited the gatehouse of the hamlet and made their way down a graveled path into the olive groves surrounding the town. Giovanni and Andrea rode side by side, each scanning the massive wall to sniff out potential vulnerabilities. Despite the seriousness of the exercise, the deportment of the two men resembled more a casual outing among friends than a military patrol.

"Is this Cordova fellow as clever as they say?" inquired Andrea, injecting a bit of gravity into their conversation, which until then consisted almost entirely of gossip and recollections of their more intemperate days among the Vatican clergy.

"He has already won back much of what our impetuous King Charles has conquered," Giovanni replied. "He is not to be taken lightly."

"When money, land, and one's reputation is at stake, I take nothing lightly, my dear Prefect," said Andrea with a droll smile.

"You could have easily said that to your previous ally, King Alfonso, good Lord Doria," Giovanni quipped. "He would have welcomed you with open arms."

"His friendship carries little weight when compared with yours."

"I see you have added diplomacy and shameless flattery to your list of skills," Giovanni said lightheartedly, but clearly pleased to hear Andrea's words.

"I have not forgotten what you have done for my brother," Andrea added.

Giovanni took a moment before responding. "It was an act of kindness any good Christian with the fear of God in his heart would have gladly done," he finally replied, trying desperately to affect an air of modesty.

"You risked your life to save him," Andrea said. "A great deal more than a mere act of kindness."

Andrea was referring to his brother Davide, who sought a life in the military after their mother's death. He sailed on behalf of one flag or another for a few years, and embarked on several random adventures in search of fortune as was wont of many young Genoese males at the time. However, unlike Andrea, a man infinitely more suited for such a life and who had decided early in his career to pursue a more reasonable path to the same goal, Davide was not a particularly judicious fellow. It just so happened that on one of these seemingly lawless exploits off the Adriatic coast, Davide's vessel was broadsided by a pirate ship of North African origin. As fate would have it, Giovanni's galley was there to rescue him.

"Don't for a minute think, however, that I have accepted this mission to repay you," Andrea said, half in jest. "I will always remain in your debt."

Before Giovanni could respond, Andrea diverted from the set path to cut through a particularly lush olive grove on the hamlet's southwestern side. His eyes flicked left and right, surveying every aspect of the field until he lifted his gaze over the recently scythed grass in the grove to the town's formidable wall, and finally to the fortress above. After traveling no more than fifty meters through the budding olive trees, Andrea pulled up on his reins, bringing his horse to an abrupt halt. He sat tall in the saddle, motionless, his head tilted upward, fixed on the towering fortress. From this particular angle, peering through the branches, it seemed not only deceptively tranquil but unusually close, even intimate, as if one could almost reach out and touch it. No one dared say a word as Andrea studied the scene. Then, after what seemed to be an eternity, Andrea turned to one of the French soldiers.

"Have every tree in this orchard cut to the ground," he ordered. Then, to answer the question he knew Giovanni would immediately ask given the immense size of the olive grove and the impact its destruction would have on the livelihood of the peasants under his patronage, Andrea quickly added, "I have my reasons."

Giovanni offered no objections. He instead confirmed Andrea's order with a quick nod to the soldier. But Andrea hadn't yet completed his thought; his mind was racing. He turned to the other soldier.

"Transfer all the falconet cannons to the fortress," Andrea said, indicating the wall. "Place them so as not to be visible. And keep the larger culverins where they are."

"Yes, sir," the soldier immediately replied.

"The illusion that the wall is liberally fortified must remain," Andrea added. His attention quickly switched to Giovanni: "Is there anyone among the troops who can converse in Spanish?"

Giovanni thought for a moment, then, evidently knowing no one who fit the description, turned to the soldiers.

"There are several I can think of," said the first soldier.

"I want to see the most reliable among them immediately upon our return to quarters," Andrea ordered.

The soldier nodded. And with that, Andrea loosened up on the reins and prodded the horse's belly with his boot heels just enough to nudge the animal into a slow trot. The four men weaved through the grove and back onto the beaten path with Andrea leading the way. They remained silent for a good portion of the trek to the main gate and throughout the hamlet, but once they entered the fortress and approached the stables, Giovanni pulled up alongside Andrea.

"I have an urgent matter in Sora and Arci," Giovanni said. "I must leave in the morning."

Roccaguglielma clearly had pressing concerns of its own, and Andrea wasted no time in addressing them to his dear friend: "There are practical matters that require your immediate attention."

"I'll send sufficient recompense for the French soldiers who fall under your command for the next six months," Giovanni quickly rejoined. "I trust you will answer for your cavalrymen's needs and stock up accordingly."

"I am of the opinion that sealing myself up in this fortress and subjecting my men, or the townspeople, for that matter, to a long siege would be unwise," Andrea declared, knowing full well that Giovanni understood the need for more resourceful alternatives in a mercenary-style war. "I would very much like to send a mobile unit out on a daily basis to raid the Spanish caravans of grain, livestock, and cheeses that supply Naples."

"Do you not think it would do more to incur Cordova's wrath than to satisfy the appetites of your men?" Giovanni asked.

"Growing fat waiting for his troops to arrive or starving to death while under siege benefits no one but the Spanish," Andrea shot back. "Fine cuts of beef, an occasional bottle of sherry, and saddlebags full of loot will keep them happy and fit for battle."

"And should they encounter Spanish troops during these missions," Giovanni inquired, "what do you propose then?"

"They will do what soldiers are called upon to do," Andrea said. "Fight."

Giovanni's smile registered his firm agreement.

After dinner that evening, Andrea and Giovanni sat in a modestly furnished library adjacent to Andrea's bedchamber. Given the crude nature of the building, erected more as an instrument of war than as a noble residence, there were more boars' heads, pieces of military armor, and paintings of della Rovere family members on the smoky limestone walls than well-worn books. The atmosphere still gave off the slight feeling of erudition and culture, however, despite the family's humble beginnings in Savona. A portrait of Pope Sixtus IV was featured prominently over the fireplace with banners displaying a simple oak tree, the symbol of the della Rovere coat of arms, on either side of it. An intricately carved bookshelf housing just enough classical poetry, political treatises, and manuscripts to amuse Giovanni and his guests occupied most of the opposite wall.

The requisite poems of Petrarch, Dante Alighieri, and the troubadours, as well as Boccaccio's *Decameron* and several books of Holy Scripture, filled an entire rack.

But this was not a night reserved for the arts or discourses on ancient philosophy, nor was it time for cheer. A liter of the local Aglianico sat half empty between the two men, and with Giovanni set to leave in the morning, there was still much to discuss concerning Andrea's mission and Cordova's unhindered advances into the territory.

A sudden rap at the door interrupted their dialogue. Giovanni appeared annoyed at first, but after the second round of knocks he finally called out for the intruder to enter. The chamber door opened to reveal three French soldiers, all relatively similar in appearance: dark curly hair, eyes black as coal, and broad, sloping shoulders. Each one sported a seventeen-inch poignard dagger in his belt and a short double-edged falchion sword at the hip.

"What is it?" barked Giovanni.

The oldest of the three, evidenced by his bushy white beard and balding pate, stepped forward: "We were told to see the captain as soon as possible," he said, snapping a military salute.

Andrea glared intently into the man's eyes, then over at the other two, studying their overall demeanor.

"*Buenas noches,*" he said after a moment. "I trust you are here to exhibit your skills in the Spanish language."

The three soldiers answered in near unison: "*Sí, Capitán.*"

"Excellent. Come, join us for a bit of wine, won't you?" announced Andrea to their surprise.

They obviously were not accustomed to this level of familiarity, especially in the presence of Giovanni, for whom they had fought in Sora a few months earlier. The soldiers gathered around the table as Andrea poured the remainder of the Aglianico into three tin cups. They didn't dare sit, but stood there waiting for Andrea and Giovanni to offer a cursory toast before taking their first gulp. For his part, Giovanni simply followed Andrea's lead, not having the slightest idea what he had up his sleeve. Andrea finally raised his cup high, holding it there until Giovanni and the three soldiers joined him.

"Into the mouth of the wolf," exclaimed Andrea, invoking the standard Italian colloquial expression for "good luck."

The other men offered the obligatory response of "The wolf should die!"

Andrea smiled and quickly added: "The wolf should die, indeed, for it is precisely into the wolf's mouth that I intend to send you."

Chapter Five

IN DEFENSE OF ROCCAGUGLIELMA

Andrea's old, aching bones throbbed under his young nephew's weight. He'd spent nearly an hour filling Giovannandrea's head with stories of his past without so much as a moment's pause. For his part, little Giovannandrea only interrupted Andrea when his curiosity got the best of him. He wanted desperately to know how far cannonballs could fly, what Andalusian horses ate, and what he'd sent those three Frenchmen to do. Otherwise the boy sat glued to his mesiavo's every word, never moving except for his eyes, which widened in awe every now and then. Fortunately for Andrea's sore bones, Giannettino had momentarily withdrawn from Gonzaga's and Figueroa's company to check on matters with his young son, leaving Ginetta to entertain the two men, and giving Andrea the opportunity to shift little Giovannandrea to his other knee.

"I couldn't help but overhear the story of the battle of Roccaguglielma," said Giannettino to his dear uncle.

"You didn't say anything about the battle, Mesiavo," Giovannandrea grumbled.

"I haven't gotten to that part yet," Andrea immediately responded to reassure little Giovannandrea that he hadn't kept anything from him.

"Then it seems I've come just in time," quipped Giannettino.

At that very moment, the chamber door opened to reveal Peretta ushering in a young, handsome gentleman of noble rearing: Gian Luigi Fieschi, a dear friend of the family and frequent visitor to the palazzo. Gian Luigi had a warm, gentle smile that endeared him to everyone at first glance, and like with Giannettino, women would often fall victim to his charm. But unlike Giannettino, the qualities of arrogance, cruelty, and womanizing escaped him. His faults more resembled those of the Young Lover in the bawdy comedies of the day, a character full of naiveté, idealism, and melodrama. Figueroa and Gonzaga straightened up and fidgeted in their seats like a pair of nervous parrots at the sight of Gian Luigi, convinced as they were of his disloyalty to the Spanish overlords, and ultimately to Andrea himself, the de facto Prince of Genoa. Their obvious frenzy caught Andrea's eye, which brought an immediate smile to his lips. *They would suspect their own mother of treachery,* Andrea thought to himself, *if there was political hay to be made of it.*

"My dear Prince," said Gian Luigi as he approached Andrea, his arms outstretched and ready to embrace him, "it warms my heart to see you again."

He greeted Ginetta and little Placidia with a particularly warm embrace, and Figueroa and Gonzaga with a formal handshake and a respectable nod. Before making his way to Andrea, he enveloped Giannettino in a friendly hug accompanied by a customary kiss on both cheeks. The two men were close in age and, despite having been natural rivals for most of their young adult lives, had always shown each other considerable civility. Gian Luigi's admiration for Giannettino's military accomplishments appeared wholehearted and genuine, and Giannettino always demonstrated great respect for Gian Luigi and his reputation as a soft-spoken, unassuming, and highly favored member of one of Genoa's most esteemed families. The Fieschi dynasty had, after all, produced over thirty cardinals and at least four hundred bishops and abbots in the last four centuries, as well as a king of Naples, a canonized saint, and two popes. In the fifteenth century alone they claimed a *signoria* in the Ligurian city of Pontremoli, and two admirals of the Genoese fleet, not to mention a visit by the king of France to their family villa in Via Lata, an event hosted by Gian Luigi's grandfather himself. As reliable allies of the French, the Fieschi were able to amass tremendous amounts of wealth, adding to their power and influence along the Ligurian coast.

"If only your father were here to witness what a distinguished man you have become," Andrea cried out as Gian Luigi approached him.

He and Sinibaldo, Gian Luigi's father, shared a long history together. Their friendship was so close that Sinibaldo abandoned a long-standing family alliance with the Kingdom of France to join Andrea in his fight against them for the liberation of Genoa. Having successfully rid the entire region of French domination, he further aided Andrea in forming a new constitution for the

Republic of Genoa, once again breaking with an old Fieschi tradition of staunch anti-republicanism. A few years later, on his deathbed, he entrusted Andrea as Gian Luigi's guardian, an act of goodwill and devotion that Andrea had never forgotten. From that day forward, any insult or accusation directed at Gian Luigi or the Fieschi family was viewed as a direct affront to Andrea himself. In his eyes, Gian Luigi could do no wrong.

Gian Luigi also made sure to pay little Giovannandrea his due. As he leaned in to gently tousle his hair and caress his cheek, he used the opportunity to greet Andrea as well, which he did with the same respect and intimacy that a young family member would show an esteemed patriarch. Their affection for one another was palpable and on clear display for Gonzaga and Figueroa to digest, as if to say that any suspicion of insurgency or revolt was shameless paranoia.

"Please sit with us, Gian Luigi, and take your mind off the political events and intrigues of our senators," said Andrea, referring to the wrangling going on behind closed doors for the election of the new doge.

"With you, good Prince, and the sage members of the Doria family to guide their hand, we have nothing worry about," said Gian Luigi as he took a seat. He was careful to acknowledge Giannettino sitting right next to him when praising the Doria family's illustrious members.

"Our dear Prince is feeling nostalgic today," Giannettino said. "And should he choose to regale us with his infamous conversation with Captain Consalvo di Cordova, he may very well be revealing a bit of gossip for the history books."

"Poæ, stop, you're giving away the ending to the story!" Giovannandrea cried out to his father.

Giannettino roared with laughter. "That was just the beginning, my son," he said. "Years before fighting pirates and defending our dear Republic, our esteemed admiral here was a brave and fearless condottiero. And as cunning as a fox."

"Not nearly as cunning as your father," said Andrea to the young boy with a laugh. "He is the one who should be telling you stories."

"No one can dispute your cleverness, this is true," said Gian Luigi to Giannettino. "If that scoundrel Niccolò Machiavelli can give tribute in his *De Principatibus* to the pope's son, Cesare Borgia, as the master of all cunning and deceit, what does that say for your dear uncle who once outfoxed Cesare Borgia himself?" he continued, indicating Andrea with a deferential tap on the knee. "That is the story I would like to hear."

"Well, with a little patience and perhaps a bit more Madeira, I may just reach that chapter in my life as well," quipped Andrea.

"Not before telling us where you sent those three Frenchmen," rejoined Giovannandrea to everyone's amusement.

"And I shall fetch the Madeira," said Giannettino.

"And more canestrelli!" Andrea cried out.

By this time, however, Peretta had already gathered up the wine and guided Ginetta and her two distinguished guests back to Andrea's bedside. Placidia followed closely with the plate of canestrelli. They all gathered comfortably around Andrea like obedient schoolchildren.

Andrea began his story by recapping portions of his meeting

with Giovanni della Rovere and his mission in Roccaguglielma, then skipping ahead several weeks to his interaction with the three young Frenchmen.

"Activity in the hamlet reached a fever pitch after we heard that Cordova's troops had occupied the hills just outside Sessa Aurunca, a mere two days' march," Andrea said.

He then went on to assert that although there was no indication that Cordova intended to attack any time soon, his very presence within striking distance set the townspeople abuzz. It had been nearly a fortnight since he'd dispatched the three French soldiers into enemy territory with orders to infiltrate their camp. He instructed them to gain vital information leading to the time, place, mode, and eventuality of an offensive. Their orders were to mingle with the troops, observe their activities, take note of their firepower, and, most importantly, find out if, when, and how Cordova intended to strike. Andrea assured the three men that the assortment of nationalities, languages, and types of combatants among the Spanish forces would serve as a perfect cover for them, and if by chance they were questioned for any reason, they were to say that they were soldiers in the Neapolitan army who had been forcefully conscripted by the French after their entrance into Naples the previous year.

As part of his preparation for the Spanish attack on Roccaguglielma, Andrea circulated freely with its inhabitants nearly every day. He oversaw minor repairs on the wall, displacement of artillery, and the rationing of provisions acquired by the daily raids of his men into the neighboring territories. His familiarity with the hamlet and its people nurtured a certain camaraderie between them that eased their anxieties and provided Andrea with a firsthand assessment of their loyalty should tensions escalate, which they inevitably would. It didn't take razor-sharp insight or an extraordinary level of experience to grasp the fact that the people's allegiance naturally gravitated toward the side promising the most stability and independence, and of course the lowest taxes. The particular customs, language, or eating habits of the occupying forces didn't matter as long as those three criteria topped the list.

Something especially disquieting, however, was stirring up the populace on this particular morning. A scaffold had been erected in the main piazza during the night, attracting a crowd of anxious villagers. Word had gotten out that two of the hamlet's wealthy land owners were arrested the previous evening for conspiring with the Spanish, and that Andrea had called for their immediate execution. With war so close at hand, Andrea didn't have the luxury of ruminating over the matter. He could not allow even the slightest defection to go unpunished; any appearance of indecision would have certainly given the wrong message. From his post at the far end of the piazza, he could see the two prisoners being led up the stairs of the scaffold by a French officer and the local priest. Within minutes the officer slipped a black hood over their heads, the priest recited a short prayer, and the hangman pulled back on the lever that opened the floor beneath them. But as the two bodies fell and the ropes went taut, their necks failed to snap, as was too often the case, causing the two men to writhe violently, gasping for air. The sea of onlookers cried out in horror as the nooses squeezed out the prisoners' last breath. The entire spectacle took no longer than five minutes, and at least for the moment, Andrea could tell himself that a minimum of order and fealty had been restored.

Andrea felt the need to keep out of sight, not for fear of being second-guessed or criticized by the townspeople, but because there were other pressing matters that weighed heavily on his mind. His top lieutenant had just informed him that one of the three French spies had returned bearing an urgent message. Wanting to debrief the man as soon as possible, Andrea made his way up to the fortress without delay. Once in his chamber and seated at his desk with a copious map of the area spread out before him, Andrea ordered the spy to be brought in.

"My Captain, I have word of Cordova's intentions," blurted the young French soldier as he stood at attention in the middle of the room next to the corporal who had escorted him inside.

"Come," said Andrea, beckoning the man to approach the desk, "tell me what you have learned."

"Cordova marches north as we speak," the man said.

"With the intention of attacking us?" Andrea inquired without missing a beat.

"He is quite angry, my Captain," the soldier said. "Our raids on his caravans are an embarrassment to him."

Despite the worrying news, Andrea took some comfort in having agitated his respected opponent. He let a faint smile slip.

"And how do you know this?"

"I was able to befriend an Italian captain who boasted that Cordova wanted desperately to lay waste to Roccagug-lielma . . . ," said the soldier, hesitating in midsentence, "and lock that brazen Genoese captain in chains for the rest of his life." The young spy looked down to the floor, clearly uncomfortable. "I beg your forgiveness, my Captain, but those were his words."

The soldier went on to reveal the size of the Spanish army, as well as the number of their cavalry and archers, the weight of their artillery, the intended date of attack, and many of the intricacies of their battle plan. Andrea quickly realized that he could not rest his entire defense solely on the power of his cannonry and the skill of his troops. His cavalrymen were professional soldiers; they fought not necessarily to win, although it was preferable to defeat, but rather to live and fight another day. Loyalty ran second to survival in their world. Andrea knew something more had to be done, and fast, to neutralize Cordova's overwhelming strength.

"What has become of your two comrades?" Andrea inquired.

The young soldier hung his head low once again, hesitant to say another word. Despite Andrea's eagerness, he waited patiently for the man to regain the courage to speak.

"They have decided, under the circumstances, to remain under Spanish protection," he murmured.

Andrea's face registered no emotion. He'd learned long ago to swallow his emotions at times like these. He stood up and reached out to shake the spy's hand.

"You have done fine work," he declared, going so far as to pat the soldier on the back. He then turned to the French officer who had accompanied the young man: "See to it that he is paid for his services, Corporal."

"Yes, Captain," replied the officer, snapping a salute. Then, in one swift motion, he turned and escorted the young soldier out of the room.

As the door closed behind the two men, Andrea found himself simply staring at the map stretched out before him, his mind racing, and at a loss as to how to proceed. He began to pace the cold terra-cotta floor, as he was wont to do when deliberating important matters. Then, he suddenly crossed to the window that overlooked the main piazza. As he watched everyone going about their daily routine—vendors, blacksmiths, and farriers openly practicing their trade, as well as children playing innocently in the streets—his gaze fixed on the carpenters dismantling the makeshift scaffold. He greeted this simultaneously commonplace and solemn activity with cold resolve, then spun around, marched purposefully to the chamber door, and opened it with a flourish.

"Lieutenant, come in here now!" he shouted. His words reverberated off the corridor's pitted limestone walls, giving them more emphasis and immediacy.

The lieutenant came running within moments. By the time he entered the chamber, Andrea was already seated back down at his desk. He immediately invited the lieutenant to join him at the table, where Andrea set out to explain what he'd just learned from the young spy. The lieutenant took note of each detail and was noticeably concerned when he heard of the enemy's strength and size, but from his body language and demeanor, it seemed clear that he was in complete agreement with the plans Andrea had laid out before him. In the end, however, Andrea wanted to address his preparation for Cordova's arrival.

"As you can see, Lieutenant," Andrea began in a cold, calm voice, "should the enemy manage to break through our walls, we would fall prey to their greater numbers and firepower."

"It is my belief that the extra cannons you had brought to the fortress from the outer wall should serve to protect us," replied the lieutenant.

"I cannot rely on your belief of what will protect us, Lieutenant—or mine, for that matter," Andrea shot back. "I must be absolutely certain."

The lieutenant shifted in his seat in anticipation of Andrea's next words. *Is he recommending an eventual surrender, or a treaty of some kind?* he thought to himself. *Surely this young captain knows Giovanni della Rovere would never accept such an outcome.*

"We must secure the safety of Roccaguglielma and its inhabitants," Andrea went on, "the woman, children, and elderly in particular." He made sure to lock eyes with the lieutenant, whom he knew to be a wise and courageous soldier. "I want them separated from the men and brought up to the fortress, where they will be housed and cared for during the battle."

The lieutenant hid his surprise and suppressed his immediate concerns as to the logistics of such an operation. Instead, he responded as a good soldier.

"Yes, Captain, immediately."

"As to the men, they will do battle alongside our troops," Andrea continued. "And let them know that they must fight not only for their *signore*, Giovanni della Rovere, but for their wives and children, whose very lives we hold in our hands."

Whether this was intended as a threat to the men of the hamlet or as a comfort to them mattered little to the lieutenant. His captain had imposed an order, and it was to be carried out swiftly and effectively. He sprang from his chair and marched out of the room.

By the next day Roccaguglielma stood poised to resist an imminent attack. All the women, children, and elders of the hamlet had been shepherded into the fortress without incident, and the remaining men, for all intents and purposes, were enrolled as appendages into the French army, and coerced into defending not only the interests of their master, Giovanni della Rovere, but the lives of their loved ones. Andrea spent a good part of that early morning accounting for his actions to the men, impressing upon them that without their assistance Roccaguglielma would surely be lost, and its inhabitants slaughtered. Every able-bodied male, of which there were few, was equipped with a weapon to confront the almost certain Spanish infiltration of their protective walls. Andrea then dispatched several mobile units into the far reaches of the valley to keep the Spanish troops continually off-balance with attacks from the rear.

Andrea passed the rest of the morning witnessing the arrival of Cordova's troops into the outlying areas from atop the fortress's highest bastion. He paid special attention to enemy movements in and around the olive grove he had razed a few weeks earlier. To his delight, it appeared that they steered clear of it and embedded their thirty-two-pound culverin cannons on the opposite side of the hamlet. Since his spy had informed him of Cordova's battle plan, Andrea felt adequately prepared. All he could do now was wait.

The first blast of artillery fire came the next morning at dawn. The rays of the rising sun beyond the Aurunci foothills had barely cast their shadow over the land when the cannonballs from Cordova's guns rained down on the hamlet like a late summer's storm. The eastern wall absorbed hours of constant battering while the Spanish infantry marched on the southernmost wall with ladders and battering rams, all with little success. The massive Norman bulwark seemed impenetrable; French gunfire and swarms of arrows met the infantry at every turn, and since the hamlet had effectively been evacuated, the only damage was structural. However, Andrea knew it was just a matter of time before a breach in the wall would usher in scores of enemy soldiers. The Normans had built a wall substantial enough to withstand any invading army with impunity, but they knew nothing of sixteenth-century technology and the havoc it could inflict. Once again, all Andrea could do was wait.

By midafternoon a minor breach had formed at the base of the eastern wall. Within minutes, hundreds of Spanish infantrymen stormed into the hamlet only to find themselves rushed by a phalanx of farmers, artisans, and shopkeepers armed with whatever blunt instrument they had been issued. Those infantrymen who managed to survive the gauntlet of pitchforks, spades, and wooden clubs were picked off nearly at will by the archers and arquebusiers perched atop the neighboring rooftops. To add insult to injury, the Spanish had to halt all artillery fire for fear of strafing their own troops while the French culverins in the fortress continued to pound the enemy outside the walls without interruption. Seeing his chances of getting a foothold inside the hamlet fading fast, Cordova ordered a hasty retreat, leaving scores of his troops lying dead in the streets. Andrea had won the day, but knowing enough not to rest on his laurels, he gathered his lieutenants in his chamber that evening in preparation for the inevitable onslaught of Spanish troops and artillery the next morning.

While the townspeople spent nearly the entire night mending the previous day's breach in the wall to stave off an early morning incursion, Andrea's mobile units struck the enemy with sporadic raids in the outlying hills. The units had already hit Spanish supply convoys the day before and continued to harass them well into the night, which completely frustrated the notoriously bumptious Spanish captain. To his embarrassment, just two days into the battle Cordova was already struggling to provide ammunition and foodstuff for his infantry and artillery units, complicating what was supposed to be a routine conquest of vulnerable feudal land. Having long ago gained the title of El Gran Capitán, owing to his shrewd military mind and impressive string of victories, Cordova found his reputation was at stake. What seemed to annoy him most was being outsmarted and outmaneuvered by a relatively unknown quantity. When he woke up the following morning and stood before his gilded mirror to trim his iconic silver goatee and map out his strategy, he swore to himself he'd have his pesky Genovese rival in chains by the midday meal.

For his part, Andrea woke up well before dawn, as he was wont to do, and after seeing to it that his troops did the same, he immediately set them to work in preparation for the day's hostilities, which he intuitively knew would be far more ferocious. He first ordered the positions of the culverins in the fortress moved in order to gain a better vantage point over the incoming Spanish forces; then he instructed the townspeople to hold off as long as possible from striking back at those who infiltrated the hamlet in the event of another breach. Andrea's logic was to use the enemy's strength against them by giving them the illusion of imminent victory and luring them into the open spaces of the piazza. He wagered that Cordova, hoping to inflict his coup de grâce and restore his good name, would then predictably order a full incursion into the hamlet, making his men easy targets for the arquebusiers and archers perched on the ramparts of the fortress as well as for the townspeople who would assemble behind them to block their retreat. With everything finally set in place and poised for action, Andrea took his position atop the fortress's southernmost bastion and waited for Cordova to make his move.

The scenario played out more or less as Andrea had planned. Once Cordova's cannons blasted a sizable hole in the eastern wall, his men poured into the streets of Roccaguglielma in droves. Meeting no resistance, they continued on through the hamlet until they reached the main piazza at the foot of the fortress. With a majority of his forces now inside the walls, Cordova called a halt to all bombardment, allowing his men to storm the French stronghold unimpeded and out of harm's way.

The cessation of Spanish artillery cued Andrea's counteroffensive. He raised his arm high into the air to ready his archers, and held it there until he saw the Spanish take their first strides up the hill toward the fortress. Then, in one swift, determined flourish, he let his arm drop to his side.

"Fire!" he shouted.

Scores of French longbow archers, together with Andrea's hired crossbowmen lining the fortress's defensive wall, unleashed a swarm of arrows onto the Spanish troops below. As was the case the day before, the Spanish found themselves virtually trapped between a dark cloud of arrows descending upon them and the arquebusiers' incessant gunfire to their backs. Also in a repeat of the previous day's conflict, they immediately sensed a massacre in the making. The men who remained from the charge up the hill quickly beat a retreat into the narrow streets of the hamlet to dodge the violent thrust of lead balls, arrows, and deadly crossbow bolts felling every third infantryman. Caught in the maze of alleyways, the soldiers then faced scattered attacks by the townspeople blocking their path back to the breach in the wall and out to safety. The day ended with Cordova once again deprived of a victory. The French could breathe easy for yet another twelve hours until the inevitable next attack.

Although Andrea's strategy frustrated Cordova's attempts to storm the fortress, the prospects of securing a decisive victory grew increasingly slim. French troops had suffered scores of casualties and nearly half of the culverins were put out of commission. Andrea took great pride in the defensive efforts of the townspeople, and to a certain extent they had made a crucial difference in the outcome, but too many of them died in the last two days fighting for the lives of their family to present a credible threat to the Spanish. Any sense of relief Andrea might have enjoyed watching the Spanish soldiers turn around and retreat to their camp in the outlying hills was quickly followed by a profound restlessness and unease. His overall strategy had its limits; he could feel it in his gut. His defense of Roccaguglielma proved to be honorable, that was true, and he'd surely earned the respect of his men as well as that of his adversaries—Consalvo di Cordova in particular. But the technical superiority of the Spanish and their overwhelming numbers made it abundantly clear that sooner or later victory would be theirs. And when that day came, Andrea was sure Cordova would move quickly to restore his ailing reputation with a conclusive and merciless trouncing.

Andrea lay in bed that night with the words of that young French spy ringing in his ears: *Cordova wanted desperately to lay waste to the village of Roccaguglielma and lock that brazen Genoese captain in chains for the rest of his days.*

Chapter Six

OUTFOXING THE FOX

Andrea did not awaken to the ravages of Cordova's cannon fire as he had predicted, but rather to an eerie and uncanny peace. Except for the faraway screeches of a tawny owl and the raspy chatter of magpies, a bone-chilling silence hung in the air, which was a nagging detail that concerned him far more than the last forty-eight hours of carnage. Andrea couldn't help but think back to the stories and superstitions he'd heard as a young boy from the town elders jabbering in the piazza. Birds portended sheer evil, they often proclaimed; their flight patterns, chirps and trills, and even their varied shapes, sizes, and colors predicted the future in one way or another. He recalled his tutor in Oneglia speaking of the ancient Etruscans and how they believed that a bird alighting on your windowsill in the morning brought misfortune to the household for the entire day, and how the Romans regarded the wise and inscrutable owl as a bitter harbinger of death. Everything about this particular morning made Andrea restless and filled his mind with rapid-fire thoughts of what could go wrong, stirring up his anxieties and stoking his most irrational fears.

The sun had barely shown itself over the far-off eastern hills, giving a pale, shadowy tint to the landscape. Andrea leaped from his bed and rushed to the fortress's tallest bastion, where, as the darkness slowly receded, he could perceive shades of movement in the Spanish camp. By this time yesterday, and the day before, Cordova's guns had already begun to wreak havoc on Roccaguglielma's eastern wall. Something different was in the works this morning. All signs led to a change in strategy, a pause in hostilities, perhaps, and the beginning of a long, drawn-out siege. Andrea had heard stories of how Cordova distinguished himself in the battle of Granada, Spain's last Muslim stronghold, while he was still a young man, and how he subsequently gained a reputation as a brave and accomplished leader during the sieges of Montefrío, Loja, Íllora, and Tajara, all otherwise impenetrable walled towns. No one had to tell Andrea that unless he could count on the assistance of more French troops marching in from the north, things did not bode well.

That simple reality stared him in the face. *The incessant chirping of the magpies and hooting of those damn owls had foreshadowed all this*, Andrea thought to himself. He immediately retreated to his chamber, where he was met by his top lieutenants.

"See to it that our mobile units continue to disrupt their supplies," Andrea commanded. "Our northern gate currently allows for ample amounts of munitions and provisions to flow freely, and it must remain that way in the event of a complete and protracted blockade. In the meantime, we cannot sit back and wait for Cordova's next move."

Then, just as Andrea was about to issue another order, a pounding shook the chamber door. The corporal who had accompanied the young spy into the room several days earlier came running inside.

"There is word from the emissary of King Charles," the corporal blurted out.

Andrea's gaze remained firmly on his lieutenants seated around the table before he finally turned his attention to the corporal. His expression did not change. Under no circumstances would Andrea allow himself to appear excitable or fleeting in front of his officers, in spite of whatever he might have felt inside. He could read the corporal's body language enough to know that whatever news he carried with him could drastically amend his plans for a counteroffensive, or dispose of them completely, and most likely call for immediate and decisive action. Since he could not tell, however, whether the corporal's announcement would be helpful or detrimental to his cause, Andrea prepared himself in that very instant, body and mind, for either of those possibilities. He straightened up in his seat and made sure to project a sense of judiciousness and authority, the fears and anxieties with which he had begun the day notwithstanding, lest he lose the confidence of his men.

"He and Ferdinand of Spain have signed a truce," said the corporal. "All hostilities must cease immediately."

A sense of relief permeated the room. True to form, Andrea didn't flinch; his carriage remained upright and firm. While some may have hazarded a smile at times like these, Andrea waited for the messenger to deliver his entire communiqué before registering an official reaction.

"On what terms?" he asked calmly.

"Both parties shall retain their conquered land," the corporal quickly replied.

As the corporal elaborated, it became clear that the conditions of the treaty did not yield Roccaguglielma to the Spanish king, but it did seem to give him rights to the territory he currently held on the hamlet's outskirts. This, of course, created a complicated and confusing political situation on the ground, which in effect diminished Giovanni della Rovere's authority over the land since the Spanish now occupied the entire region from the northern border of the Kingdom of Naples to Roccaguglielma's doorstep.

"I see," Andrea replied, doing his best to mask his mild disappointment.

Being an ambitious man, Andrea had set his sights on total victory, despite the odds being so obviously stacked against him. He did realize, however, that he had far exceeded the expectations of his dear friend Giovanni, who in all probability had given up hope of sustaining his rule over the territory. The more Andrea thought about the corporal's words, the more he recognized the weight of his accomplishment: He'd managed to keep Cordova's forces at bay for the last two days, which, it turned out, made all the difference in the world to the final outcome. On a geopolitical level, France maintained a foothold in the corridor running from the Kingdom of Naples north to the Papal States, and on a personal level, Andrea's reputation as a military man would grow exponentially.

This explained, perhaps, why he experienced only a mild and temporary disappointment upon hearing the news of a truce, rather than complete disillusionment. In the split second that all of those conflicting thoughts raced through his mind, his facial expression went from inscrutable to one of conveying modest relief. His lips may have even curled into a faint smile for a moment or two, but definitely not long enough for anyone to notice, or so he hoped.

In the days that followed, a strange and somewhat encouraging atmosphere took hold: The troops of the opposing forces, buoyed by the recent truce, gathered in the fields outside the walls for long nights of feasting and merriment of all sorts. With Andrea's consent, many of the Spanish fighters would mingle with the French soldiers and townspeople in the hamlet itself. Cordova was so impressed with the conviviality shown by his former adversaries, and by Andrea's liberality in particular, that he decided to return the favor. Curious to meet the young Genoese captain who had displayed such surprisingly bold and clever tactics in battle, Cordova sent a message to Andrea inviting him to his quarters for an afternoon of fine wine and true Spanish hospitality. Much to Cordova's surprise, Andrea replied with a gracious note of acceptance.

The following day, with the noon sun blistering overhead, Andrea paraded into the Spanish camp sparing no expense to make an excellent first impression. He appeared in a fully armored breastplate over a shirt of Egyptian linen, red-and-white striped breeches, and knee-high riding boots with rowel spurs of gilded copper. Rounding out this showcase of elegance and reverence for his host, Andrea chose a select squad of his most trusted, and handsomely dressed, cavalrymen to accompany him.

Having been alerted well in advance of Andrea's arrival, Cordova went out of his way to personally greet him at the entrance of his tent. He, too, put his entire military regalia on display. The two men stood face-to-face, peering intently into each other's eyes, both allowing a warm smile to surface as they addressed each other. Being the guest, Andrea was first to pay his respects.

"It is an honor to meet you, Gran Capitán," he said, bowing his head ever so slightly.

Andrea's towering height, physical vitality, and regal demeanor so captured Cordova's immediate attention that the Spanish captain let several moments of awkward silence slip before responding.

"Rarely have I witnessed a man's outward appearance so handsomely match his lofty reputation," Cordova replied, grinning from ear to ear. "The honor is, of course, all mine."

Cordova respectfully stepped aside and welcomed Andrea into his quarters with a slight flourish of his hand. He joined Andrea as he crossed the threshold, and together they made their way to a spectacularly long oak table lavishly prepared for the midday meal. What made the milieu even more noteworthy, besides the table's enormous size, was that it was only set for two people.

"Make yourself at home," Cordova said, once again gesturing with a swish of his hand for Andrea to take a seat.

Cordova wasted no time flattering his guest with snippets of favorable gossip he'd heard about him. And for his part, Andrea responded with words of sincere admiration and respect, never hesitating to refer to his host as Gran Capitán, and always deferring to the Spanish captain's knowledge and expertise throughout their conversation. Although Cordova had recently turned forty-two, he had the appearance of a wizened military man. Streaks of gray blended with a mane of jet black hair that was pulled tightly away from his face. Not a whisker of his goatee and pencil-thin moustache appeared out of place, which, together with his rigid posture and the habit of wearing his chin high, gave him the air of a pompous Spanish gentlemen, a trait he masterfully counterbalanced with an endearing smile and an aversion to ever talking about himself. His eyes burned with vigor and met Andrea's equally determined gaze head-on. They spoke of war and episodes of valor in tones befitting a leisurely afternoon meal. Cordova seemed particularly interested in Andrea's experience in the Franco-Aragonese War several years earlier.

"Is it true you fought in Faenza against the invading French army?" he asked.

"In Rome and San Germano as well," Andrea added.

He was about to say more, but was interrupted by a flurry of entrées and wines being rushed to the table. It didn't take long for Andrea to realize that his gastronomical conditions in Roccaguglielma were considerably less luxurious than those of his Spanish counterpart. Not one dish being set before him even remotely resembled the banalities produced within his own modest kitchen. The servants wheeled out one gastronomic specialty after another, all recipes gleaned from the most fashionable culinary book of the period, *De honesta voluptate et valetudine*, a guide highlighting foods that ranged from warm, soothing broths and roasted meats to fanciful candied fruits and fine aged cheeses. A large *girarrosto*, or rotisserie, featured a suckling pig seasoned with rosemary, fennel, and fresh-squeezed blood oranges. Platters of veal loin, grilled lamb, *anatra all'arancia* (duck in orange sauce), and El Gran Capitán's personal favorite, *piccione crostata*—a tart of spit-roasted pigeon tempered with a creamy *agresto* paste made of green grapes, prunes, almonds, garlic, parsley, and bread crumbs—occupied nearly every inch of table space between the two men.

"I was spared the Battle of Capua when King Alfonso called me to Naples," Andrea finally said as a young servant filled his bowl with beef consommé laced with milled cinnamon.

"And what did you make of the efficiency of our Aragonese troops?" Cordova inquired.

Andrea shifted in his seat. Although Cordova's tone had so far given Andrea no reason to feel scrutinized or pressured, this line of inquiry required ample doses of seat-of-the-pants diplomacy and tact. After all, he was sitting across from one of the most illustrious military captains on the continent. Each word he uttered or idea he espoused, every movement of his body or facial gesture, right down to the subtle rise of an eyebrow, spoke volumes. Men's reputations lived or died on much less.

"There was no comparison between the two sides," Andrea replied, locking eyes with Cordova. "We were all undistinguished infantrymen reinforced with courage and valor, but we had no strategy and precious little tack other than trying to scare the daylights out of the French by virtue of our overwhelming numbers."

"They, on the other hand, had an infantry, cavalry, and artillery that marched according to a well-thought-out plan," Cordova was quick to interject. "Am I wrong?"

"It was their artillery that made the difference," said Andrea.

"How so?"

"First of all, there seemed to be no end to the French culverins and heavy mortars, and they were mounted on wheeled carriages pulled by horses that were exceptionally robust and swift," Andrea replied without hesitation. "Never have I seen an artillery advance with such impetus."

"Which was also seamlessly incorporated into their infantry and cavalry, I am told," Cordova added.

"We never expected such discipline and precision," replied Andrea, not even bothering to hide his admiration of the French in front of his Spanish host. "Their iron cannonballs blasted right through our protective walls, making retreat our only option," he lamented. Then, perhaps fearing he'd gone too far, Andrea made sure to give Alfonso's son, Ferdinando, his due: "Thank God for our condottiero. Despite his youth and the gravity of our losses, his dignified character and courage filled me and all the Aragonese forces with confidence and the willingness to keep fighting."

Given the shift of the discussion toward a decidedly weightier subject, Cordova reached across the table for entrées carrying more substantial nutrition.

"I suspect you would have been doomed without him," Cordova said dutifully as he slid the salvers of veal and grilled lamb in Andrea's direction. "Eat up," he said. "Your nettlesome mobile units failed to abscond with any of our more precious livestock during their raids, so there's plenty of it to go around."

Andrea thought it wise not to respond directly, only letting a faint smile surface, and decided instead to continue the previous conversation while lifting a handful of lamb chops and several hefty slices of veal onto his plate.

"The slow, humiliating retreats after Faenza and Rome took their toll," Andrea said, his voice easing into a storytelling rhythm. "And the faster the French snuck up behind us, the more men unfortunately deserted our ranks."

"As a man and a soldier, I can share in your pain," Cordova replied with only the slightest touch of emotion. He was beginning to lose interest in reliving those French victories. He'd analyzed and reanalyzed the performance of the Aragonese troops during Charles VIII's descent into the Kingdom of Naples countless times, and being the discerning and meticulous student of war that he was, he came away with all the lessons in military strategy he needed.

What seemed to be stirring up Cordova's curiosity now was

how this young, relatively inexperienced Genoese captain sitting across from him managed not only to stay alive in the wake of a devastating assault, but essentially thrive. What could he have done differently, Cordova kept asking himself. Surely, Roccaguglielma should have fallen within the first few hours.

"Tell me, Captain . . . ," Cordova said, hesitating a moment before completing his thought.

The moment had arrived for which this entire occasion had been created, and Andrea could feel it. The intensity in Cordova's eyes set Andrea's adrenaline racing.

"What did you think of my decisions, or the comportment of my soldiers, in battle?" Cordova finally said in a calm, subdued voice.

The directness and outright sincerity of the question astounded Andrea; it left him speechless at first, with his mind flipping through all the possible answers, and anticipating Cordova's myriad reactions in return. Was this a test, perhaps? An interview of sorts? A trap? In the end, Andrea fielded the inquiry the only way he could: honestly, but with a healthy amount of discretion.

"There was little you could have done much differently," Andrea said. "Our solid defense was a product of the bravery and determination of our soldiers, and of course the configuration of Roccaguglielma itself, a fortress extremely difficult to penetrate without a considerable loss of life."

Appreciating Andrea's unwillingness to displease, but eager to understand what went awry, Cordova asked again: "My dear Captain, do not hesitate to speak your mind. I ask in all candor, gentleman to gentleman, because I have never encountered such a tenacious and brilliant resistance to such overwhelming superiority in all my career. I implore you to state the bold truth. Your words will not offend. In fact, I would be extremely grateful."

This was no test, nor was it a trap of any kind. The secret to Cordova's success was revealing itself to Andrea in stark and quite practical terms. If his years in Rome awakened a youthful Andrea to the cynical and scheming ways of the world, and his time at Guidobaldo da Montefeltro's court in Urbino fashioned him into a fine young gentleman, then it could be said that his experiences on the battlefield fighting for both the Spanish and the French molded him into a formidable and respected condottiero. And now the legendary Consalvo di Cordova was deeming him worthy enough to share in his insights on how to become an astute and refined military strategist: First, delve dispassionately into past strategies and maneuvers, then identify the outcome of those military actions, examine them, learn from them, and move on.

With all of this in mind, Andrea was careful to craft his response to Cordova's request with all the finesse of a diplomat and the wisdom of a true leader.

"What I have already answered with respect to the fortitude of my soldiers, and the disposition of Roccaguglielma's fortress, I can confirm once again with confidence. However, there was perhaps one thing that you might have overlooked."

El Gran Capitán's curiosity was suddenly piqued. He reached for the terra-cotta ewer of Tempranillo wine he had brought with him from his native Spain and filled Andrea's cup to the brim.

"There was one detail that, if you had detected it, would have tilted the odds decisively against us," Andrea added.

"And what may that be?" inquired Cordova.

Despite having already determined that the Spanish captain's intentions were pure, Andrea struggled with what he was about to reveal. He feared coming across as demeaning, or that his words would be misinterpreted, but most of all he wanted to avoid any damage to the man's pride. Andrea lifted the cup of wine to buy some time, and let it hang there until Cordova did the same. After an awkward pause, they clinked cups, and drank.

"Had you stationed your guns in the wooded area around the olive grove on the southwestern slopes, you would have found it easier to break through our defenses," Andrea finally blurted out. "Entering from that angle, you would have met less resistance, and would have succeeded in dividing our forces irreparably."

"My lieutenants determined that area to be too barren and unprotected for our culverins," replied Cordova.

"The trees would have provided the perfect cover for your artillery and rendered them impervious to our archers," Andrea added. "Knowing that a man of your caliber would immediately realize the grove's strategic importance, I had all the trees cut to the ground several days before your arrival."

"Which forced us to plant our cannons on the wall's northeastern side," Cordova grumbled, suddenly realizing he'd been outsmarted.

"Where we waited fully prepared for your assault," said Andrea as if finishing the sentence for him.

Cordova sat stone-faced, letting Andrea's words sink in. Andrea could only wonder what his Spanish counterpart was thinking as he locked eyes with him. Had he revealed too much? Should he have nuanced that last phrase a bit more? In any event, Andrea felt prepared for the worst. After a moment, he noticed a faint smile begin to surface on Cordova's face. *An encouraging sign*, Andrea thought to himself. The smile then grew into a toothy grin, followed by a giggle, and finally an all-out belly laugh. The lightheartedness of Cordova's reaction dispelled whatever fears or misgivings Andrea might have had. In fact, he felt compelled to join in on the amusement. Within seconds, the two men were in stitches.

"Brilliant!" bellowed Cordova, hardly able to control his laughter. "Absolutely brilliant!"

Chapter Seven

DEATH IN SENIGALLIA

Everyone at Andrea's bedside grew increasingly intrigued as the story of Roccaguglielma unfolded. Figueroa fixated on Cordova's beard, evoking fits of laughter every time he inquired as to its length, shape, and color; Gonzaga repeatedly asked about the fortress, its size and dimensions, and its configuration with respect to the hamlet itself; Giannettino wanted to know all the details regarding the mobile units; and little Giovannandrea's interest in the Spanish thirty-two-pound cannons knew no bounds—his eyes went agog with each mention of them. Even Ginetta floated a query or two. Only Gian Luigi appeared a bit restless with the thrust of the narrative, staying conspicuously disengaged throughout Andrea's account, almost to the point of distraction.

"Cat got your tongue?" asked Giannettino.

"I apologize for being too enthralled in our Prince's heroic exploits to speak," quipped Gian Luigi.

"I thank you for the compliment," Andrea said with a smile,

"but if I'm not mistaken, I believe I saw you a bit too interested in tasting Peretta's canestrelli to truly speak your mind."

The room broke into laughter.

"Guilty as charged," Gian Luigi replied, chuckling along with the crowd. "But allow me to add, dear Prince, that your knack for shifting effortlessly from warrior to diplomat—and matching wits with the great Consalvo di Cordova, whom I have heard could not be outdone in both savagery and sophistication—filled me with admiration. I can only dream of possessing such talents. But truth be told, it is your meeting with the infamous Cesare Borgia that genuinely provokes my interest."

Andrea's encounter with Cesare Borgia, known to many as Duke Valentino, had all the earmarks of a truly flattering story, but Andrea shied away from telling it at every turn. Although the episode revealed clever facets of his personality, and illustrated a resourcefulness and strategic acumen few men could claim, it also dug a bit too deeply into Andrea's emotional side, a part of him he rarely allowed others to see.

People had long since learned that delving into Andrea's personal life carried certain risks, especially in matters concerning his relationships with women. When it came time for his friends and associates to settle down and get married, for instance, or to stop their endless carousing from brothel to brothel, Andrea refused to follow their lead. Marriage was not his cup of tea. He'd made up his mind on that issue long ago, partly due to the intimacy required of it, something that always caused him discomfort, but mostly because of his unquenchable thirst for success. He had no time for women. Not out of a lack of appreciation—far from it. He simply believed that the life of a soldier constantly going off to war, or that of a ship's captain forever seeking adventure, stood in stark contrast to maintaining a healthy marriage and negotiating the responsibilities of a family. And since the story of his meeting with Cesare Borgia took place in the prime of his life and involved a woman—a very special woman, in fact—Andrea preferred to keep it to himself.

"There was no shrewder, more devious, or more unscrupulous man alive than Cesare Borgia," Gian Luigi reiterated.

"Except, perhaps, his father, His Holiness Pope Alexander VI," Andrea replied. "But allow me to set the record straight," he was quick to add. "Borgia and I never actually met face-to-face."

"In any event, it is said that you, my dear Prince, got the best of him," said Gian Luigi.

Andrea answered him flatly and without a hint of bravado: "Both he and his father were sworn enemies of the della Rovere family, and therefore no friends of mine."

"Forgive my ignorance," said Figueroa. "I, of course, have heard tell of the Borgia pope's infamous deeds, but as to his son—how, if I may ask, has he gone about earning such a notorious reputation?"

"You have your youth as an excuse for your unfamiliarity with the man," Andrea responded. "Let me only say that Gian Luigi speaks the truth when he labels Cesare Borgia, the infamous Duke Valentino, the most duplicitous and cunning prince of his time."

"Our good friend Count Fieschi seems particularly interested in the underhandedness of it all," interjected Gonzaga, giving Gian Luigi a side-eyed glance, "and I, quite frankly, would love to hear you tell it."

"As would I," said Giannettino, playing into Gonzaga's hidden allegation of the Fieschi family's disloyalty to the Spanish.

Irked by the insinuation, Andrea was about to issue a mild rebuke when his wife chimed in.

"As would I," Peretta said, slipping Andrea a playful wink to free him of any guilt for airing one of his early *affaire de coeurs*.

For his part, Andrea felt inclined to change the subject entirely and frustrate everyone's expectations, but little Giovannandrea insisted he tell the story. Evidently, Consalvo di Cordova wasn't nefarious enough to capture the boy's imagination, but Cesare Borgia seemed to fit the bill perfectly.

"Why was he called Duke Valentino?" Giovannandrea asked.

Andrea bit his lip, regretting ever getting himself into this mess, but a good mesiavo couldn't disappoint his young nephew. He took a deep breath and launched into his tale.

"Cesare Borgia was the son of Pope Alexander VI," Andrea began. "When his oldest brother was killed, some say by Cesare himself, he abandoned his robes as a cardinal of the Church to become a ruthless condottiero."

"Can a man just stop being a cardinal?" asked little Giovannandrea.

"When your father is the pope, all is possible," his mesiavo replied.

Andrea then spoke of Cesare Borgia's plans to carve out territory in the Marche and Romagna regions of central Italy, a scheme he and his father cooked up, ostensibly to increase the power and influence of the Church. In reality, they wanted to form principalities over which the Borgias, and in particular Cesare himself, could rule with impunity.

"But how did he get the name 'Valentino'?" Giovannandrea insisted.

"I see you have your father's impatience," quipped Andrea, shooting Giannettino a quick smile.

Giannettino reached over and lovingly ruffled his son's hair, calling on him to settle down.

"I'm sorry, Mesiavo," whispered Giovannandrea.

"No need to apologize, my son," Andrea replied. "With the proper guidance, that restlessness of yours will mature into valor and strength, also just like your father."

Now that the air had cleared, Andrea felt compelled to slake Giovannandrea's boyish curiosity by describing how Cesare Borgia curried favor with King Louis XII of France, and was conferred the title of Duke Valentino shortly thereafter. The byname of Valentino stuck with him ever since. With the money put at his disposal by the French king, who had even more appetite to keep a foothold in Italy than his predecessor, Borgia set out to recruit an army of Italian and transalpine mercenaries to launch his military adventures. His campaign of terror began in the Marche region in 1500, and there seemed to be no stopping him. Italy had perhaps found its savior, some thought, the perfect leader to keep the interminable flow of foreign armies into the peninsula at bay, a man whose brutality was equaled only by his natural cunning and skullduggery.

Providing an example of the young Borgia's masterful trickery, Andrea recounted the conquest of Urbino. Given the strong connection Andrea felt to the city and its ruling family, he told it with a tear in his voice. Borgia had made the wise decision from the outset of refraining from the use of force against the city, knowing full well that the popularity of its leader, Duke Guidobaldo, would inspire the people of Urbino to come to his aid. Instead, Borgia went out of his way to create a false sense of friendship and confederation with Guidobaldo by asking for his help in attacking the neighboring signoria of Camerino. Guidobaldo agreed, but immediately after he had begun to dispatch infantry, artillerymen, and supplies, not to mention mule drivers to navigate the region's precipitous cliffs, he discovered that it was all a ruse: Borgia and his troops were marching on Urbino at that very moment. With no time to assemble a credible resistance, Guidobaldo decided to abandon the city.

After his conquest of Urbino, Borgia turned his wrath on Camerino, imprisoning its ruler, then having him strangled, along with his three children, by his insanely ruthless henchman, Michelotto. Borgia then set his sights on Senigallia along the Adriatic coast, a powerful city that had been ruled by none other than Giovanni della Rovere for many years, which is where Andrea's story of outsmarting Borgia—the infamous Duke Valentino—actually began.

Andrea's descriptions of Borgia's uncanny ability to attack like a lion while also weaving delicate webs of deceit fascinated everyone in the room. But Andrea refused to plow forward with the more sensational parts of the story, opting instead to ponder the fateful day when he stood at Giovanni della Rovere's side as he lay dying in his chamber bed. It was 1501, nearly five years after the battle of Roccaguglielma. Andrea had remained in Giovanni's service ever since, following him into the Marche region, where he was contracted to maintain the peace over the vast della Rovere territory in and around Senigallia. The entire area had become a dangerous hunting ground over the last year as Borgia moved northward from Rome, leaving a trail of blood and destruction in his wake. It was just a matter of time before Senigallia fell into his crosshairs, and everyone knew it, most of all Giovanni, who feared his imminent death would leave his wife, Giovanna, and young son, Francesco, defenseless against a merciless conqueror. Word had already gotten out regarding the defeat and imprisonment of Caterina Sforza, a woman as beautiful and refined as she was brazen and intrepid, who ruled over the neighboring city of Imola, and Giovanni wanted to avoid the same fate for his dear Giovanna at all costs.

Andrea stood at Giovanni's bedside holding his hand in silent support, turning every so often to gaze at the starless night sky that darkened the eastern window of the Rocca Roveresca, Senigallia's noble fortress and della Rovere family residence. Giovanna and Francesco had just left the room weeping uncontrollably, accompanied by the local cleric who had administered last rites. Giovanni lay motionless, eyes staring straight up at the raftered ceiling, fixed on nothing in particular. Movement was minimal and clearly painful as evidenced by the occasional grimace, which now seemed to be his only form of expression. As his final moments approached with a suddenness and intensity that startled even Andrea, the lines on his face hardened into an apparent death mask. Seeing Giovanni's lips quivering in an attempt to speak, Andrea leaned in to hear what could very well have been his friend's last words.

"I'm right here, my dear Giovanni," Andrea whispered.

Sweat poured from the dying man's brow, betraying a mortal fever that ate away at him piece by piece.

"You have served me well, Andrea," he said in a voice cracking with sorrow. "Before I leave you, I must ask for one final act of service."

"Whatever you wish, my friend," Andrea replied.

Giovanni struggled to utter his next words, pausing a moment to gather whatever fragments of strength he had left.

"The Republic of Venice had long ago agreed to provide a safe haven for my family in times of need," he finally said. "But the della Rovere are no fools. We know full well that the doge and his senators must tend to far more important matters than the guardianship of a widow and her young son."

Giovanni tried to say more, but words failed him. He let his head fall back onto the pillow and closed his eyes, praying for the energy to finish his thought. Andrea said nothing. He simply waited . . . trusting, hoping that his friend would find the wherewithal to continue. A few more moments drifted by before Giovanni's eyelids eased open, this time with more spirit and focus. He seemed reborn, but it soon became painfully clear that Andrea was witnessing his dear friend's final burst of lucidity.

"I know of your profound sentiments for Giovanna," he eventually mumbled, "and hers for you."

Andrea breathed deeply. He wanted desperately to avert his eyes out of shame, even go so far as to deny Giovanni's claim, but the truth was evident, and always had been. Ever since their first encounter in the hallowed halls of Urbino's Palazzo Ducale nearly fifteen years earlier, neither Andrea nor the young and nubile Giovanna managed to hide their deep-seated feelings for one another. At the time, however, Andrea's dreams of adventure were quite vivid; they fueled his existence and kept the notion of serious courtship far from his mind. But perhaps more importantly, Andrea's sense of unworthiness reared its ugly head. *How could I possibly presume to marry into wealth and power without first possessing those very qualities myself?* he always thought to himself. It was that same ambition that spurred him forward from an early age, often snuffing out his emotions, and directing his passions toward the only thing that seemed to matter to him: success, which for Andrea meant not only fame and fortune, but also a fulfillment of his destiny. Pursuing affairs of the heart, therefore, remained out of reach, compelling him even more to persist in the achievement of those goals.

Giovanni meant in no way to upbraid his friend, particularly in these crucial moments. Andrea saw the spark of wisdom and nobility in his eyes, as well as a look of pure compassion and understanding that comes from knowing you have nothing left to lose. This soothed Andrea, relieving him of any guilt he might have felt for harboring sentiments of affection all those years for the wife of his dearest friend. It moved him to speak with candor and to reveal what should have been confessed many years sooner.

"Forgive me, my friend," said Andrea.

It became instantly apparent, however, that Giovanni sought no apologies or any recognition of guilt, and he certainly intended no rebuke. He wasn't thinking of himself or of his earthly possessions, whose value, or non-value, often came into stark focus at times like these. He only desired the well-being of those closest to him—his dear wife and child—and in keeping with the noble condottiero that he was, he understood the imminent threat to their safety and wanted desperately to protect them from harm.

"God has brought you to me at this critical moment, dear Andrea," Giovanni said. "You are my loyal and most precious friend, and the only man I can trust to carry out this last request."

Giovanni drew in a deep breath, hoping to find a bit of strength, and perhaps a few more moments of life, from within its vapors. His next few attempts to speak were hampered by an uncontrollable fit of coughing that Andrea managed to assuage by propping him up higher against the goosedown pillows that supported him.

"The Devil has taken hold of our peninsula," Giovanni said at a volume no higher than a whisper. "He has devoured the surrounding cities and shall soon come for my dear Senigallia." He paused momentarily to clear his throat before issuing his next few words: "I beg of you to protect our city and the lives of our townspeople."

Andrea remained silent, showing his acceptance of Giovanni's wish with a slight nod, sensing that the crux of Giovanni's request was yet to come.

"But the Devil's thirst for power is great and can only be

quenched with the blood of my Giovanna and my dear son," he said, his voice cracking with emotion. "And for this I must ask you, as my dying wish, to act as a tutor to Francesco, my heir and proud bearer of the della Rovere name." Giovanni took another strong, determined breath before continuing. "And to defend my sweet Giovanna with your life, which I trust you would do even without this bold request of mine, such is your love for her."

As Giovanni uttered those last words, a faint smile appeared on his face, casting a spell over Andrea—a smile that accompanied his dying breath, and which no doubt he carried with him into the afterlife.

Chapter Eight

A GRAND ESCAPE

Giovanni della Rovere drifted off peacefully, in stark counterpoint to the life of violence and aggression he lived as a proud condottiero. Andrea remained at his side, and although he rarely indulged in such things, he prayed for his friend's soul for a good portion of the evening. He also asked God for guidance in carrying out the task Giovanni had placed on his shoulders. The charge of defending Senigallia against Cesare Borgia and his band of six thousand French and mercenary soldiers concerned him even more than Cordova's Spanish troops twice in size, and Charles VIII's twenty-five thousand men and blitzkrieg-style artillery before that.

He now saw Borgia through Giovanni's eyes: a devil, a man freed from the restraints of morality and gentlemanly conduct, and whose authority sprang from an unholy alliance forged between the sacred and the profane—that is to say, the Church of Rome and the Kingdom of France. Where condottieri of the past might have seen themselves as professional soldiers fighting for a cause, their king, or simply for glory, the young Borgia saw it all as a game whose rules were conjured up as he went along, and done in the name of no one but himself. He projected the aura of one smarter, more vicious, and far freer in spirit than anyone else alive, and whose powers of destruction, as fiercely antipathetic as they were, appeared to many as a positive force for change. His persona as a disciplined but ultimately unpredictable madman served to terrorize all those who stood in his way. And although Andrea's unease over Borgia's intentions never rose to the level of terror, the words "fear" and "respect" would not be too far off the mark.

Giovanna assumed the role of feudal mistress over Senigallia in the months that followed her husband's death, with Andrea acting as the city's commanding officer. The limited number of men at his disposal, and the threat of an attack by Borgia's increasingly more powerful armies, convinced Andrea that he could only secure the city from within the confines of the Rocca Roveresca. The specter of war had few debilitating effects on the psyche of a seasoned soldier like Andrea. In fact, it served as an impetus and honed his instincts, but this entire situation presented a different, more complex challenge, one he'd never had to cope with before, and in reality had always nimbly avoided. Having the additional complication of preserving the integrity and honor of a woman to whom he also felt so emotionally attached played havoc with his mind. *Will these sentiments blind me to the truth I see before me?* he wondered. *Will they compromise me, or induce me to be unwise in the heat of battle?* Andrea couldn't shake the feeling that Borgia could somehow anticipate his feelings for Giovanna, as if the man possessed superhuman powers and would ultimately exploit them.

Many nights passed with Giovanna and Andrea dining in the great hall without ever uttering a word of their first encounter in Urbino. Besides being a member of the ruling Montefeltro family, Giovanna was known as the *prefettessa*, or madame prefect, of Rome. Their meeting in the grand hall of Urbino's Palazzo Ducale was surely a magical moment, at least for Andrea, who, except for the occasional visit to a brothel during his wilder days in Rome, had little experience with women. She was thirty years old then, and had been married to Giovanni for nearly fifteen of those years without having yet given birth to a child. Like all wives of condottieri, she spent a good portion of her time alone. To alleviate the sense of solitude, she traveled from Senigallia to Urbino to visit her family when Giovanni ventured off to war. It was only a day's ride through the gently rising plains east of the Apennines into the harsher, more precipitous edges of the mountains that housed the city of Urbino to the west. Being a woman who enjoyed music and the arts, it was a journey she made happily. She was accustomed, after all, to the culture and refinement of the court of her father, the renowned Federico da Montefeltro, who sponsored many artists and writers, among them the young Raphael in the years before he ventured off to Rome.

It was no wonder, then, that the equally elegant and highly entertaining environment of her brother's court held a deep attraction for Giovanna. During the last decade of the fifteenth century and the beginning of the sixteenth, her brother Guido-baldo hosted great men of letters and esteemed literary theorists who celebrated the beauty of Italian language and literature. Giovanna loved sitting in the company of these men as they discussed classic Roman and Greek philosophy, literature, and history, not to mention more contemporary subjects such as *sprezzatura*, the fine art of gaining power and influence within the court system.

Of course, the merriment and civility of Guidobaldo's court was a thing of the past ever since Cesare Borgia took control of the city of Urbino. And as for Senigallia, all but the fortress of Rocca Roveresca was occupied in a surprise raid one morning by five of Borgia's captains, who, knowing he would one day betray them, had formed a secret alliance to thwart his advances into their territory. The five men then offered the city of Senigallia to Borgia as a form of appeasement, but more importantly, as a demonstration of their strength. Only the Rocca Roveresca in the heart of the city remained to be conquered, leaving Andrea, Giovanna, and the young Francesco virtually captive within its sturdy ramparts with only a few thousand soldiers to protect them.

Borgia, meanwhile, told the five captains as well as two brothers of the esteemed Orsini family, who were also secretly part of the conspiracy against him, to gather in the hills outside Senigallia, where together they would storm the fortress and take control of the entire city. What the conspirators did not know was that Borgia was aware of their pact against him and had assembled an army of two thousand cavalrymen and ten thousand foot soldiers who were approaching the city from along the riverbank, descending from the mountains. When they all met on the outskirts of the city and proceeded together into Senigallia with the expectation of overtaking the fortress, Borgia had them all seized and thrown into prison. Two were strangled to death that very night, and the Orsini brothers met the same fate shortly afterward. Borgia's intricate scheme had been executed to perfection.

With this in mind, and with little or no chance of defeating the young Borgia, Andrea could do nothing but peer from the window of his bedchamber perched on the third floor in the Rocca's northwestern corner, and watch the enemy troops surround the Palazzo Ducale, which Borgia had set up as his headquarters. For all intents and purposes, Borgia had already assumed control of all the centers of power within the city, and it was only a matter of time before he made his move on the fortress. To give off an impression of strength, Andrea ordered twice as many men as usual to line the battlements, and to sustain that image, he had all the culverins placed strategically along the wall and atop each of the Rocca's circular bastions. The idea was not to intimidate the enemy, knowing full well it would be absolute folly, but rather to set the stage for a peaceful settlement, one that would spare the lives of Giovanna and her young son.

From his vantage point, Andrea witnessed no activity in the city that seemed out of the ordinary, nothing to suggest an imminent assault, or a shift of strategy. But his gut told him differently. There was something about this night and all the circumstances surrounding it that spooked him. Perhaps it was the arid sirocco winds carrying the crimson sands of the African desert with them, turning the night sky to a deep purple, that made him feel uneasy, or the unnerving silence that seemed to haunt him wherever he went, but no matter the reason for his discomfort, Andrea knew he had to take action, and fast. A sudden knock at the door snapped him out of his reverie.

"Come in," he said after a moment's hesitation.

He remained glued to the activities, or the lack thereof, on the streets below, unable to bring himself to turn around when Giovanna made her entrance into his chamber. She ignored his reticence and sidled up close to him. Andrea kept his eyes straight ahead, not sure how to navigate the flood of conflicting emotions welling within him. With the specter of Giovanni's death seeming to linger endlessly and the threat of war becoming a day-to-day reality, any expression of love—or feelings other than grief or fear, for that matter—seemed entirely out of place. And yet, love was exactly what they both wanted desperately to proclaim.

"Our meager show of force may only encourage him further," said Andrea, his eyes still fixed on the Palazzo Ducale across the way. "He will no doubt bring more cannons into the city by day's end tomorrow."

"The son of this dreadful Borgia pope has stolen my beloved Urbino and humiliated our family," she said, her voice trembling with rage. "We cannot permit him to do the same to Senigallia."

Andrea allowed his gaze to turn ever so slightly in her

direction, then responded coolly and calmly to her appeal: "I'm afraid we haven't a chance against him, my dear Prefettessa."

"You have always been a bit too sensible for your own good, Andrea," she said, forcing him to lock eyes with her. "As have I," she added with a touch of sadness.

Giovanna's allusion to Andrea's levelheadedness had more to do with their history together than the military situation on the ground, and he knew it. Back when Andrea served as palace guard in Urbino, his undeclared affection for the young Giovanna often overwhelmed him. At times, he thought he would burst at the seams. Giovanna, too, felt her true impulses restricted by the chains of decorum. Andrea's regard for her husband and friend, Giovanni, and his deference to Giovanna's rank and title went a long way toward holding him in check. But it was her free spirit that prompted her to take the first step; it was her loneliness that sought out his company; and her natural desire for intimacy that made their *affaire de coeur* an inevitability.

Like many men and women born into nobility and destined to rule, or to lead soldiers into battle, Giovanni had entered into a marriage to Giovanna that met a political and dynastic imperative. The notion of love never entered into it. Infidelity, therefore, was more or less to be expected. But, of course, societal restraints dictated that the accepted bounds of decorum always be maintained. Discretion ranked supreme, and any talk of leaving one's spouse to run off with their lover was treated as nonsense. Marriages, therefore, were rarely destroyed; families remained intact and the status quo preserved. Ironically enough, it was precisely the unfeasibility of taking these relationships any further that encouraged them and secured their longevity.

But this was not the case for Andrea. He and Giovanna spent one night of sheer bliss together while Giovanni was off fighting for the French in the southern region of Campania. Soon afterward, however, Andrea decided to terminate the affair, not for lack of affection—his love was pure—nor was it out of fear of Giovanni's vengeance or retribution. In fact, Giovanni's deep respect for his wife tempered whatever jealousy or bitterness he may have harbored. He simply turned a blind eye. Andrea's reluctance to indulge in his feelings for Giovanna sprang, instead, from a firm belief that his future was written in the stars, a future that could only be fulfilled by exercising the freedom to live life to its fullest. Adhering to such a philosophy burdened him emotionally, he was the first to admit it, but as time went by, he grew increasingly more practiced at sidestepping that part of himself in the name of destiny.

"We have no allies to come to our assistance," Andrea replied, sticking to the matter at hand and purposefully avoiding the deeper implications of her branding him too sensible for his own good.

"The Republic of Florence is no friend of this pope, nor of his bloodthirsty son," she said. "We can count on their aid."

"I am afraid it is too late," Andrea was quick to respond.

Footsteps approaching from down the hall caught his attention, followed by a robust knock at the door.

As he turned to address the matter, Giovanna's eyes finally

met his, eyes that still managed to bewitch Andrea as they always had, only this time they signaled fear and vulnerability.

"We must save Francesco," she whispered, reaching out to take his hand. "He is our future."

Andrea felt the full weight of those words. He took her other hand in his, and drew in close, never averting his gaze.

"You shall both be safe," he said. "I promise you."

A second knock, this time with even more force and conviction, prompted Andrea to straighten up and assume the air of Senigallia's commanding officer.

"Come forward!" he barked.

The door opened to a stout, barrel-chested young officer who rushed in with deadly urgency. He carried a folded sheet of parchment in his left hand, and saluted his captain with his right.

"What is it?" Andrea asked.

"This comes from Cesare Borgia himself," the officer said, handing the letter to Andrea.

Andrea broke the waxed seal without hesitation. His eyes narrowed as he read, then looked up suddenly, pausing a moment to absorb the weight of Borgia's roughly scrawled words before addressing the officer.

"That will be all," he murmured in a soft, reserved voice, doing all he could to mask his concern.

The officer spun around and left the room.

"Borgia claims to want no bloodshed," Andrea said, "and says that you and the people of Senigallia have nothing to fear." Turning away from Giovanna, unable to look her in the eye, he threw the letter to the ground in anger and paced the room madly.

"What is the matter, Andrea?" she said. "This is good news, is it not?"

Andrea stopped at the window. He stared into the starless sky as he spoke: "He asks only that you surrender to him personally, and that Francesco be at your side."

Giovanna remained silent, not sure how to react. Andrea, on the other hand, grew even more irate.

"Does he take me for a fool?" he shouted, breaking into another round of pacing. "After the deadly tricks he played on his captains right here in this city, and his numerous displays of savagery, the man is incapable of acting honorably."

"If you say we have no hope of surviving a confrontation with him, then for the good of Francesco, I shall present myself to him as he asks," Giovanna said.

"If you surrender, he will kill you both, Giovanna," Andrea shot back.

Giovanna took a step back, shocked by his straightforwardness.

"And if we do battle with him, we shall perish, that much is certain," he added.

Those words struck like arrows to Giovanna's heart. The defiance she had expressed a moment ago in the face of Borgia's threat now turned to resignation and an acceptance of death, which she bore with the strength and nobility of a true scion of the Montefeltro family.

"If we are to die, then let us fight and go down with honor

and dignity," she said, holding her chin high while peering straight into Andrea's eyes.

Andrea's listened closely to Giovanna's heroic exhortation. His was not a binary mind, however. There were always choices to be made that went beyond the obvious or even the reasonable. A few moments passed without anyone saying a word.

"We shall accept Borgia's offer of peace," he finally announced, taking Giovanna by surprise.

Without waiting for her response, he ran to the door and called for assistance at once. Within moments the same barrel-chested officer arrived.

"At your service, Captain," said the officer upon entering the room.

By this time Andrea was already at his desk penning a response to Borgia's proposal. Giovanna stood beside him, both too angry and astonished to speak as Andrea signed the letter with a flourish, then set his feather quill back into the inkpot, folded the parchment, sealed it with beeswax, and handed it to the officer.

"See that Cesare Borgia receives this straightaway."

A surge of indignation grew within Giovanna, her face flushed with anger. "Would you so readily send me and my poor Francesco to our death?" she cried.

"My missive asked that Borgia send a representative in the morning so that you and Francesco may surrender to him," he replied. "But, of course, we will do no such thing. You shall both be on the road to Florence before the Compline bells ring this very night."

After a moment's pause that registered a host of expressions on Giovanna's face, ranging from disbelief to anxiety to elation and back to disbelief, she finally responded in a tone that betrayed a tinge of trepidation: "And what is to become of you?"

Andrea's mischievous grin revealed an absolute confidence that Giovanna recognized all too well, and offered her some comfort.

"I promise to tell you all about it when we meet again," he replied, doing his best to wipe the smile from his lips.

When pushed to such extremes, Andrea's inner strength and valor saw him through to the bitter end, virtues he had no doubt gleaned from his father's natural contempt for the rules of the game, and his dear mother's tenacity in the face of adversity.

"For now, you must gather up Francesco and whatever belongings can fit within your stallion's chap leather bags and meet me in the stables."

Shocked by the immediacy of it all, Giovanna stood frozen before finally snapping to her senses. Then, without so much as another word, she spun around and headed for the exit.

"And one more thing," Andrea cried, stopping her in her tracks. "Find the scullion and her son before they retire for the night, and exchange clothes with them. No one from the noble house of Montefeltro must be seen leaving here tonight."

Giovanna absorbed the directive with the composure of a seasoned soldier and hurried out the door.

In the stables later that evening, Andrea prepared two horses for the long trek through the Apennines, a mountain range whose vertiginous cliffs presented a considerable level of danger, especially on the Tuscan side, where mudslides, falling rock, and shifting masses of earth occurred with relative frequency. This piece of the Tuscan-Romagna road separated the peninsula between the rolling hills of Latium and Tuscany to the south, and the vast plains hosting Italy's largest waterway to the north, the Po river. Fortunately, the initial portion of the trip offered fewer perils since the grassy slopes on the eastern side of the mountains, composed primarily of sedimentary rock, rolled ever so gently skyward. Andrea had summoned a foot soldier from his native Genoa, a man he trusted with his life, to accompany Giovanna and her son on their journey. He, too, had disguised himself as a commoner, and would pose as Giovanna's husband to alleviate any suspicion, in particular during the early stages of their trip, while still within the grasp of Cesare Borgia's men.

Giovanna showed up just as the Compline bells signaled the start of the evening prayers. Andrea hardly recognized her in her tattered sack dress and sleeveless tunic. He couldn't help but eke out a laugh. She wore a soot-encrusted sheepskin cloak that had been dampened in a recent downpour, causing it to reek so badly of mildew and dung that she had to pull her linen wimple up from under her chin and over her nose to stifle the foul smell. Francesco stood alongside her, looking no less awkward. His loose-fitting pants were laced at the lower leg and tied with a hemp rope at the waist. The faded damask jerkin he had retrieved from the scullion covered a white tunic large enough to fit a boy twice his size, and his woolen cap drooped well over his eyes and ears. Both he and his mother wore leather boots with heavy wooden pattens to keep their feet dry.

"You may want to look a trifle more at home in your outfits if you intend to fool anyone," Andrea joked.

"Let us get on with it, shall we?" Giovanna replied, too frightened and uncomfortable to hazard a smile.

Andrea gave Francesco an endearing bear hug and imparted a few ennobling words before helping him onto a stout cart horse he had taken from the blacksmith's stable. Andrea then pulled Giovanna aside as the foot soldier secured the saddle bags on her packhorse.

"Be safe," he said. "I shall join you sooner than you think."

They both stood speechless for a long, impassioned moment, unable to do much more than gaze into each other's eyes. Inhibited by the presence of the foot soldier, a veteran under Giovanni's command for many years, and her son, who looked on with curious eyes, Giovanna had to content herself with a formal embrace. Andrea, too, already somewhat tongue-tied and emotionally conflicted, did all he could to contain himself as they locked into their goodbye hug. Outwardly it appeared decorous, even routine, but on the inside their blood coursed through their veins with unbridled desire.

When they finally disengaged, Andrea held the packhorse steady for Giovanna to mount. She slid her foot firmly into the stirrup and lifted herself into the saddle. Andrea then watched Giovanna, Francesco, and the foot soldier ride out of the stables, through the bailey, and finally to the ten-foot-tall oak door at the gatehouse, which opened for them without so much as a squeak. With the lanterns doused for the evening, they filtered into the street cloaked in darkness, and continued on through the western city gates without raising the slightest suspicion among the night guards.

Andrea awoke well before sunrise the next morning to carry out the second half of his scheme. Everything was set in place by the time the Rocca opened its gate to Borgia's representative, a spindly skeleton of a man flanked by two burly henchmen armed with lances and suited in steel-scale armor. Andrea waited in the grand hall where he welcomed the representative, who, without even extending the courtesy of a formal salutation, called for the prefettessa's immediate surrender. Andrea took a moment to size up his adversary and discerned instantly that the man's over-refined and effete manner would play neatly into his hands.

"The duchess has had a difficult night," Andrea said matter-of-factly, doing all he could to suppress a smile. "I think it only proper to warn you."

The representative, however, was no fool. He knew enough to hide his bewilderment, which he did quite well.

"The quality of her sleep, or lack of it, is of little concern to me," he said with a slight upturn of an eyebrow, demonstrating just the right amount of superciliousness and condescension Andrea was hoping for.

"Perhaps it would be best if we proceeded to her chamber straightaway," Andrea replied without missing a beat.

He led them up the stairs and down the narrow, tapestry-lined hall to Giovanna's bedchamber. But when arriving at her door, Andrea stopped and turned to address the representative. He then feigned a nervous cough to give the impression that he was about to proclaim something either awkward or potentially embarrassing. The representative, of course, interpreted it as anxiety or perhaps humiliation for having to surrender, and was quite surprised when he heard the real reason for Andrea's behavior.

"You see, the prefettessa had taken ill last evening with an intestinal infection of some sort," Andrea began. "The pain was excruciating." Seeing the representative's impatience mounting, Andrea continued without hesitation: "The laxative her physicians prepared for her of flax seed, marjoram, and nutmeg did little to evacuate her bowels. In fact, the pressure to relieve herself only grew. Not until she ingested a fair amount of antimony pills while lying in her chamber bed did the volcano finally burst, so to speak."

"In her bed?" mumbled the representative, doing little to mask his disgust.

The mere mention of antimony, a silvery metal fashioned into pastilles the size of plump raisins, was enough to sicken the poor man. The pills irritated the intestines to such a degree that the body's need to expel them, along with a good amount of excrement, was immediate and usually quite explosive.

"In her bed," repeated Andrea, rubbing it in even deeper.

At that moment a chambermaid exited Giovanna's room toting soiled swathes reeking of waste matter, and a tin bucket loaded with feces and urine. The odor emanating from the room nearly knocked the representative over. The two guards at his side didn't withstand the stench any better, doing all they could to stop from gagging, including breaking their position at attention to take a few steps back and cover their mouths with the palms of their hands. The chambermaid hurried off without saying a word.

"I presume that once the nurse finds the pastilles in the prefettessa's feces, she will return to administer them again," Andrea said to the representative, who, in the meantime, had retreated to join his two guards.

Andrea was referring to the practice of reusing the antimony pills by searching for them in the stool. The ability to recover these pills, and thus administer them numerous times over many years, made them quite popular.

"The prefettessa doesn't appear to be the least bit prepared to surrender," said the representative, clearly annoyed by the experience.

"Surely Cesare Borgia, the good Duke Valentino, must understand that the code of honor and decorum would frown heavily upon subjecting a woman of such stature to public humiliation," Andrea quickly replied. "It would no doubt sully the duke's good name and cheapen his victory. But, of course, if you insist," he added, pulling the representative closer to the chamber, "we can approach the prefettessa and assess her condition for ourselves."

The representative's body language said it all. He recoiled at the mere suggestion of it and stood his ground, not venturing another inch toward the chamber door.

"I see no reason to bring disgrace upon the Lady da Montefeltro and saddle her with any more discomfort than she has already suffered," he said.

"And I presume her son, Francesco Maria della Rovere, can

postpone his surrender as well?" Andrea asserted, confident of the representative's consent.

"Such matters of intestinal health are usually quite brief," said the representative, attempting to regain some control over the situation. "I shall return tomorrow at the same hour. See to it that the prefettessa and her son are prepared to proffer their surrender no matter the circumstances. I shall relate what has occurred this morning to the duke straightaway." He bowed respectfully, then added: "And allow me to speak on his behalf and wish her a speedy recovery."

No sooner had the representative issued his blunt reproach than he spun around on his heels and marched down the corridor, eagerly followed by his two guards.

Andrea waited until they passed through the gatehouse door and crossed the footbridge ushering them into the main piazza before he ran back to Giovanna's bedchamber, where he promptly dismissed everyone who had participated in the charade. Besides the chambermaid, this included the young stable groom, who had lugged shovelfuls of fresh horse dung into the room and added ample amounts of excrement from the castle's cesspit to provide just the right level of pungency. Andrea had thought of everything. He even enlisted the Rocca's laundress to lie in bed, tucked well beneath the satin-covered quilts, to pose as the prefettessa should the representative withstand the stench and venture into the room.

As promised, the representative arrived bright and early the following morning. He not only found Giovanna and her son gone, but Andrea as well. Andrea had disguised himself as a monk and ridden out of Senigallia on a donkey in the dead of night. It cannot be confirmed as absolute truth, but a rumor quickly circulated intimating that in his rage at being outmaneuvered, Cesare Borgia had discharged his henchman, Michelotto, to strangle the representative to death that same day, and no one doubts that Michelotto did just that.

Chapter Nine

THE FIESCHI CHARM

Despite the tale of Cesare Borgia's humiliation concluding on a fairly gruesome note, the room exploded in spontaneous laughter. Even Andrea, who struggled through the more intimate parts, couldn't hold back a smile, even with his dear wife, Peretta, peering into his eyes. Giovannandrea continued giggling well after the general laughter had died down. Not only did the scatological nature of the story tickle his eight-year-old sensitivities, but the thought of the snooty representative getting his scrawny little neck wrung like an old dish rag sent him into hysterics. And like most children who have just experienced a cheap thrill, he begged Andrea to tell the story all over again. Of course, this brought on another round of laughter since everyone knew it was the last thing Andrea wanted, or would ever consent to.

"Here's what I shall do," said Andrea. "I'll tell you the same story next year for the holidays."

"It should be a family tradition," quipped Giannettino.

"Just like the canestrelli," Peretta quickly added. "Which, by the way, I noticed no one ate during the last part of that story."

"For good reason," joked Figueroa.

"I'm hungry," Giovannandrea cried out spontaneously, without the slightest hint of irony.

"Me too," said Placidia.

Although Andrea had been enduring a throbbing in his knees for the last several hours, he managed to laugh along with everyone else at the children's comments. He did, however, finally allow himself to wince in pain. The aching in his lower spine and the burning sensation in every other joint in his body only added insult to injury. The joy of sporting Giovannandrea on his lap had overshadowed the discomfort for a while, but his eighty-one-year-old frame could only take so much. Luckily for him, Ginetta and Peretta detected his unease and jumped to his aid.

"Perhaps it's time to give your mesiavo a little rest," said Peretta as she reached over to lift young Giovannandrea from Andrea's knee.

"And sit on your father's lap," added Ginetta, sidling over to assist Peretta.

At this point, Gian Luigi also leapt to his feet to help out. "If I may be so honored, perhaps he wouldn't mind taking a turn on my knee," he said.

Gian Luigi had been a welcomed member of the family ever since his father, Sinibaldo, died nearly fifteen years earlier. He and little Giovannandrea had shared many hours together, and given Gian Luigi's natural likability, their relationship flourished over the years. And for his part, Giannettino felt perfectly at ease with Gian Luigi's friendly gestures. In fact, he sprang up to lend Gian Luigi a hand in helping Ginetta, who had gone to Peretta's aid in the first place. All these arms reaching out to relieve the family patriarch of his misery formed a tableau that eloquently symbolized the cohesiveness of the Doria lineage. In the end, Giovannandrea climbed atop Gian Luigi's lap of his own accord, and all was calm again.

As if on cue, Tonino opened the chamber door carrying a tray of freshly baked *focaccia*, a traditional flat bread that originated with the ancient Etruscans of central Italy and was modified over the centuries to satisfy distinct Genoese tastes. It was the ideal afternoon *merenda*, especially the three versions that Tonino had prepared for the occasion: focaccia *rosmarino*, an oily, heavily salted bread sprinkled with sprigs of fresh rosemary; focaccia *col formaggio*, a paper-thin bread covered with *stracchino*, a soft, spreadable cheese made of cow's milk, typical of the city of Recco to the south; and finally a biscuit-style focaccia from Camogli, another seaport on the Ligurian coast. All three varieties of flat bread doubled as the perfect companion to the plate of sliced meats Tonino balanced in his other hand: *salame di* Sant'Olcese, a mixture of pork and beef salami with black pepper and garlic; *mostardella*, a raw beef and pork sausage; and a fine *prosciutta castelnovese*, Andrea's personal favorite, a cured ham brought in from the mountain towns east of the city, and known to all the locals as the "prosciutto's happy wife." After placing the food on a serving table in front of the fire, Tonino opened a bottle of Rossese di Dolceacqua, a red wine from Andrea's mother's place of birth, and a regular fixture on the Doria dinner table when he was a child.

"I cannot speak for the rest of you, but a bit of focaccia and a warm fire are too hard to resist on such a frigid January afternoon," Andrea said, rising to his feet. "Feel free to join me."

Ambassador Figueroa's passion for Italian cured meats nearly matched his fascination with the peninsula's convoluted political scene. He got up immediately, as did Gonzaga, along with Ginetta and Peretta, who began pouring the Rossese for Andrea and his two guests to set the mood. Giannettino stayed behind with Gian Luigi and little Giovannandrea sitting leisurely on his knee. It wasn't long before Placidia hopped onto Gian Luigi's lap as well, across from her brother.

"Well, well, I must be the most fortunate man alive!" cried Gian Luigi.

The two children giggled mischievously as they rocked back and forth, which threw Gian Luigi into a fit of laughter, and brought a smile to their father's lips as well. The atmosphere couldn't have been more playful.

"It pleases me to see their sincere love for you," Giannettino said.

"The pleasure is mine, dear Giannettino," Gian Luigi replied. "I have watched them both grow into beautiful children from the time they were born."

Over by the fire, Andrea sat in his trusty curule seat, an X-shaped folding chair inlaid with strips of ivory and bone, and upholstered in soft green velvet. He sat there quite often as of late, usually positioning himself as close to the fiery hearth as possible in a desperate attempt to soothe his aching bones. Today would be no different except for the large sliver of focaccia and Sant'Olcese at his side, a treat he reserved for special occasions such as these. The Rossese, however, was an almost nightly indulgence. As it turned out, despite his stoic nature, his many years at sea had nurtured a special appreciation for the comforts of home and the simple joys of family life. As he leaned back and took a hearty gulp of wine, he couldn't help but notice the children on Gian Luigi's lap as happy as larks, a fact he immediately pointed out to Figueroa and Gonzaga.

"Does that look like a man about to betray me and his beloved Genoa?" Andrea asked, more confident than ever that his two guests were natural-born muckrakers and conspiracy theorists.

Andrea was self-reflective enough, however, to realize that a good part of his confidence in Gian Luigi's loyalty to him, the Doria family, and the Spanish was grounded in the city's commercial success, a feature that inspired good will among its perennially warring families and went a long way toward soothing the ills of the general populace. The unquestionable dominance of the Spanish military also helped persuade him of Gian Luigi's acceptance of the status quo, as did his belief that the Fieschi family in general would be insane to risk their good name and everything they owned for such a treasonous endeavor.

But Andrea's longevity as a military officer and political leader obviously depended on more than simply clinging to his personal opinions; they required extensive inquiry and thoughtful analysis, which Andrea had done as soon as he heard whispers of unusual French activity along the Ligurian border several weeks ago. The numerous military men frequenting the Fieschi palazzo in Via Lata also concerned him, as did Gian Luigi's recent acquisition of four private galleys, one of which had recently moored in the harbor, but in the end it all failed to raise any real suspicion. Andrea considered himself a formidable judge of character, and in his eyes Gian Luigi seemed beyond reproach.

Without the lure of a good war story to keep him entertained, or at least an unintentionally amusing one like Andrea's Senigallia incident, Giovannandrea began to grow restless, and of course he couldn't survive too long without eating. Watching everyone by the fire feasting on the freshly baked bread eventually got the best of him. Placidia, too, couldn't resist the focaccia *col formaggio*. She loved anything and everything with soft, buttery cheese on top. They both slid off Gian Luigi's lap and joined the other circle of grownups by the fire, leaving Giannettino and Gian Luigi to their own devices.

"Would you mind if I asked you a question?" asked Gian Luigi, leaning in close to Giannettino as if about to whisper something salacious.

"What is it, my friend?"

"We all know that deriving wealth from one's feudal land is no easy task," Gian Luigi began. "It is slow and unpredictable. One cannot build dreams on such things. And without dreams to sustain you, life itself would be unbearable, would it not?"

Giannettino said nothing. He waited for Gian Luigi to

formulate his next thought, studying his face the entire time—a technique Andrea had taught him at an early age.

"That is why I am now looking to the sea for my future," Gian Luigi continued. "I have decided to come to our Holy Father's defense in Rome with three of my galleys, but I hope to sail the fourth one into the high seas on my own, fighting the Turks, our mortal enemy, and seeking the celebrity and fortune that so many of our fellow citizens have found."

Gian Luigi paused, giving Giannettino the opportunity to weigh in. But Giannettino betrayed no emotion one way or another.

"Of course, I could also embark on a far nobler pursuit by offering my services to Charles V, and sail on his behalf and that of our fair city," Gian Luigi went on. "I must ask you in all humility, dear Giannettino, what do you believe is my wisest choice?"

By soliciting his opinion on such a matter, Gian Luigi was showing his friend a considerable amount of respect, a gesture that pleased Giannettino a great deal. As a rule, Giannettino restrained himself when dealing with Gian Luigi, holding back his deepest feelings and never speaking with the candor and straightforwardness a true friendship really deserved. As far back as they could both remember, a deep-seated rivalry existed between them. Their competitiveness was perhaps most evident when they were both actively courting the same woman, Ginetta Centurione, Giannettino's current wife. She was, at the time, not only the most sought-after and prestigious young woman

THE PIRATE PRINCE OF GENOA

in all of Genoa, but also happily betrothed to Gian Luigi. With Andrea's intervention, however, Adamo Centurione, Ginetta's father and arguably the wealthiest man in all of Italy, switched his preference to Giannettino.

Given Gian Luigi's affection for Ginetta, and the wealth and influence their union would have brought to the Fieschi family, this came as a devastating blow. For the critics of Giannettino, and there were many, it once again confirmed his inordinately privileged status, and only served to enhance the antipathy toward him. Giannettino couldn't care less what the people thought of him on many issues, but with Gian Luigi, given their tangled history, he always went out of his way to soften his normally high-handed stance.

"I haven't a firm idea how to answer you, my friend," said Giannettino. "And I do not presume to be an authority on such things."

"You are a comrade and the most expert man I know regarding the high seas," Gian Luigi replied. "Except for our dear Prince, of course," he added, indicating Andrea with a slight nod of his head. "Your advice would be a precious gift to me."

As deferential as Giannettino may have been toward his dear friend, he was first and foremost a proud scion of the Doria family and staunchly dedicated to its interests. It would have been unthinkable for him to advise Gian Luigi to offer his services to Charles V and the Kingdom of Spain. This responsibility, and privilege, belonged to the Doria family, and to them alone. It was an open secret that a substantial part of Andrea's power rested in his ability to keep other Genoese families in check, never allowing them to gain too much influence with the emperor and thus someday grow strong enough to pose a threat to Andrea's authority. This tactic proved quite tricky. It required striking a tender balance between keeping the rival families prosperous while simultaneously curbing their power. Giannettino understood this dynamic intuitively; it governed his every move.

"Since you look to me for guidance, my dear Gian Luigi, I feel obliged to present my thoughts on the matter," Giannettino began. "There can be no doubt that throwing your support behind a large power like the Empire is a safe course of action. It increases your likelihood of monetary gain and keeps you in the emperor's good graces. But the process is a long one, and although the rewards can be great, they unfold at a slow and extremely frustrating pace, since you are subject to the whims and political strategies of men far more powerful than you. Aligning yourself to these powers will effectively guarantee that you cover your costs, of which you will have many, as you surely know, but the rest remains quite unpredictable. Sometimes they leave you free to roam the seas and attack enemy merchant ships—a lucrative endeavor, to be sure—but more often than not, you will find yourself sitting idly for months waiting to be called into service."

Giannettino paused to gauge his friend's reaction, or to field his response, but Gian Luigi said nothing. Instead, he sat back in his seat, a grin pasted on his face, waiting to hear more, a wish Giannettino promptly satisfied.

"On the other hand, setting out on your own in search of booty, attacking Turkish cargo ships or any random vessel deemed to be an enemy of Spain and the Empire, may involve higher risks to your safety and to your purse strings, but it offers far greater freedom and countless material rewards. The choice is yours."

The smile that crossed Gian Luigi's lips as he listened to Giannettino's words of advice was hardly one of smugness or conceit. As a matter of fact, by answering as he did, Giannettino was in essence giving Gian Luigi permission to proceed, which in itself was a huge step forward. Regardless of whether Gian Luigi ventured out on his own or served powerful entities such as Spain, the pope, Florence, or the Republic of Venice, he would have had to receive Andrea's blessing before doing so. Such was Andrea's authority over the citizens of Genoa, in spite of his holding no formal position within the government.

"I cannot tell you how much it pleases me to hear your thoughts on this matter, dear Giannettino," Gian Luigi replied. "As you have certainly noticed, my galley in the harbor has a full crew of men ready to sail. In fact, we have set tomorrow as our departure date."

Giannettino was only partially taken by surprise by Gian Luigi's last statement. The steady flow of men in and out of Villa Vialata had been held under scrutiny for some time, and naturally gave rise to some mistrust, but nothing out of the ordinary given Genoa's ongoing military commitment to Spain and its strategic position on the Mediterranean, both of which had turned the harbor into a beehive of activity. What caught Giannettino slightly off guard, however, was his friend's decision to leave so soon.

"Well then," he said, slapping Gian Luigi on the back, "into the mouth of the wolf."

"The wolf should die," Gian Luigi shot back, stretching his smile even wider. "Then, of course, you will not find it strange to hear more ruckus than usual on the docks tonight as we ready for our departure."

"I shall consider myself duly warned," Giannettino quipped. "And by the way, there is no need to repeat all this to Andrea," he added. "I shall inform him myself this evening at dinner."

"You are a good friend," said Gian Luigi. "I cannot thank you enough."

Placidia then arrived with two huge platefuls of focaccia and assorted meats. "Mamma said you must eat something," she giggled.

Giannettino leaned over to give her a kiss on the forehead as he relieved her of one of the plates.

"Tell your lovely mamma she is an angel," said Gian Luigi, taking the other plate from her.

Placidia scooted back to Ginetta without saying a word, and hopped on her lap. Giovannandrea sat next to her on his own chair, trying his best to follow the animated discussion between his mesiavo and his two guests regarding the upcoming election for doge. The days between the first and the fourth of January represented a kind of limbo for the Genoese citizenry, since no one actually occupied the top spot in government during that brief period. The jockeying for position among factions, the political wrangling, and downright strong-arming of friends and foes ran rampant. It was as if having no leader, no one to hold responsible for whatever catastrophe might befall the city, created a kind of mass psychosis where the simple notion of "anything was possible" both excited and terrified the general populace, especially men like Andrea and members of the senate whose fortunes rested on the outcome.

On the other hand, Genoa had long borne the reputation as an incurably volatile state and was often regarded as a "state without a state." In fact, that single quality could be considered Genoa's primary characteristic, one that differentiated it from all the other political bodies on the peninsula. Unlike them, Genoa's seafarers and merchant class generated a highly competitive system of commerce that eclipsed the sovereign state in terms of power and influence. In essence, Genoa was a republic of merchants whose authority was both political and military, and whose affairs so masterfully intertwined with those of the city, the government, and the people that it became increasingly difficult to distinguish them. The figure of Andrea as nobleman, admiral, and revered prince perfectly embodied that fusion of interests, and as a result, when Andrea spoke, people listened.

Once again, however, Giovannandrea's boyish curiosity sidetracked the conversation. Frustrated that he couldn't follow the complex analysis and tangled stratagems being bandied about, he decided to throw himself headlong into the exchange. He latched on to something Gonzaga said earlier about Andrea's distinguished naval career and blurted out a question on the topic that derailed the discussion's logical flow.

"But why do they call you Admiral?" he asked.

The innocence and sheer enthusiasm of the question

stopped the conversation cold. *Surely he must know know the answer,* Gonzaga mused to himself. *His father is one of Genoa's most renowned admirals thanks to Andrea!* What went on in Figueroa's head followed much the same reasoning. Only Andrea understood what his young nephew intended to say. But rather than provide a cursory response to what seemed to be a simple inquiry, Andrea remained silent just long enough for the focus of the discussion to fall back onto little Giovannandrea, according him the same platform, respect, and responsibility to explain himself as his guests. The boy wasted no time in doing just that.

"You were an officer of the guard in Rome, a captain in the hills of Roccaguglielma, and in Senigallia you never had to leave the fortress. Don't admirals fight their battles at sea?"

Figueroa and Gonzaga both sat up straight in their chairs, curious to see how Andrea would field the boy's indelicate but perfectly understandable question.

Andrea didn't hesitate. "You want to know if I truly searched for treasure out on the high seas and fought the Barbary pirates, don't you, my son?" he asked calmly.

The boy's eyes widened, which Andrea took for a yes.

"Surely you have heard of my exploits with Barbarossa?" Andrea asked.

Giovannandrea lowered his eyes, suddenly ashamed that he'd spoken so carelessly. Of course he knew of his mesiavo's confrontations with the infamous pirate.

"But you were a captain, too," he replied in an effort to amend for his lapse. Then, judging by Andrea's dark stare, the boy realized he needed to say more in order to save face, which

149

he artfully did by utilizing an old trick he'd gleaned from his father and his beloved mesiavo, as well as from literally every Doria aunt, uncle, and cousin he'd ever met: He resorted to simple flattery.

"Shouldn't we also call you Il Gran Capitano?"

It was all Andrea could do to keep from laughing out loud, not out of mockery or scorn, but sheer pride. He saw so many traits in the boy that reminded him of himself. Of course, Giovannandrea's attempts to negotiate his way out of these tiny missteps were naive and embarrassingly transparent, but he knew instinctively which diplomatic techniques to apply and which to avoid, and he did so with great confidence.

"I believe it is time for more wine," Andrea proclaimed, reaching out for the bottle of Rossese. "Or would you rather the Madeira?" he added, staring straight at Figueroa, whom he knew, being Spanish, would prefer it.

However, being the well-mannered ambassador that he was, Figueroa didn't say a word, opting instead for the Rossese out of deference to his host. Gonzaga followed suit, sliding his cup right up next to Figueroa's for Andrea to fill.

"Good," said Andrea, replenishing everyone's glass as well as pouring a splash for Ginetta, who signaled she only wanted a sip or two.

Andrea even poured a thimbleful into a cup for Giovannandrea, then topped it off with a sufficient amount of spring water from the Calizzano region of the Maritime Alps to give the Rossese di Dolceacqua a faint rosé tint, more clear than crimson, but just opaque enough to make the boy feel like one of the adults. Giovannandrea raised his cup to meet Andrea's in a toast.

Andrea smiled. "To Giovannandrea Doria, Genoa's soon-to-be greatest admiral of all time," he declared. "Who, if he practices a bit of patience, may even hear his old and weary mesiavo tell of how he became Admiral Andrea Doria, Prince of Genoa and the Genoese Republic."

It didn't take long for Giannettino and Gian Luigi to vacate their posts by Andrea's canopy and join in on the toast.

"Hear, hear!" they all cried out in unison.

After a hearty gulp of Rossese, they set their cups down and waited quietly for their prince to continue his life story. But before he could get a word out of his mouth, Giovannandrea hopped out of his chair.

"Wait, I must eat something before it is all gone."

Being accustomed to such impulsiveness, Ginetta unfurled a slice of prosciutta castelnovese on one of the last remaining pieces of focaccia, handed it to her son, and sat him back down, all within a few seconds. And being the thoughtful mother that she was, she made sure to satisfy Placidia's nutritional needs as well. A sideways glance from Giannettino was all the warning Giovannandrea needed to realize it was time to remain quietly in his seat.

"Ah, to be young again," Andrea quipped, inducing a laugh from everyone present, especially Gonzaga, who had seven children of his own, all under the age of ten.

"His vitality is a sign of good health," Gonzaga remarked. "I recognize that same spirit in all my sons. Like the young Giovannandrea here, they will go quite far in life."

"As will your sweet daughter," Peretta rejoined, "who, no doubt, shall find the power and success commensurate with her Gonzaga name."

"Our dear Ambassador Figueroa, however, seems to be following in my footsteps," Andrea pointed out, slapping him on the knee like an old friend. "Remaining free of romantic entanglements for as long as possible." He then turned to Gian Luigi: "And you, of course, my dear young Fieschi, have only recently tied the knot of holy matrimony, and shall undoubtedly raise a son as clever and unruly as Giannettino's little boy."

Gian Luigi replied with a proud smile: "Eleonora and I have plans to extend the Fieschi name far and wide."

"I pray God you will," said Ginetta, peering warmly into Gian Luigi's eyes. "It would please me greatly to see you and dear Eleonora happy."

Gian Luigi's lingering sentiments for Ginetta made it nearly impossible for him to meet her gaze for fear of either breaking into tears or crying out in a fit of rage. Instead, he bolted to his feet, and with a slight nod of his head in Andrea's direction, indicated his intention to leave.

"Don't tell me you intend to go home so soon," Andrea said, clearly disappointed.

Before Gian Luigi had a chance to respond, Ginetta and Giannettino stood up alongside him in an attempt to allay any further awkwardness. Ginetta had never really made peace with her father's abrupt annulment of her betrothal to Gian Luigi, and as a result she continued to hold some feelings for him, albeit now mixed with sympathy and regret. Touted as the handsomest young couple in all of Genoa, she and Gian Luigi stole the show wherever they went. Their passion for one another burned for all to see and kept the gossipmongers of the city busy for years—but unfortunately not as busy as when their engagement eventually dissolved and Giannettino entered the picture. He was every bit in love with Ginetta as his dear friend, Gian Luigi, and she, after a shaky beginning, couldn't help but fall deeper and deeper in love with the raffish young Doria.

The two were wed shortly afterward, which closed the door to Ginetta's heart for Gian Luigi forever, throwing him into a deep depression. A few years later, however, his fortune turned for the better. He married Eleonora Cybo Malaspina, a woman as erudite and sophisticated as she was provocatively charming. Her love for Gian Luigi was so intense it overcame her mother's stern disapproval as well as that of Andrea, who was the young man's legal guardian after Sinibaldo's death.

"I'm afraid I also have guests this evening, my Prince," Gian Luigi said after an awkward pause that kept everyone on edge. "Imagine the impression I would leave if I weren't there to greet them." Then with a droll smile, he added, "And the earful I would hear from my dear Eleonora."

"Of course," said Andrea. "Please send our love to everyone and wish them all a happy and prosperous new year."

Gian Luigi accepted Andrea's auspicious words with yet another nod and a muted thank-you. Ginetta was the first to give Gian Luigi the traditional goodbye kiss on both cheeks, followed by Peretta, Giannettino, and finally Andrea. After bidding Gonzaga and Figueroa a formal adieu with a flourish of the hand and a slight bow, he embraced Placidia and Giovannandrea, planted a kiss on their foreheads, and crossed to the chamber door, offering everyone a final wave before leaving.

The room fell into an uneasy silence. Some of those present inevitably sat pondering notions of romance, unrequited love, and the institution of marriage in general. Others scrutinized the young Fieschi's behavior, wondering whether they had just observed further evidence of his plot against the Republic or had indeed witnessed his complete exoneration. Andrea's thoughts began to straddle both camps.

Chapter Ten

ADMIRAL ANDREA DORIA

The raven-hued limestone that embellished the fireplace in Andrea's bedchamber gave off a wave of intense, dry heat that radiated throughout the room. It proved no match, however, for the encroaching January wind swirling through the city as the night drew near. It froze everything within its reach. Raw arctic air rushed through Genoa's *caruggi*, the city's narrow medieval walkways, like an icy squall before a winter storm, chilling even the warmest of homes. The enormity of Andrea's palazzo—with its broad corridors, lofty ceilings, and walls of cold, dispassionate stone—seemed to welcome the bleakness of it all.

Andrea huddled closer to the fire as he launched into recounting the next phase of his long and turbulent life. He didn't tire at the rate of normal octogenarians. Far from it. In fact, he grew in strength and determination with each word, fueled by the admiring eyes of his dear nephew and the respect of his guests, not to mention the love of his dedicated wife, who knew that occasions like these brought him renewed vigor and soothed his busy and tempestuous mind.

Peretta hadn't seen him so untroubled in ages, so tranquil, and so willing to reveal himself. Over the years, she had grown accustomed to worrying about whether he would live or die each time he went off to battle, and she grew to accept her anxiety as a fact of their marriage. Seeing him return home safe and sound from his various conflicts with more energy than when he left eventually inured her to the myriad perils he faced. She often joked that like so many of her fellow citizens, she actually started to believe in the myth of his invincibility in combat, as if he were the mighty Achilles himself. But, unlike the celebrated Greek warrior, it would ultimately require a slow, painful deterioration of his vital organs to take Andrea down, which is why the severity of this latest bout of rheumatism and gout gave her pause. With his mortality beginning to rear its ugly head, each and every day mattered. And if one of those days happened to bring him pleasure, as this one certainly did, she would do everything possible to make it last.

"After venturing far from home in the service of the French, the Aragonese, and the Holy Mother, the Church," Andrea said, "and after seeing those who longed for peace and liberty being so callously subjected to the whims of foreign powers and the ruthlessness of men, I thought it time for me to return to our beloved city in hopes of freeing it from those very same ills."

As the sun dropped below the horizon, the crackling fire provided the room's sole light and, except for Andrea's commanding voice, its only sound. As he recounted the death of the Borgia pope, the glimmer of a smile crossed his lips, which the flickering orange and red flames transformed into a devilish smirk.

"The journey back to Genoa took me through the Republic of Florence, where a new *gonfaloniere* had recently been elected, and Niccolò Machiavelli served as his noble ambassador," he continued. "Theirs was a government bent on the dignity of man, an honorable pursuit which I promised myself I would one day bring to fruition within our own hallowed walls."

"And become our pater patriae!" shouted little Giovannandrea at the top of his lungs.

"Which only took me another twenty-five years," Andrea added.

The abruptness of the boy's tribute jolted everyone at first, and then, almost in the same instant, hurled them into spasms of laughter. The more Andrea spoke of his exploits, the more it became clear to him that he was already well on his way to living out his elusive dream of becoming the "father of the country."

The pursuit of this dream had come at a dear price. After his success as the city's commanding officer at Senigallia, and with the safety of Giovanna and her son assured, it was time for Andrea to continue fulfilling his destiny. Giovanna, too, had been entrusted with a higher purpose in life: preserving both the Montefeltro and della Rovere family names. As it turned out, her late husband, Giovanni, had appointed her regent of all his territories as his dying wish. That honor would then pass on to her son, Francesco, upon reaching his sixteenth birthday, provided Giovanna did not remarry. In addition, when Guidobaldo da

Montefeltro, Duke of Urbino, recaptured Urbino following Cesare Borgia's sudden demise in 1503, he saw fit to designate Francesco as his rightful heir, a responsibility the young boy would be called upon to assume just a short time later. In the five years between Giovanna's harrowing escape from Senigallia and her son becoming Duke of Urbino, she had her hands full, to say the least, as did Andrea, whose goal of finding freedom and independence for Genoa kept him far from the hills of Urbino and the gentle shores of Senigallia. Giovanna and Andrea simply drifted further apart.

Upon his reentrance into Genoa in 1503, Andrea found the city of his forefathers still embroiled in the same destructive infighting between noble families as twenty years earlier. And, once again, he knew that in order to succeed, given his limited resources and influence, he had to venture outside the confines of the city, only this time he would endeavor to do so in the name of Genoa's economic and political interests. It frustrated him that he was nearly forty years old and he still hadn't attracted the attention of a major political figure on the continent. He'd spent too much time serving the interests of a single family to be duly noticed on a global scale, and for nearly a decade the keys to his advancement had been intentionally kept from him by Alexander VI, the Borgia pope, in Rome.

But on August 18 of that year, the winds of change began to blow a bit more favorably for Andrea. Alexander VI died of "Roman fever," meaning arsenic poisoning. It was believed that his son, Cesare, had sprinkled a lethal dose of *cantarella* on his food, mistakenly thinking it was meant for a troublesome dinner guest. Soon afterward, the conclave of cardinals elected a pope who assumed the name of Pious III, but given his advanced age, he died twenty-eight days later, opening the doors of the Vatican to Giuliano della Rovere, who soon thereafter ascended the Throne of Saint Peter as Pope Julius II. Once again, a fellow Ligurian had been handed the reins to Italy's most powerful city-state.

A second event during that same year proved equally auspicious for Andrea. The people of Corsica, an island 250 kilometers south of Genoa, had risen up in revolt against the Bank of San Giorgio, a financial institution founded in the Genoese Republic that had evolved over the years to become the island's de facto overlord. Originally created nearly a century earlier to consolidate the sprawling public debt, the bank had grown in influence over the years, functioning almost as a state, and eventually taking ownership of vast territories throughout the Mediterranean and beyond. The bank purchased Corsica from the Republic of Genoa in 1453 once it became evident that the Republic could not guarantee peace among the island's inhabitants. In order to resist Corsica's continuous state of rebellion, the bank finally organized an armed expedition in 1503 led by none other than Nicolò Doria, who had enrolled Andrea into the Vatican guards some twenty years earlier. Nicolò did not hesitate to enlist Andrea again, this time as his second-in-command. Their undertaking was simple: penetrate Corsica's rugged hinterlands; track down Ranuccio della Rocca, the rebellion's notorious and hugely charismatic leader; and bring him to justice.

"With Nicolò in command, we scaled the mountains throughout the entire island in search of Ranuccio," Andrea said. "And we trudged the malaria-filled marshes and its ungodly forests, all to no avail. The brutal conditions we faced on a daily basis shattered our morale, and the hostility from the island's inhabitants who supported Ranuccio's struggle proved more formidable than we had ever imagined. And suffice it to say that the constant ambushes and surprise raids did little to calm our nerves. Not until Nicolò sailed off to Rome to pay homage to our new pope was I able to assume full control of the operation."

"Well, did you capture Ranuccio?" Giovannandrea blurted out in his typical impetuous fashion.

Andrea took the question in stride this time, responding without any further comment: "The bank put me in command of a fleet, and we policed the coastal regions with impunity. But we failed to have any effect on the heart of the rebellion hidden deep in the hinterlands."

"Once you entered the island's harsh interior, it has been said that you carried out a ruthless and merciless policy against the villagers who protected him," said Gonzaga. "A laudable tactic indeed, and one that more often than not finds success."

Andrea recoiled at the left-handed compliment. He, of course, did not view his actions as heartless or brutal in any way, but merely necessary remedies for the malady of insubordination infecting the island.

"We fought according to the hallowed traditions of war," he responded, "as did our enemy. And in the end we were victorious."

"I intended no manner of disrespect," Gonzaga was quick to respond.

"None taken," said Andrea, offering a sincere smile. "Ranuccio grew ever more isolated from his base of support due to our tactics and was finally captured."

"I have heard much of this Ranuccio della Rocca," said Figueroa. "He is heralded as a champion by the Corsicans to this very day."

"And perhaps rightfully so," Andrea said as he stared into the fire, lost in thought. "Despite his gruff and unseemly appearance when captured, I found him to be a man of noble character, quite proud and courageous as well. I understood his hatred of his Genoese lords. He sought freedom for his people, an independence that I craved as well, and he was willing to do anything to achieve it. But the whims of fate were against Ranuccio and the Corsican people. Caught between the shores of the Italian peninsula, the Kingdom of France, and the growing Spanish empire, the island proved too vital to the preservation of our Christian heritage for it to fall prey to the Turks. I am sorry to say liberty can never be a lasting option for Corsica."

"Perhaps the Corsicans can take comfort in the thought that their defeat served a greater good," Figueroa said.

"It, of course, soothes our souls to believe such things," Andrea responded solemnly, "and yes, the subjugation of the Corsican people to French and Genoese rule helped safeguard our Christian traditions, but I find it difficult to believe that the people ever found much solace in it. There can be no substitute for liberty."

"Living under French rule has always left much to be desired, this is true," Gonzaga chimed in. "We must thank the Lord that our freedoms are safe with our Spanish protectors," he added, deferring to Figueroa as their noble ambassador.

"Hear, hear!" said Andrea, lifting his cup in tribute. "It took many years to free our beloved Genoa from the yoke of French dominance. Spain was, of course, our enemy back then, but the treatment we endured from our French allies at the same time, and from their king in particular, could not be sustained. It lacked due regard and a proper appreciation of our service." Andrea raised his cup even higher. "Long live Charles V, King of Spain and Holy Roman Emperor."

After they all drank and set down their cups, Giovannandrea tried his question once again: "What happened to Ranuccio?"

Andrea's face grew dark, not out of anger for anything that poor little Giovannandrea might have said or implied, but again because of how the French, Genoa's supposed ally at the time, handled the issue. The lack of respect they paid Andrea irked him to this day.

"What happened did not exactly do justice to my efforts and those of my men who fought bravely for the French flag," Andrea said, shaking his head in disgust.

He was referring to the fact that upon Ranuccio's arrival in Genoa, rather than trying the rebel for treason and promptly hanging him by the neck, the French prevailed upon the current rulers of the government to set him free. As it turned out, the French king had proffered a secret deal whereby Ranuccio would be enrolled into the Order of Saint Michael, the highest dynastic order of chivalry in France, awarded a substantial sum of French *livre*, and escorted unmolested out of the city, all under the condition that he cease all hostilities toward the Kingdom of France. Andrea walked away from the event dispirited and understandably disillusioned. As he recounted this sad episode to his guests, he realized more clearly than ever that the incident was, in fact, the first straw of many that would eventually break the camel's back with regard to his relationship with the French Crown.

"Meanwhile, the infighting between the nobles and the popolari in our city grew more vindictive and bloody with each passing day," said Andrea. "In the end, as you all know, the people's representative, Paolo da Novi, was elected doge in 1507, a political reality that our French friends simply could not tolerate. Within months, their troops descended onto our peninsula and found refuge in the neighboring Lombardy. With the French fleet anchored safely off the coast of the lighthouse and poised to strike, their infantry marched through the Giovi Pass and quickly assumed full control of our dear city." Andrea paused to recall the grueling events of those turbulent days, then continued his account, not bothering to hide his aversion to what followed: "Paolo da Novi was captured while fleeing the city, then summarily beheaded in the piazza outside the Palazzo Ducale."

"The French gave the people their martyr that very day," Gonzaga quickly added.

"Quite true," Andrea replied. "His memory lived on for years afterward, strengthening the will of the popolari against the rule of the nobles."

"An antagonism you settled when you formed the new republic," Giannettino said, eyeing his dear uncle with pride.

"The infighting affected our constitution, this is quite true," said Andrea, who suddenly turned his attention toward little Giovannandrea, who was shifting restlessly in his seat, clearly needing to get something off his chest. Andrea leaned over to whisper in the boy's ear, his tone warm and caring: "Has my story upset you?"

Ginetta joined in, running her fingers through the boy's long, dark curls to comfort him. Giannettino, too, became concerned. He locked eyes with his son, hoping to instill strength and confidence in him through a simple man-to-man gaze.

"What is it, son?" he asked.

Giovannandrea just shrugged his shoulders, leaving it unclear whether he was at a loss for words or simply reluctant to speak his mind.

"Come now, my boy," said Andrea, "there is no shame in feeling compassion for your fellow man if that is the reason for your hesitation."

Giovannandrea took a deep breath. "He was elected by our people, wasn't he?" he asked timidly.

"The French wanted an excuse to install a governor in our city," Andrea replied. "They also sent troops to occupy the fortress they had constructed."

"The Briglia?" Giovannandrea asked.

"Indeed, my son," Andrea said. "They called it the Briglia, 'the bridle,' thinking they could rein us in like obedient mules."

"But they didn't have to kill the man," Giovannandrea howled.

Andrea took a moment to ponder the proper response. He knew enough about the boy to recognize his resilience and indomitable spirit. Revealing the raw truths of the world would certainly not corrupt his innocence or drain him of his passion for life, but at the same time this was supposed to be an enjoyable family gathering. *Why burden him with more bone-chilling realities about our city's troubled history than necessary?* Andrea thought to himself.

Giannettino felt differently, however. Noting Andrea's hesitancy, he jumped in with a few cold facts of life.

"One day when you are a leader of men, my son, whether in battle or in the halls of government, you will undoubtedly come face-to-face with such cruelty," Giannettino said, his eyes still fixed steadily on his young son, "and perhaps you, yourself, may have to inflict such pain on your fellow man in the name of justice. This, I am sorry to say, my dear Giovannandrea, is the world we live in."

The gruesome events following Paolo da Novi's decapitation had become legendary among the people of Genoa, and therefore Andrea was essentially recounting his story for the benefit of his two guests. But Giannettino believed that it was time for Giovannandrea to become aware of it as well, morbid details and all. Before uttering a word, however, he reached over and covered his young daughter's ears to make sure her delicate sensitivities weren't violated. He then turned and addressed his son.

"After Paolo da Novi's execution, the nobles of our fair city cheered as his headless body was tethered to a horse and dragged through the piazza, where it was eventually chopped into quarters."

Feeling the need to lend some ethical and emotional weight to Giannettino's impassive delivery of events, Andrea quickly added: "What the French did to that poor man with the consent of many of our city fathers, the Fieschi in particular, is a blemish on our city's good name. I want you to remember that."

Giannettino did not relent, however, intent on driving home his message of life's tyranny. "It wasn't enough for the man to be beheaded, drawn, and quartered," he rejoined. "A stark lesson had to be beaten into the heads of Genoa's citizens." Then after an emphatic pause, Giannettino got to the meat of the issue: "The four hacked parts of his body were dropped at each of our city gates, and his head, after being impaled on a soldier's lance, was placed on display atop the Grimaldina Tower for the entire population to witness."

The room went silent, prompting Giannettino to finally drop his hands from Placidia's delicate ears.

"If I am ever a leader of men," said Giovannandrea, "I shall see to it that such things never happen."

Upon hearing those words, Andrea reached over and caressed Giovannandrea's blushed cheek. For a man like Andrea who understood the complexities of the city's social fabric and cared for its well-being, unlike so many of his fellow noblemen, the situation at the time had presented him with a glaring crisis of conscience. The old noble class that had built the city's institutions in the thirteenth century was being rendered virtually powerless under the popolari regime. They held only one third of the seats in the Grand Council. As a member of this class, Andrea's basic sentiments nearly always sided with them, but his intelligence, judiciousness, and natural inclination as a fair leader afforded him a much wider perspective. He could see clearly, for instance, that the alternating dogeship between rival families, a trend that had begun over a century ago, contributed heavily to Genoa's internecine battles, and was simply not sustainable in the long run.

Over the years, the nobles, the rich merchant class, and the kings, princes, and dukes of the continent relied upon Andrea's military prowess, but Andrea knew he had more to offer. He genuinely believed that his acute and powerful intellect set him apart from all the rest. It wasn't enough to be a captain of war or a distinguished general in the present environment. Andrea was convinced of that. He had to hold sway over the administrative and financial sectors as well. And the time was right for him to make his move.

"Although traditionally a friend of the French, Pope Julius II was above all a Ligurian; he wanted them out of the region at all costs," Andrea said. "A few years after the da Novi incident, he managed to chase the French governor from our shores with the able support of the Fregoso family. They left only a small contingent of his soldiers in the Castelletto fortress. The warship they positioned beneath the Briglia, however, presented the real problem. Its cannons were pointed straight at our city."

"The Fregoso were loyal friends of the Doria, were they not?" asked Gonzaga.

"Indeed," Andrea affirmed without a moment's hesitation, then just as quickly, he turned his attention to little Giovannandrea. "The Fregoso doge appointed me prefect of the port at the urging of Pope Julius, no doubt, as well as commander of the entire Genoese fleet. The mission I'd been assigned was a nearly impossible one, but—"

"But he had finally earned the title of admiral," interjected Giannettino.

"At the ripe young age of forty-six years old," Andrea added ironically. The smile on Giovannandrea's face filled Andrea with nearly as much pride and satisfaction as receiving the admiralship all those many years ago. "I hope that answers your question," he said to the boy.

Giovannandrea furrowed his brow, looking a bit confused. "But you haven't told us what the mission was."

"By God," Andrea cried out, nearly bursting into laughter, "you are more difficult to impress than the Holy Roman Emperor himself. And to answer your question, besides a host of other things, our mission included kicking the French from our shores."

"By all accounts, the giant cannons aboard the French warship could have wreaked real havoc on the city," said Gonzaga.

"And what about the troops in the Castelletto?" Figueroa

asked. "Did Genoa possess an army strong enough to fight them?"

"Our first objective was to limit the damage their warship could inflict on us," Andrea said. "We knew that if we succeeded in chasing them from our harbor, their troops would have to abandon the Castelletto."

"And what you did was brilliant, if I may say so," interjected Giannettino. "Only someone like David could have killed Goliath, and that's exactly what happened," he added with pride.

Andrea was quick to elaborate, and careful to remain objective and technical in his explanation for fear of appearing overly boastful, which undoubtedly would have characterized Giannettino's rendition of events.

"We decided to use our 'sparrowhawk,' a much smaller, lighter, more agile, and infinitely quicker vessel than the French ship," Andrea said. "With me on the forecastle setting the course, and my master boatswain, we were fortunate enough to play the winds to perfection. Since we were familiar with the currents and had already calculated the ship's draft, we were able to ride the narrow divide between the promontory below the Briglia and their warship without suffering so much as a scratch. Once we moved in too close for their massive cannons to be effective, I gave the order to our oarsman to plow full speed ahead. Almost in that same instant I hollered, 'Avast!', hoping to stop close enough for our grappling hooks to pull us alongside them."

"To board their ship?" Giovannandrea shouted in a near frenzy. "To fight them face-to-face?"

"Man-to-man," his father chimed in.

"And man-to-man it was," Andrea reiterated. "But first, with the hooks firmly in the enemy's hull, we dragged them to shallower waters, where we both went aground. We then leapt onto their ship, swords in the air, ready to fight to the very last man. Of course, being a palm taller and wider than everyone else, and leading the charge onto the French ship, I was an easy target. An arquebusier's lead ball caught me straight in the chest the instant I boarded. I stumbled backwards and hit the deck like a sack of potatoes."

At that point, Andrea stopped short of saying anything further, an action that bewildered and frustrated Giannettino, who immediately jumped in to fill the void: "Our dear Prince is too modest. He refused to be distracted by the blood saturating his doublet and seeping through the slits of his metal cuirass. And despite the pain, he picked himself back up and fought alongside his men to the very end."

"You say it as if I'd performed one of the labors of Hercules," interjected Andrea. "I felt no pain. In fact, I felt nothing. And as for the blood, I hardly had the luxury of noticing it while my men fought so bravely around me, shedding so much of their own blood."

"But when all was said and done, victory was yours," said Gonzaga.

"Indeed it was," Andrea replied. "The French withdrew their men at once, and Genoa remained free of foreign intervention."

"Thanks to our admiral," proclaimed little Giovannandrea with a wide, toothy smile. "Thanks to my mesiavo."

Chapter Eleven

MARCH TOWARD LIBERTY

The walk from Palazzo del Principe to his home in Villa Vialata took Gian Luigi down to the port at the foot of the palazzo, through to the center's tangled caruggi, then up the steep Carignano hill and along the ancient Roman walls, where a handsome procession of orchards, olive groves, and stately villas led to a commanding view of the city and the endless Ligurian sea. At the very summit stood the Fieschi villa, its façade adorned with alternating slabs of pitch-black Portoro marble and milky white blocks from the quarries of Carrara. Two imposing towers studded with plaques of the Fieschi coat of arms flanked each side of the villa. An olive grove encircled it and continued down the southern slope as far as the San Giacomo district, home of one of the city's oldest churches. Rare plants, fountains, and two artificial lakes, the envy of all Genoa, embellished a botanical garden to the rear.

On cold winter evenings like this one, Gian Luigi would normally complete the trip in less than thirty minutes, with the frigid *tramontana* winds from the north helping to quicken his pace. But tonight was different. He stopped in a dozen houses along the way to welcome in the new year with friends and relatives alike, some of whom he invited to pay him a visit in Via Lata later that evening. Before cutting away from the shipyard along the port to navigate the city's narrow caruggi, he met with a few associates integral to the proposed departure of his galley in the morning. Like many crewmembers, sailors, and paid oarsmen, they were unsavory in appearance and certainly not the types of men that someone of Gian Luigi's social class would normally visit, but on Genoa's port, all manner of interactions were within the bounds of accepted behavior when dealing in affairs of adventure and commerce.

He spoke first with Gianbattista Verrina, a man of remarkable spirit and forcefulness. They nestled in a dark alcove in the Loggia della Mercanzia in Piazza Banchi, away from the port's icy currents, to exchange vital information concerning the crew that was scheduled to ship out in the morning. When the winds grew too cold to bear, Gian Luigi bid Verrina a fond farewell and moved on to the house of a fellow nobleman who at the time was hosting a gathering of prominent Genoese figures. Tradition dictated that the twelve days between Christmas and the Epiphany on January 6 be celebrated with nightly social events that typically included an excess of food, wine, music, dance, and long hours of card-playing, which, of course, involved a fair amount of gambling. Even the children were allowed to partake in certain games of chance during this period, such as *biribissi*, a form of roulette. In a city like Genoa where banking, trading, and financial transactions of all sorts defined much of its culture, and where risk-taking was an integral part of everyday life, such activities were viewed quite favorably. They revealed a person's true character, the Genoese believed, and provided a place where one's inclination to avarice, anger, and dishonesty could be tested.

Gian Luigi encountered Raffaele Sacco next, a man of dubious means, but loyal to the Fieschi family and an experienced seaman. They spoke while promenading through the caruggi among the holiday crowds. Sacco assured Gian Luigi that he would see him at Vialata later in the evening—not in the grand salon, where the invited guests would be enjoying their food and drink, but in the villa's kitchen where his dear friend, Vincenzo Calcagno, worked as a trusted servant. Gian Luigi had grown fond of both Calcagno and Sacco in the last few months, and despite the chatter of a few uppity aristocrats who felt that the young Fieschi's liberality was in poor taste, he would often venture into the gardens just outside the kitchen door to share a flask of homebrewed wine and discuss topics too sultry and indecorous to broach with his peers. Gian Luigi's reputation as a "man of the people" was well warranted and benefited him greatly in his recruitment of men for his latest undertaking.

When Gian Luigi opened the massive wrought iron gate at Vialata and stepped onto the path leading to his front door, he felt the sudden urge to stop at one of the many *taggiasche* olive trees that covered the grounds. This particular tree had held a special meaning for him ever since he was a ten-year-old boy, the year his father, Sinibaldo, passed away. Being rather slight in stature when he was young, he would often climb atop the tree's sturdiest branch, which provided a panoramic view of the sea below, and take in the spectacle of it all. Like many boys his age, he daydreamed of finding out what lay beyond the horizon. He'd heard stories of fellow Genoese citizens who had explored the western coast of Africa, and of Christopher Columbus, a seafarer in search of far-off eastern lands, as well as John Cabot, who, under the auspices of the king of England, ventured to the New World. It was during one of these reflective moments on an uncharacteristically warm afternoon in February that young Gian Luigi received word of his father's death. Ever since that day he would sit beneath that tree when the mood struck him, not so much to imagine a brave and adventurous future as he did in his younger years, but to recall the many times his loving father joined him in the shade of that very same olive tree to share the Fieschi family's daring exploits and long, noble history.

The air on the Carignano hill blew in violent gusts whenever the icy winds from the Alpine north merged with the milder coastal breezes. The battle between the two opposing currents would often erupt into a near tempest. Gian Luigi had grown so accustomed to these frequent squalls that, oddly enough, they calmed him down even in the most stressful of times. They mirrored his inner turmoil, a part of himself he rarely shared with his adoring friends, who viewed him as the new standard-bearer of the Fieschi family, a reputation he took to heart. His wife, Eleonora, knew of his demons firsthand, and she, too, along with the winter winds, could placate his troubled mind with her soft and loving words that rang like the verses of troubadour poets to his ears. But tonight, on the eve of an endeavor he had planned and dreamt about for so long, he wanted nothing of the sort. The cold, dispassionate presence of the same olive tree that kept him sane and happy throughout his youth was all he wanted.

Gian Luigi peered out over the rooftops into the starless distance, where the tall and stately *Lanterna* beamed its golden light out to sea, and where a far-off ship revealed the flicker of a solitary gaslight in the captain's cabin as it sought refuge in the dead of night. His eyes scanned the port, finally coming to rest on the hazy silhouette of his private galley hidden in the frosted mist. Although the distance from Vialata to his galley below stretched much too far to detect any human activity, he knew in his heart that all the preliminary measures had been set in place. His men were simply awaiting his authorization to trigger phase two of the preparations, an undertaking that would last long into the night. But, despite Giannettino having cleared him for departure, Gian Luigi hesitated to give his final go-ahead until he could sit comfortably beneath the freshly pruned branches of his chosen tree and properly contemplate all the risks and benefits of his venture.

The thoughts rustling around in Gian Luigi's mind brought him back, once again, to his father's sobering words as a boy: *We must put our faith in a man of strength if ever we wish to free our great city from those who threaten our liberty.* The man of rising power and influence to whom Sinibaldo would continually allude was, of course, his dear friend and rival, Andrea Doria. The story of Andrea's heroic victory over the pirate Godoli off the shores of the Tuscan archipelago never failed to hold young

Gian Luigi's attention. Godoli's commandeering of Genoese merchant ships had the city's bankers, investors, and government officials up in arms, prompting them to dispatch Andrea with a fleet of ships to hunt him down—and hunt him down he did! The pirate's sudden capture, which came on the heels of Andrea's success against the French in the battle of the Briglia, etched his name into the hearts and minds of the Genoese citizenry.

Even Andrea's fellow noblemen, covetous and envious by nature, could not deny the magnitude of his deeds. Word had quickly spread that he had boarded Godoli's ship and gone toe-to-toe with the enemy, despite having once again suffered a severe wound, this time to his shoulder, from a pirate's mighty scimitar. The part of the story that had evolved to near mythical proportion for much of the general populace was how Andrea, without missing a beat, tore the shirt from a fallen corsair to stanch the spurting blood, and went on to fight alongside his men until victory was assured. He returned home with the leader of the Barbary pirates humiliated and bound in chains, and with his future as Genoa's prince within reach.

Sinibaldo's admiration for Andrea and the Doria family shined through with each tale he spun of Genoa's march toward liberty. *Valor and courage in the face of defeat shall always be rewarded*, Gian Luigi could still hear his father say. He was referring to the generous gift of two newly constructed galleys that the Republic awarded Andrea for his triumph over the French and his capture of the pirate Godoli. The gesture, of course, came with a list of responsibilities, but it also afforded Andrea the privilege of taking possession of all booty he appropriated from the enemy while in the course of his service to the Republic. This age-old tradition of reaping the spoils of war while sailing in the name of powerful city-states, kingdoms, and empires obviously carried with it the potential for enormous wealth. *And with his reputation as a soldier, sailor, and a man of military genius came great financial gain*, Sinibaldo would repeat to his son ad nauseam, hoping to infuse in him the same thirst for power and prosperity that he had so jealously witnessed in Andrea. *It is how we can keep the Fieschi name alive*, he would inevitably say.

Having been awarded two lethally armed galleys inflated Andrea's political, military, and financial status almost over-night, despite the ambiguity over who actually held the rights to these vessels. In one sense, Andrea owned them outright, which allowed him to utilize the ships in *asiento*, a system by which he could charter them, and his services, to other political or private entities. At the same time, however, a small percentage of these galleys also belonged to the city of Genoa, which required Andrea to protect Ligurian shores against Barbary pirates and Turkish ships, an activity that handed him a handsome salary as well. Of course, such a system often had Andrea, and other seaman who sailed in asiento, serving two masters. Although it seemed questionable in principle, the system was consid-ered fair game and quite legitimate at the time, as long as it presented no real conflicts of interest. Over the long term, this type of arrangement tended to favor limited hit-and-run forays and quick ambushes over long, drawn-out battles where too many lives could be lost or, more importantly, where the galleys themselves were at risk.

No naval victory, no matter how big or small, was worth sacrificing the source of his wealth and power. Andrea understood this dynamic from the very outset, and adopted it as a military tactic. Ironically, this mode of combat also formed the cornerstone of a corsair's military philosophy, which is why so many of Andrea's compatriots saw him as their "Pirate Prince," a term intended to be both commendable and degrading.

Sinibaldo's unceasing message of liberty made itself particularly clear when he spoke of the years immediately preceding the city's great reforms of 1528, and it was precisely on those events that Gian Luigi wished to concentrate as he leaned against the olive tree's twisted trunk. The gravity of his impending enterprise weighed heavily on his shoulders, and he welcomed these few moments of time to reflect on its many ramifications. Taking comfort in the fact that the evening meal was still a few hours off, he curled the fur-lined collar of his cloak tightly around his neck to brave the blistering cold, and continued to bask in the memory of his father's sage advice. He was a well-cultured man and had enough understanding of recent history to put Sinibaldo's words into proper political context. He took into consideration that leadership on the continent had changed dramatically in the decade before his birth in 1520, which severely influenced the subsequent course of events, and Genoa's future in particular: France, the Holy Roman Empire, and the Vatican had all installed new rulers. *These men would have had almost absolute control over our city's future if it weren't for Andrea's cunning, bravery, and expertise in assuring our ultimate independence* were the words Gian Luigi remembered most clearly from his father's discourses. They lay at the heart of the respect he bore for his current prince and protector.

Being a keen observer of events, Sinibaldo narrated his adventures and daily experiences as if imparting valuable lessons in history. He spoke in great detail of the time between 1513, which marked a violent uprising against French domination, and 1522, when the Spanish brutally sacked the city of Genoa, destroying everything in sight and burning it nearly to the ground. Even now, all these years later, Gian Luigi could see the image of his father's face contorted with rage as he recounted how the Spanish seized control from the French with lightning speed, forcing Andrea to abandon the city. It wasn't long before King Francis I offered Andrea a six-year contract to work exclusively for the Kingdom of France. The terms were simple: Bring Genoa back within the French sphere of influence. But in actuality, Andrea's long-term goal, one that he never dared express to his French patron, differed considerably: put an end to the political infighting within Genoa's city walls and drive all foreign interlopers from Ligurian shores. Andrea didn't hesitate to accept the king's offer with that secret objective ruminating in the back of his mind. *I may have worked against Andrea Doria's interests at first, aiding the Spanish in their violent takeover,* Gian Luigi recalled his father saying, *but I quickly realized he was our only hope.* Shortly afterward, in fact, Sinibaldo joined forces with his old rival to liberate the city.

Except for the northern winds bustling through the leaves on the trees like swarms of locusts, the world around Gian Luigi remained hushed and unusually still. Out of the corner of his eye, he could see the light from a recently kindled lamp in the window of the grand salon. This, of course, meant that within the hour he would have to put on his best face and greet the incoming guests with all the charm and gentlemanliness for which he had become so well known. There was so much of his father's wisdom he still wanted to explore, and so much peace of mind he still needed before he could clear all the discursive thoughts from his head. Gian Luigi's forays into the past, seeking the wisdom of his deceased father on how to become a man of virtue and integrity, helped provide him with the proper direction, or so he hoped. He'd always admired Andrea's ability to concentrate and Giannettino's razor-sharp attention to details, and wanted desperately not only to emulate them, but to surpass them in every way. However, something inside him always told him he wasn't up to the task. He despised that feeling, and over the years what began as a benign, almost natural, form of jealously, albeit born of true admiration and respect, grew dark and malicious, transforming his genuine esteem into envy and even hatred.

Of course, being no more than ten years old when Sinibaldo shared his stories, much of what his father said was lost on the poor boy. Only now, after having witnessed Andrea in action, and having understood the breadth of his political and military acumen, could Gian Luigi assess the true weight of his father's stories, and the reason behind his telling them. Was Gian Luigi being primed to take command? *Was that why he told me all those things,* Gian Luigi thought to himself, *why he asked Andrea to be my guardian? If so, I still have so much to learn.*

But perhaps the most pressing question Gian Luigi kept asking himself was: *What actions must a future leader take to ensure a city's freedom when the current prince is old and at the end of his tenure, and when the man in line to succeed him, although quite capable, is prone to tyranny and roundly hated by the people?* Gian Luigi had reflected on these issues hundreds of times over the course of the last several months, and on this cold and starless night he found himself no closer to an easy answer. *Certainly, armed rebellion cannot be the only solution,* he thought to himself.

As the candles in the windows of the grand salon lit up one by one behind him, throwing the entire *piano nobile*, the main floor, into sharp relief, Gian Luigi sighed with resignation knowing his time for reflection was up. He turned and shuffled to the massive oak doors at the villa's entrance, none the wiser. But, of course, the night was still young.

Chapter Twelve

ROAD TO REFORM

Andrea's recollection of events following the Sack of Genoa by Spanish troops differed slightly from Sinibaldo's somewhat panegyrical account. He broached the subject when Gonzaga asked him the indelicate question of how he liked working for the French all those years. Andrea chuckled at first, then followed up with some rather strong words.

"It was a disaster," he said flatly. "The war between Emperor Charles V and King Francis I was tearing the peninsula apart with France suffering the majority of defeats." Andrea then turned and stared straight at little Giovannandrea with a glimmer in his eye. "But as admiral of the French fleet, my ships were the only ones inflicting any lasting damage on the Spanish."

"His name resounded throughout the Empire," interjected Gonzaga, addressing his words to the young boy as well. "Your mesiavo's seventeen French galleys pounced on our thirty-six ships like a lion devouring a tiny mouse. I know because I was there." And with that, Gonzaga spun around to Andrea with a mischievous grin. "My question, however, still remains: How did you like fighting for the French?"

"Had you allowed me to finish, you would have gotten your answer," Andrea rejoined with a smile. "As I was saying, during my six-year contract with them, I fought in Marseille and Savona, and I even captured several Spanish captains, among them an esteemed prince, for whom King Francis promised me a ransom of twenty-five thousand ducats!"

"Twenty-five thousand ducats!" Giovannandrea cried out. "That sounds like a lot!"

"It would be if I were ever paid," Andrea shot back. "But like that scoundrel Louis XII before him, who released Ranuccio della Rocca of Corsica, King Francis saw fit to free the prince without so much as a thought of me or my men, and the danger we encountered on his behalf."

"It was money that would have gone to pay for wages and armaments for the king's own ships, was it not?" said Gonzaga.

Andrea nodded in agreement. "Which led me to believe that France's coffers were dry, and that Francis had likely kept the ransom for himself," he said, shaking his head. "A sign of bad things to come."

"The capture of the French king at the Battle of Pavia a short time later was no better an augur," Gonzaga said with a laugh.

Andrea agreed. "Even his dear mother predicted their demise," he said. "King Francis had lost the battle of all battles."

"But with his honor intact," Gonzaga cried out, his tone gushing with irony. "Or so they would have us all believe."

"You attempted to rescue him, did you not?" Giannettino asked.

"I did," Andrea replied. "But King Francis himself forbade it for fear of being killed. Something Emperor Charles would never have done due to his high moral character. The recently elected Pope Clement VII picked up the mantle after that by forming a vast alliance against Spain and the Empire. The League of Cognac was his monster."

"And the rest is history," Gonzaga cried out, alluding to the Empire's decisive victory.

"I sense gratification in your voice, dear Lord Gonzaga," Andrea replied. "Although the wars of that period ended kindly for Spain and the Empire, as a native of this Italian peninsula, I must confess that the means to achieve those ends filled me with much sadness."

"Allow me to respectfully remind you, dear Prince, that despite your being on the losing side during those wars, they ended quite kindly for you and your city," Gonzaga shot back.

The governor of Milan's candor did not ruffle Andrea in the least. In fact, he preferred the tough talk of condottieri over the lilied language of dignitaries and diplomats. He saw Gonzaga's plain-spoken outburst as an opportunity to add his voice to the events of history. He may have previously referred to Pope Clement's alliance with France, Florence, and Venice as a monster, but the pope had chosen Andrea to lead the Vatican's eight galleys against the Empire, which Andrea happily accepted for a fee of thirty-five thousand *scudi* a year. The mission played into the scheme that Andrea had been pondering for years:

finding peace and independence for his native city while also feeding his insatiable desire to accumulate great wealth and power. He had already begun construction on what was to become his sumptuous Palazzo del Principe, but his dream of building the largest and most prestigious villa on the Riviera needed more funds, and his ever-expanding sense of self-worth required a formidable upgrade in rank and influence. He, therefore, went about fashioning his participation in the League's war against Spain and the Empire in his own image. After embarking on a mission to occupy La Spezia and Portofino along the southern Ligurian coast as well as Savona to the west, he set his sights on ridding the Spanish from his native city with France's help.

The crusade to free Genoa did not go well for Andrea at first, with the Duchy of Milan, Genoa's northern neighbor, thwarting Andrea's efforts to capture the city from the Spanish at every turn. Andrea's later attempts proved more successful, however, but in the end only served to pique the emperor's ire further, prompting him to unleash twelve thousand soldiers onto the Italian peninsula to hasten a victory. The overwhelming ferocity of his troops, made up mostly of German mercenaries known as lansquenets, instilled fear into the hearts of the League of Cognac. Leading the defense for the League was none other than Francesco Maria della Rovere, son of Giovanna da Montefeltro, whom Andrea had rescued from the clutches of Cesare Borgia some twenty-five years earlier. Francesco had succeeded his grandfather, Guidobaldo, as Duke of Urbino in 1508, and was subsequently appointed captain general of the Church by his uncle, Pope Julius II. By 1526, at the time of the Empire's descent into Italy, Francesco was heralded as the "Italian Hercules" and the peninsula's best protection against the conquering hordes from beyond the Alps.

Despite Pope Clement VII having recruited some of the most skilled condottieri to lead the charge against the Empire's German and Spanish mercenaries, as always, the Italian city-states had their own separate and often conflicting agendas, which allowed the Imperial troops to plow forward and reach the walls of Rome in early May of 1527. By that time, the lansquenets were hungry, tired, and, most importantly, furious at having been deprived of any compensation for all their efforts.

On May 6, with Andrea's ships poised off the shores of Civitavecchia near the mouth of the Tiber river, Emperor Charles V's lansquenets, almost entirely made up of Lutherans scornful of the Vatican's power and corruption, descended on Rome with all the righteousness of avenging angels and the savagery of infernal beasts. There was nothing Andrea and his fleet of seventeen ships could do. The lansquenets' thirst for plunder, destruction, and depravity took three days to slake. No convent, monastery, household, or female inhabitant escaped their wrath; no window or door remained intact, nor did any Roman statue survive decapitation or demolition. Nearly a thousand Swiss guards, Rome's last line of defense, were slaughtered. Fires sprang up everywhere, corpses covered the streets and alleyways, and disease eventually blanketed the city and nearby country-side. Deaths numbered in the tens of thousands, mostly women and children, and pillaging ran rampant into the winter of the following year. Pope Clement VII was able to find refuge in the Castel Sant'Angelo with three thousand of his guards to protect him. Only after months of waiting for the lansquenets' fury to dissipate was the pope able to escape to Orvieto, a city on the banks of the Tiber, a hundred kilometers to the north. Rome hadn't experienced such devastation in over a thousand years.

The circle of listeners around Andrea tightened as he told of Rome's awful fate.

"Despite all the chaos and uncertainty, the time was ripe for an assault on Genoa," Andrea cried out. "And the liberation of our beloved city!" he quickly added with even more emotion. "The first thing I did was reestablish my alliance with that scoundrel, King Francis of France. Then I sailed to Portofino, where I met Cesare Fregoso to plan our attack. My cousin Filippino joined us as well."

At the mention of his cousin, Andrea shifted his attention to Giannettino, peering straight into his eyes with all the weight and severity of his position as prince, admiral, and family patriarch.

"Before you stood at my side, dear Giannettino, Filippino was there with me," Andrea said. "Look at where he is now, my son, praised as one of Genoa's greatest heroes, just as you shall be one day."

"As he already is," Figueroa chimed in, obviously an admirer of Giannettino and an avid supporter of his succession to Andrea as prince and de facto ruler of Genoa.

Andrea acknowledged Figueroa's compliment with a slight nod. "I could not have captured Godoli without my faithful cousin Filippino," he went on. "Just like without my young nephew here, that crafty pirate Dragut would have slipped between our fingers," he added, slapping Giannettino on the knee.

The capture of the infamous corsair just a few years ago took Genoa by storm. Giannettino seized nine of Dragut's vessels off the coast of Corsica, two of which were heavily armed galleys. He liberated two thousand Christian prisoners and delivered the pirate to Andrea within days of his first commission as commander of his own fleet.

"But, of course, I digress," said Andrea with a laugh. "Let us return to our saving the Republic, shall we?" He waited for the snickering to die down before adding, "Now, where was I?"

"Off the lovely shores of Portofino," Figueroa replied.

"Ah, yes," Andrea said, reaching for his cup of Rossese.

"Actually, you were telling us how you liked working with the French all those years," insisted Gonzaga. "Did you know at the time that you would eventually abandon them?"

"I knew they could not be trusted," Andrea shot back.

"But first let us hear how he and Fregoso drew up their strategy," contested Giannettino. "I have heard many stories of those days, but never from our Prince himself."

"There is much he never reveals about those days," Peretta blurted out before anyone else could utter a word.

The room went silent. Everyone waited for either Peretta to explain herself or Andrea to reply.

Peretta and Andrea locked eyes. She betrayed the glimmer of a smile, while he remained stone-faced for as long as he could before he would allow himself to do the same.

"When one talks of war, I suppose it is only appropriate to speak of love in the same breath," he said sarcastically. "Both being equally interesting and as dangerous."

"Hear, hear!" quipped Ginetta, raising her cup in mock tribute.

"I concur that love can be as dangerous," said Peretta, poised and self-assured. "But as to it being as interesting, I must admit, I have my doubts."

All the men in the room, including little Giovannandrea, nodded in agreement, confident that nothing could hold a candle to the fascination of war, although none of them knew precisely why Andrea had suddenly embraced the topic of love in the first place. Peretta's mischievous grin grew even wider, making it clear she had more to say.

"War lacks the clever nuances of love," she said. "Love can drive men into battle as it did the ancient Greeks against the Trojans, or induce them to peace as our Christian faith instructs us. Love can be war's greatest weapon as well," she went on to proclaim in a calm, steady voice, "because it has the power to subdue the enemy without so much as a fight."

"Hear, hear!" Ginetta repeated, this time in all seriousness.

By this point, Peretta had certainly succeeded in piquing everyone's interest. What, indeed, was Andrea hiding about those days? Ginetta's smirk revealed her awareness of Peretta's true meaning, as did Andrea's. And as for the rest, all they could do was wait for clarification, except for little Giovannandrea, who couldn't care one way or another; he simply wanted his mesiavo to get on with his war story.

It now remained up to Andrea to respond to his dear wife's provocation, which he did straightaway: "Peretta de Mari Usodimare, daughter of the great Gerardo Usodimare and Teodorina Cybo, and I were married without much ostentation or pageantry."

"Which is to say in secret," interjected Peretta.

Andrea hid his nervous smile behind an even more nervous cough. As it had been made abundantly clear throughout the evening, he hated bearing his soul, especially regarding the intimacies of his life.

"In secret," he repeated in a near whisper. "We announced it publicly, as you may know, in 1527, shortly after taking Genoa from the Spanish." Andrea forced out another anxious cough before continuing. Not even the arquebusier's lead ball lodged in his chest at the battle of the Briglia pained him as much. "In reality, of course, our wedding took place several years before that, and given our advanced age, we . . . ."

Andrea stopped himself right there. The look on Peretta's face told him he'd already started off on the wrong foot. He corrected himself without hesitation.

"Given *my* advanced age," he said, "I decided . . . I mean to say, *we* thought it best . . . to dispense with formalities. Our little wedding was quite beautiful, actually."

"Can we go back to saving the Republic now?" inquired Giovannandrea.

The boy's bluntness and the series of giggles it provoked managed to clear the air of any awkwardness. No one was more grateful for Giovannandrea's interruption than Andrea himself.

He rewarded his little nephew with a quick wink that no one but the boy actually caught, a gesture that filled Giovannandrea's heart with pure joy. And, of course, the fact that his mesiavo would now continue his tale of war and freedom was icing on the cake.

"Fregoso and Filippino sat at my table in the *Capitana* off the coast of Portofino," Andrea began. "I had already conceived of the plan and simply needed Fregoso to concur. Filippino trusted me blindly, so I knew he would carry out whatever orders I gave him."

Andrea's eyes burned with resolve as he recalled the scene in his head. For a moment he felt as if he were actually there, twenty years earlier—already an old man by some standards, but clearly at the beginning of his life, his real life, the one he had always envisioned for himself. The image stood out in his mind as pristine as a reflection in a limpid pond and conjured up emotions he hadn't experienced since that very day. He lost himself in that thought, staring idly into the fire, letting the images take him wherever they needed to go. And in that moment, he remembered word for word his address to the officers gathered around him in his admiral's quarters; it was a soulful rallying cry.

"Captains!" he bellowed from his seat at the head of the long oak table. "We are about to alter the destiny of our beloved city, our precious Republic." The admiral then turned his attention away from Fregoso and his trusty cousin, and focused on the squad of officers and ship's company that had been recruited for the venture, all of them loyal to the Republic's cause. "The Kingdom of France is with us," he went on, "but no Frenchman will descend from the mountains into our great city to rid us of the Spanish; no Frenchman shall sail with us or storm our Ligurian shores. Only true and virtuous Genoese soldiers shall have that privilege. When the order is given, Captain Fregoso will lead his army into the city. Captain Filippino Doria's men will infiltrate the feudal lands along our southern shores, those loyal to the Adorno family and our adversaries, while my galleys engage Spanish ships in the harbor, leaving them with no way of escape. By then, the people of Genoa, unable to forget the brutal Spanish attack of six short years ago, will rally to our cause. Once we rush ashore to join Captain Fregoso's troops, victory will be ours."

As with all plans and strategies, things did not unfold exactly as hoped. Andrea hesitated a moment to gather his thoughts before moving forward with his narrative.

"Of course, you all know the end result of our efforts, but the particulars of the battle, the minor mishaps, miscalculations, and surprises, tell the true story. Filippino found himself surrounded in the hills north of Portofino and was captured, and Adorno's army caught Fregoso unawares on the outskirts of the city. So, rather than engage the Spanish fleet in the harbor as planned, we went ashore and rushed to Fregoso's aid, the real threat of being surrounded notwithstanding. But what happened next filled me with more hope and brought me more joy than I'd ever experienced in my life."

Andrea found it interesting that despite knowing how events eventually turned out, everyone seemed to be sitting on the edge of their seats and waiting for more. Being soldiers themselves,

Giannettino and Gonzaga appreciated the details of combat and devoured Andrea's every word; Figueroa sat spellbound by all the political intricacies, mentally working out possible truces, compromises, and treaties; and little Giovannandrea's imagination ran rampant with romantic images of warriors in the heat of battle. Even Peretta, Ginetta, and little Placidia couldn't help but surrender themselves to the suspense of it. Peretta, however, also had her own memories of those days. They resonated deep in her gut. After all, she had just married her dear Andrea back then, and hadn't the slightest idea whether she would ever see him again.

The tension was thick. The simple question "What in heaven's name filled you with so much hope and joy?" sat on the tip of everyone's tongue, but no one dared speak it. Their body language said it all, however, prompting Andrea to finally get on with it.

"As our troops fanned through the city calling for the overthrow of the Adorno government and the ouster of the Spanish, the people rose up in near-unanimous support. They rushed out into the streets to join our ranks," he cried, his voice rising with emotion. "The battle was swift, casualties were few, and victory came within hours. A truce was offered, and I readily accepted; the Spanish vacated the Castelletto; and I entered the Doge's Palace that very afternoon as the people chanted 'Pater Patriae!' in the piazza below."

Andrea sat back in his chair and closed his eyes to better savor the memory. It had taken him sixty-one years to arrive at that moment, which was decidedly just a starting point for him.

"Although Cesare Fregoso wanted to proclaim the birth of the new republic right there and then, I felt it was premature, which indeed it was, as history has proven."

"How did you know to wait?" asked Gonzaga.

"I'm not sure I did, exactly," he replied. "I knew, first of all, that we had to transcend the traditional dualism of electing either an Adorno or a Fregoso as doge. I insisted on choosing an outsider to govern our city. He was from Milan and therefore above the fray, which seemed to please nearly everyone. Secondly, I was convinced that it was not yet time to ruffle those delicate French feathers. Not yet. I studied the situation at hand: King Francis wanted to keep us under his thumb while carrying out his protracted war against Emperor Charles. And for his part, Charles wanted control of Genoa because he needed a safe passageway between Spain, where he resided and administered his empire, and the territories of Austria, Bohemia, and Germany under his command. In both cases our beloved homeland would most likely have become the final battleground. I decided, therefore, it was best to remain under French dominion for the time being in order to preserve our institutions, and then patiently and judiciously plan our next move."

Chapter Thirteen

BIRTH OF THE REPUBLIC

By spring of 1528 France and Spain had rekindled their hatred for one another. This time, however, Andrea could clearly predict the winner, and unfortunately, France, Genoa's present protector, had lost its luster. Andrea's relationship with the French had, in fact, been deteriorating over the past few years for a number of reasons. Militarily, France's ground troops betrayed considerable weaknesses and lacked an overarching sense of strategy and discipline. On a purely personal level, Andrea mistrusted the French king. Despite Andrea's victories in Naples, Corsica, and Salerno, and his continued loyalty to the French cause, King Francis almost systematically neglected to pay Andrea his due, both in salary and in respect.

Meanwhile, Spain's supremacy on the continent grew exponentially, especially following their successful campaign the previous year, culminating in the Sack of Rome. And, as it turned out, Emperor Charles' needs and objectives intersected neatly with Andrea's. Their affinity for one another blossomed, with both men intuitively recognizing the personal and political advantages of their friendship. As opposed to France's egocentric plan for Genoa and its role in the Mediterranean, the emperor's vision benefitted both parties. The Spanish had no interest in hegemony over the region and would have wholeheartedly welcomed Andrea as their admiral, while France's proud and insanely jealous military refused to accept the idea of a foreigner like Andrea as their leader. But what raised Andrea's hackles most was King Francis's hidden strategy of assuming absolute control over Genoa and the Riviera.

Over the years, Genoa had profited little from its partnership with France both in political and economic terms. Genoa and Spain, however, had been doing business for decades, and now that the Spanish were enjoying a virtual monopoly on all products from the New World, the attraction for Genoese merchants was considerable. Spain had much to gain by aligning itself with Genoa as well. Always in need of hard cash, Emperor Charles liked the idea of having easy access to the Bank of San Giorgio and wealthy Genoese bankers. And in order to properly shelter its financial interests, Spain needed a reliable Mediterranean fleet like Andrea's to defend it against the French and the increasing threat of piracy. Knowing, therefore, that Andrea's six-year contract with the French king was about to expire, Charles V made him the proposal of a lifetime: a free and independent Genoa. And in contrast to France's ubiquitous presence in the region, the emperor guaranteed that no Spanish soldiers would occupy the presidio in the Castelletto or the Briglia. He also made it clear that the internal affairs of the city did not interest him in the least, either politically or economically. In essence, the emperor championed a free, prosperous, and self-governing city.

In August 1528, a secret agreement was signed tying Genoa's fortunes to Spain and the Holy Roman Empire. The contract added twelve galleys to Andrea's fleet, doubling the number of ships under his command while substantially increasing his salary. It also went a long way toward consolidating Andrea's position as condottiero of the sea, making his future task of ridding the French from neighboring Savona and regaining control of Genoa relatively painless.

Just a few weeks after the contract was signed, Andrea sailed into Genoa's harbor. He stood tall at the helm of the *Capitana*, looking out over his beloved city as the throngs on shore chanted "Long live the Republic!" He finally came ashore on a brisk September morning to further chants of "Doria and liberty!" and "Death to the French!" At the age of sixty-one, after years of service to many masters, but with the goal of presiding over a free and autonomous Genoa, Andrea Doria had finally entered the Doge's Palace hailed as the city's prince and liberator.

On September 12, the day after entering the city, Andrea met with his cousin Filippino in the office of the doge in the Palazzo Ducale. He was joined by his most trusted officers as well as several of the most distinguished representatives of Genoa's popolari and noble class. The important business of constructing a new republic awaited everyone's attention, but what stood first and foremost on Andrea's mind was his desire to apprise Genoa's citizenry of the current political situation. A handful of nobles were privy to Andrea's clandestine meetings with Spanish emissaries, and were later made aware of Genoa's secret transfer of allegiance from the French to Charles V and the Empire, but the general populace enjoyed no such privileges. They had to be told. All thoughts of political stratagem fell by the wayside in Andrea's mind and gave way to gallantry and clear-eyed statesmanship. Now that the torment and confusion of war lay behind him and a modicum of peace was at hand, at least for the time being, he wanted desperately to focus on a vision for Genoa that included the needs and desires of all of its citizens.

He turned to Filippino with fire in his eyes. "Send out heralds telling the people to gather in the piazza before the noonday bells."

"At once, Admiral," Filippino replied, rising from his seat at Andrea's right hand. He relayed the message to his confidant, who then turned and hurried dutifully out the door.

Andrea crossed the room to the elegant French doors that opened onto the balcony, his mind racing with ideas. He straightened his back, standing tall as he gazed into the relative emptiness of the streets below. Despite the welcome news of French troops being severely weakened in the Castelletto and the Briglia, he could feel the people's chronic unease. "They deserved nothing less than the truth," he whispered to himself. Liberty came at a price; this much he would have to concede to them. He would tell the multitudes that freedom without the protection of one of Europe's major powers was impossible. This was simple reality. And only Spain offered a sustainable alliance.

His biggest challenge would be convincing the people of the wisdom of his decision, albeit one that tended to merge his personal goals with those of the city. And, no doubt, the primary question on everyone's mind was about the nature of the new republic, especially among the city's oldest families, who were suspicious of the kind of government he would see fit to build, given the power, respect, and enormous influence he had amassed in the last two decades. *Surely he would proclaim himself leader of the new government,* Andrea imagined them saying, *and plant the seeds of a long-lasting Doria dynasty.* Andrea's astute political sense, however, warned him of the pitfalls of harboring such authoritarian notions. He understood that Genoa's people, like those of Venice, another maritime state, would frown on a monarchical system; in time, the city's noble families would most likely rise up against the new masters.

He kept all of this in mind as he studied the gathering crowd through a slit in the white linen drapes that graced the balcony doors. The wild chanting that had greeted him the previous day had abated, and the unease he sensed earlier had now grown into something quite tangible. And this worried Andrea. He had always been accustomed to finding the straightest line between himself and victory, then pursuing it to the very end.

The process was quite straightforward, really. It demanded the requisite amount of input from his advisers and aides, but in the end, the correct path to success rose directly from the pit of his gut. That was his secret. The final decision rested solely on his shoulders, which suited him just fine. And his subordinates, bound by a sense of duty and an unbending military code of conduct, executed his orders without question.

But the situation in which he found himself now presented

a completely different set of variables, causing him to question his ability to navigate all its snares and booby traps. In the political world, danger usually percolated from within, often without notice, sometimes from the depths of the *popolo minore*, or common people, but most frequently from the heights of the noble elite. Chants of praise would transform into cries of contempt in the snap of a finger. Opposition was a much stealthier beast. Victory could no longer be Andrea's sole objective. Notions of fairness, civility, prosperity, peace, and well-being would also have to come into play. For a moment, he truly doubted whether he was up to the task . . . but only for a moment.

Andrea stepped out onto the balcony as the noon bells in the Grimaldina tower echoed throughout the city. The people stood elbow to elbow, filling the immense piazza to the brim. The cheers that greeted him signaled a deep admiration and respect, but given the size of the crowd, it fell short of a resounding welcome, not so much because of Genoa's time-honored tradition of stoicism and reserve, but more out of a sense of trepidation. Genoa had experienced radical changes in leadership in the past, that was true, which the citizenry took in relative stride, but this was discernibly unlike anything before it. Usually, from the point of view of the average merchant, fisherman, and servant, all that really changed in these circumstances were the faces of those in power. Life carried on as usual. This time, however, Andrea had identified the factors stifling Genoa's path to freedom and dealt with them with meticulous and exhaustive tenacity. Everyone realized that the hour for making a clean start had arrived.

Andrea needed absolute silence in order for his voice to reach the perimeters of his vast audience. He waited for the hum of excitement to ease. Then, sensing that the right moment was approaching, he took a deep breath, gathering enough steam to deliver his opening words of appreciation to the thousands who had assembled to hear him.

"Citizens of Genoa," he cried out, "today, the twelfth day of September of the year 1528, I declare that our great city has been liberated from the chains of foreign domination."

A thunderous roar lifted from every corner of the piazza, stopping him in mid-sentence. It took a full minute for it to subside.

"And they shall never return to our shores," he continued, "at least for as long as I have the strength to resist."

Cries of "Liberty!" spread throughout the crowd.

Andrea pressed on: "I could not remain indifferent to our city's disintegration and the suffering of our people who could no longer walk our streets and precious caruggi safely, by night or by day."

He paused to gauge the level of support in the crowd, which, again, although robust and sincere, lacked the enthusiasm he had expected. *They are still filled with suspicion*, he told himself.

In the next instant, he cried out with a tremor in his voice: "On this day, from the halls of our beloved Doge's Palace, I swear to you upon the soul of my dear *moæ* that we shall never lose the integrity of our republican institutions ever again; never fall under the dominion of foreign troops or lose our independence; and never again serve another master. This I guarantee to you!"

Vigorous chants of "Long live the Republic!" followed. This, too, required several emotion-filled moments to subside. Andrea drew in another deep breath.

"From this day forward we shall become free citizens of the Holy Roman Empire," he went on to say. "You may ask why the Empire, and why not the Kingdom of France? Why become a friend of Charles V when we have served King Francis for so long? And I say to you that France can never guarantee our freedom. She will never relinquish her desire to annex our beloved territories, and never promise to leave the city of Savona free of her troops. This simply cannot stand! Savona has always been part of Genoa, and always shall be!"

As the cheers escalated to a fever pitch, Andrea looked out over the masses with more pride than he ever thought possible. He'd never sought this level of adoration, or ever cared to acquire it. His was the ambition of a man who wanted to break free of the confines of his social, political, and economic condition. Transcend them. He longed for the respect of his fellow man, not his adulation; his loyalty, not his praise; and his camaraderie, not his mindless subservience. But their cries of "Doria and liberty!" warmed his heart and tempted his latent cravings for honor and glory.

He could see now how easily one could fall victim to the tentacles of power. Many in his entourage had indeed encouraged him to seize the moment. "Who better to rule over us?" they would routinely say. Up until now, however, he resisted their appeals, knowing full well that the vast majority of Genoese citizens suspected that he would do just that. But what really drove his decision to step away from the role of Genoa's official head of state grew out of the same set of goals that had motivated him his entire life: personal freedom and adventure, two objectives he knew to be incompatible with the often-tedious responsibilities of running a government.

"The solemn oath I swore with Charles guarantees our independence as well as our political and economic sovereignty!" he trumpeted at the top of his lungs. "I swear it to you, so help me God!"

Andrea nodded ever so slightly, signaling the end of his address, then stepped away from the parapet to wild applause and chants of support that continued well after he had retreated back into the doge's office.

Once inside, Filippino's approving smile caught Andrea's attention, which immediately soothed him, and several members of the city's highest-ranking families, including Sinibaldo Fieschi, expressed their satisfaction with a simple bow of the head.

I've done it, Andrea thought. He breathed a sigh of relief as if he'd just fought the most punishing battle of his life. Then, rather than revel in his achievement, he quietly called for a horse-drawn carriage to escort him to the Palazzo del Principe on the outer edges of the city. It was finally time to go home.

He slept like a newborn that night, a deep dreamless sleep that he hadn't experienced in years. He rose to the sound of children playing in the palazzo's recently frescoed corridor that ran the entire length of the structure. He could distinguish Giannettino's voice as well, who seemed to be conversing with Peretta's son, Marcantonio, both growing boys primed to follow in Andrea's footsteps. He couldn't have awakened to a sweeter sound.

Moments later, Peretta burst into the room accompanied by her handmaid carrying a padded doublet of black silk. The handmaid folded it delicately over his X-shaped chair at the foot of his bed and hurried off. Peretta approached Andrea's side, but stopped short of what could be considered an intimate distance. Her smile was warm, but fleeting. She had come to wish him well regarding his planned meetings in the Doge's Palace later that morning, but was clearly too busy managing the household to linger.

"The doublet has just come back from the tailor," Peretta announced. "It is of the finest mulberry silk from China."

"Have Tonino bring me the *farinata* this morning, will you please?" Andrea said as he sat up in bed, obviously not the least bit interested in his Chinese silk doublet. "And the good wine. I feel I need the strength of a bull to see me through the day."

Peretta leaned in and bussed Andrea on the cheek. "Anything for my Prince," she whispered in jest.

As opposed to the routine dark bread that greeted Andrea each morning, and nearly every waking household in the region, farinata offered an added kick. An oily, flat bread made with chickpea flour and sprinkled with coarse sea salt and fresh rosemary, it married well with the local Vermentino wine. Andrea preferred this particular wine's fruitiness during the summer and early fall months to the more astringent reds that kept his belly warm during winter.

"Wish me well," he replied. "I shall do everything possible to dissuade them from calling me their prince."

"It is too late, my dear Prince," she quipped. "People have tired of calling you Admiral."

"Oh, stop this nonsense and find me Tonino at once," he laughed. "I could eat a horse."

Peretta took a step backward, twirled around with the same poise and grace that had enchanted Andrea all those many years ago, and flitted across the room—but not before offering her dear husband a heartfelt grin, which provided him far more support than the river of flattering words that gushed from the mouths of his colleagues.

"And don't forget to wear your doublet," she said as she stood at the door. "The sheer blackness of it suits you, and with your sable hosen and beret you shall make quite the impression on those stuffed shirts in the senate."

A moment later she was gone. As usual, she got the last word.

One thousand five hundred citizens, all members of Genoa's most esteemed professions, filled the grand hall of the Doge's Palace: bankers, artisans, merchants, and nobles of all the oldest families. Their purpose was either to accept Andrea's proposal of aligning with the emperor to form a new republic, or dismiss it outright. As expected, it passed with the greatest of fervor, after which Andrea stood before his fellow Genoese to advance his idea for resolving the political issues that would surely arise in the coming months. He cleared his throat and straightened his handsome silk doublet.

"I suggest we form a group of twelve men to forge our new constitution and certify our much-needed reforms."

"The infighting that has plagued our city must be the first item on the list!" shouted an unknown voice.

Andrea's response was quick: "And eliminate the distinction between our old and new nobility. They must have an equal chance at the dogeship."

Once again, his words won the overwhelming support of the crowd. In fact, the remainder of the day continued to go smoothly for Andrea, who, by now, enjoyed almost godlike status.

In the days that followed, the twelve Reformers worked closely with Andrea to put his ideas into effect. Sinibaldo Fieschi sat across from Andrea on several occasions to lend his advice and support, as did Andrea's cousin Filippino. They all met on October 12 to finalize the reforms, a month after Andrea's celebrated speech to the people. After everyone had settled around the table, one of the twelve Reformers kicked off the meeting.

"Our doges are chosen for life!" he shouted. "That must change!"

"I propose we limit their tenure to two years," Andrea chimed in.

"Excellent idea, but we mustn't allow just anyone to assume that title," Sinibaldo rejoined with an air of conceit. "Now that merchants, bankers, and mere artisans may join the ranks of nobility, we must show prudence in our choice of doge."

Andrea tried his best to hide his unease, but apparently he

failed miserably since all eyes turned to him for comment—which he refused to offer.

Realizing that Andrea had no intention of responding, a second member of the Twelve broke the silence: "There should also be a fair number of governors to work alongside our doge."

"I believe we have all discussed that the appropriate number of governors should be eight," a third Reformer said. "Also appointed for two years."

"Agreed!" all twelve shouted in unison.

"And a Major Council of four hundred citizens and a Minor Council of one hundred to deliberate our city's most pressing issues," said a fourth Reformer.

"And whose role it is to nominate the governors and other members of the signoria," added a fifth member, addressing his words directly at Andrea as if his dogeship, and membership in the signoria, were a foregone conclusion.

Andrea, once again, remained stone-faced, careful not to show a preference one way or another.

"Agreed!" they all cried.

"Perhaps it is time to vote on the composition of this new nobility of ours before continuing any further," said a sixth Reformer.

Sinibaldo jumped in again: "We need to establish definite criteria for entrance."

"I agree," snapped Andrea.

Everyone chimed in their approval.

"Of course those owning homes in our city must be represented," said a seventh member of the Twelve.

"Agreed," said Andrea in the same definitive tone.

"Just how many homes?" asked another. "And I daresay it must be a substantial number or we shall be burdened with more members of the nobility than commoners."

Andrea glanced over at Sinibaldo before commenting on that last statement. He'd given this subject a lot of consideration, and what he was about to suggest would surely displease his dear friend, but before he could say a word, Sinibaldo interjected: "The amount of land one owns in our city's outskirts must also be included."

"Genoa is a strong and vibrant city," Andrea said in a calm, measured voice. "Commerce is our primary strength, and I believe that those who contribute to that strength within our city walls must be fully represented."

Andrea's words met with near-unanimous agreement, prompting yet another member of the Twelve to comment: "The number of homes for each family must reach at least ten in order to be taken seriously."

"That is ridiculous!" said Sinibaldo.

"Five, I believe, is a fair and just number," Andrea said, speaking directly to the Reformers.

He knew full well, however, that they had discussed this particular issue countless times in the past month, and not one of the Twelve felt it reasonable to establish a quota lower than seven. He also knew that certain families who depended on their feudal holdings to maintain their noble status possessed very few homes within the city walls, and the Fieschi were just such a family. Therefore, Andrea may have been demonstrating qualities of fair-mindedness and diplomacy by suggesting a number of five, but he was also knowingly weakening the Fieschi family's position vis-á-vis Genoa's new political order. This was the motive for Andrea's look of concern earlier, and for his reticence. There was no way around it: His old-time rival and recent comrade in arms against the French was losing his grip on power.

The twelve Reformers assembled later that afternoon to flesh out the issue of how to blend the old nobility with the new one and place them on equal levels. Andrea, Sinibaldo, and distinguished representatives of Genoa's prominent families sat in attendance, but were deprived of the power to intervene. The Reformers' first order of business was to create distinct groups, called *alberghi*, that would house all of the city's most important and influential families, no matter their lineage. Then, as a nod toward Andrea's earlier suggestion, it was further resolved that any kindred group owning six or more homes within the four walls of the city would qualify.

At that point, Sinibaldo stomped out of the assembly. Although his holdings in terms of land and castles were extensive, he fell short of the requisite six homes, as did the Adorno and Fregoso families, who, however, refrained from abandoning the grand hall, despite their words of vehement opposition. In the end, twenty-eight such alberghi were formed. Families who failed to meet the quota yet possessed great influence due to their wealth or noble birth could merge with one of the existing twenty-eight alberghi. This was seen by many as a giant step forward since it put the newer, merchant-based families on par with the older nobility, but it also separated the citizenry into two distinct categories: members of the alberghi versus the common people.

At day's end, Andrea garnered the accolades he deserved, and more. He, together with Filippino and all the members of the Doria clan who risked their lives for the Republic against the Spanish, and subsequently to oust the French, received exemptions from their taxes in perpetuity. Andrea was also awarded a whole host of extra benefits. The Reformers presented him with an elegant palazzo in the Piazza San Matteo, directly across from the church. They believed he would use it as his residence while serving as their doge, a position everyone assumed he would eventually request.

But Andrea appeared to have other plans. After the assembly, as the Reformers and their assistants exited the grand hall, Andrea pulled several members of the Twelve aside to request another short, and very private, meeting.

"You have been most kind with me, dear sirs," Andrea said, huddled into a corner with two of the Reformers. "And I accept your most gracious gifts with great humility. The plaque you plan to hang in my name in the courtyard of San Matteo pleases me in particular. I am most appreciative."

"It is the least Genoa can do to honor you," replied one of the Reformers with a lifeless smile. Throughout the assembly he came across as a behind-the-scenes leader of the Twelve, but only in as much as it pertained to the legality of things. Otherwise, he had little else to offer.

"We thought we could write something referring to your dogeship on the plaque," added the other Reformer, clearly the more enthusiastic of the two. "Perhaps 'Dux Andraea de Oria, Patriae Liberatori—"

Andrea interrupted him in mid-sentence. "I have no interest in becoming a doge. Do not use the word *dux*," he said flatly, which left the two men somewhat befuddled.

The more enthusiastic of the two quickly responded. "But—"

Andrea cut in again. "Have you not created a commission of supreme censors? Whose role it is to find fitting candidates for the dogeship?"

"We have," replied the Reformer, "but the censor's role is chiefly ceremonial, and we thought—"

"Yet it stands above the other institutions," said Andrea, interrupting the Reformer a third time.

"But has no other powers," said the first Reformer. "I daresay you must have a title befitting your stature in the city or it will appear we are ungrateful for all you have done."

"Then proclaim me Censor for Life, for the love of God," cried Andrea. "I don't care."

The eyes of the more enthusiastic of the two Reformers lit up, clearly sold on the idea.

"*Censore Perpetuo*," he said aloud, as if testing the sound of it. He looked over at his colleague, whose crooked smile signaled his approval.

"*Censore Perpetuo* it is," pronounced the other Reformer. "I shall present it to the Twelve."

A mischievous grin crossed Andrea's lips. What more could he ask for? Not only would he get to keep his fleet, his contract with Charles, and his freedom to sail in asiento, but he also had fashioned a position for himself that assured him influence over the Republic and its policies in perpetuity.

"Good," said Andrea as he strode off. "I am pleased to have been of service."

Chapter Fourteen

CONSPIRACY IN THE AIR

A knock at the bedchamber door interrupted Andrea's rendering of the free Republic's war-torn beginnings. Tonino entered with a flourish, toting another round of drinks. The unusually tall and slender bottle he balanced so effortlessly on his tray contained a clear, translucent liquid whose appearance seemed to puzzle Andrea's two guests. Six miniature glasses were neatly huddled around the bottle.

"Ah, a little something to warm your bellies before your journey across town," Andrea said as he cleared some space on the table by the fire.

"You are so kind, dear Prince," said Figueroa, "but I have guests at the embassy this evening and must take my leave soon." He eyed the bottle with skepticism. "However, forgive me for wondering how water in a thimble-sized cup could possibly warm up my insides."

Andrea, of course, did not want to seem condescending or insulting in his reply, but his laugh erupted too quickly and much too spontaneously to appear otherwise. He glanced over at Gonzaga, who appeared equally perplexed at first, but had quickly deduced by examining the elaborate shape of the bottle, the daintiness of the glasses, and the liquid's crystalline cast that yet another form of alcohol had entered their midst.

"We can thank the enterprise and imagination of our friends in the Levant for this extravagance. They have developed an excellent process of filtration," said Andrea. "And let us not forget our brave crusaders, who not only protected our faith against the infidels, but quite often brought back with them precious gifts such as these."

"This offering of yours possesses the power of magic if it can so easily disguise itself as pure spring water," said Gonzaga.

Andrea laughed. "The mighty Persians have helped us find a way to render the skins, stems, and seeds of the grape useful, and quite enjoyable."

"This is no wine I have ever seen," said Figueroa.

"It has the fiery soul of wine," Andrea replied, gesturing to Tonino to fill the glasses. "Taste it. I assure you, you will thank me for it."

All eyes followed Tonino's careful movements as he poured. Peretta and Ginetta made it immediately clear they wanted no part of it, however, knowing all too well the nature of this spirited liquid. Andrea doled out glasses to Giannettino, his two guests, and one for himself, which he quickly rose in a toast.

"To our great Republic," he said. "May we choose an honest and virtuous doge in the coming days."

"Hear, hear!" everyone responded in unison, including little Giovannandrea, who pretended to have a glass of his own.

Andrea, Giannettino, and Gonzaga swallowed the contents in one gulp, while Figueroa could barely gather the courage to wet his lips, which was apparently enough to throw him into a wild coughing jag. His eyes welled up with tears and sweat rolled down his brow. His delicate palate had never taken such a beating.

"Good Lord, I'm afraid I've been poisoned!" he cried, only half in jest.

"I have seen this before," replied Gonzaga, "and even heard tell of its strength. What do you call it?"

"*Grappolus*," said Andrea flatly. "I have heard it referred to as *grappa* by the peasants in the mountains not far from your beloved Lombardy, Lord Gonzaga."

"I daresay it is endowed with the powers of healing," Gonzaga quipped.

"I could have used it ten years ago off the island of Paxos," Andrea growled. "A slither of shrapnel as sharp as a fisherman's blade nearly cut my leg in two. I never felt such pain."

"A fisherman's blade! Tell me, mesiavo, tell me more!" cried Giovannandrea.

"I intend to do just that," exclaimed Andrea with a laugh. "I know you have been waiting for mention of Barbarossa all evening."

"Tell us the story of the fisherman's blade!" he called out again.

"First you must know about Suleiman the Magnificent," Andrea replied. "As ruler of the Ottoman Empire, he realized quite quickly he needed the likes of a pirate like Barbarossa to deal with Emperor Charles's navy."

"And with you," Giannettino quickly added.

"Please excuse me, dear Prince," said Figueroa, getting up from his chair. "As much as I would enjoy hearing of your exploits against that wicked pirate, as I have mentioned, affairs of some import await me at the embassy."

Gonzaga rose to his feet soon afterward. "Allow me to release you of the burden of my company as well," he said. "The hour has grown late."

Wanting to show his appreciation for his guests' kind visit, Andrea struggled to his feet, bearing the pangs in his inflamed knees and sore back in silence. He'd sat idly for much too long, causing his joints to stiffen terribly. Each movement, no matter how small, sent shooting pains throughout his body.

"I trust I haven't bored you with my silly tales," whispered Andrea to Gonzaga at the door.

Governor Gonzaga had shared some history with Andrea and had fought in many of the same wars against one foreign invader or another, making him quite conversant with much of what Andrea had revealed.

"Always a pleasure to hear your learned point of view, my Prince," Gonzaga replied as a parting salute.

Figueroa, too, nodded his farewell, and together they stepped out the door.

Andrea called out to Tonino: "See to it that our guests are shown to the gate properly."

Tonino jumped to their side and dutifully escorted them down the hall. Andrea shut the door and shuffled back to the fire. He lowered himself carefully into his chair and continued to regale his young nephew with tales of love and war.

"I trust I'm not boring you as well," quipped Andrea to little Placidia. "Your feisty little brother steals all my attention."

"Do you have a scar on you leg where you were hit?" the little girl asked.

"I do," Andrea replied with a wry smile.

He bent his aging frame at the waist and reached down to grab the hem of his linen nightshirt, which he wore smartly beneath his chamber coat. He rolled it up to just above his shin to reveal a coarsely healed gash running on an angle from his knee down to his upper calf.

Before Placidia and little Giovannandrea could react, there was a knock at the door. Tonino entered and stood at attention.

"I have been told that dinner will be served shortly," he announced.

Andrea let the hem of his nightshirt drop and turned to Giovannandrea. "I think it best if we finish this story over some hearty food, don't you?" he said. Looking around at everyone, then finally locking eyes with Peretta, he added, "I shall be down in no time. I can hardly show up in my nightshirt, can I?"

On the other side of the city atop the Carignano hill, a dinner of a far more extravagant nature was underway. Over fifty men—all from the upper echelon of Genoese society, members of the old nobility and popolari alike—were gathered in the Villa Vialata. The nobles wore long, bright-colored togas, while the merchants, artisans, bankers, money changers, and military men had all donned the traditional clothing of their guild, nearly all of which glittered with inlaid silver and gold threads. Armored guards met them at the villa's gate and escorted them into the grand hall. Each guest heard the same cryptic message uttered by the chief guard as they entered: "No one is permitted to leave this evening without the explicit permission of Count Gian Luigi Fieschi."

The atmosphere bewildered them, to say the least, but their intuition had warned them from the outset that this dinner would differ from the rest. It had an air of secrecy about it, which intrigued them, but also had them quite worried. Gianbattista Verrina, the man Gian Luigi had encountered near the docks on his way home from Andrea's villa, had contacted everyone personally over the past few days, acting as Gian Luigi's representative. He invited them to join the Fieschi family for dinner, alerting them in no uncertain terms of a long night ahead. Some invitees foresaw wild festivities, but most suspected an event of a more factious nature. After all, a large portion of Genoa's populace viewed Gian Luigi as their city's future and, to a large extent, so did he. Most of the guests likely thought the dinner had something to do with the appointment of a new doge in two days' time—and perhaps that the young Fieschi planned to throw his hat into the ring.

The suspicious undercurrent that defined the ambience was soon reinforced by the realization that the tables had not been set for dinner, and no food appeared anywhere. And where were the myriad servants necessary for a successful dinner party?

Pewter tankards of red wine from the Fieschi's private vineyards, however, made the rounds with great frequency, as did the cupola-shaped cakes of *panettone*, a holiday sweet bread filled with chips of citron, lemon zest, candied orange, and dried grapes. Although this placated the crowd for a while, serving as an aperitif of sorts, it didn't take long for the rumors to start, and for the quiet but forceful demands to know what in God's name was going on to reach Gian Luigi's ears.

For those who knew the young count and his dear wife, Eleonora, the clearest indication that something irregular was afoot came instantly upon entering the villa. First of all, there were soldiers everywhere; secondly, and most importantly, Eleonora was nowhere to be found. There was no denying that a fair percentage of the fifty esteemed guests came primarily to be greeted by her at the door and to engage in her company throughout the evening. She often regaled her invitees with verses from Francesco Petrarca's book of love sonnets, the *Canzoniere*, as well as Dante Alighieri's *La Vita Nuova*, and even from her own collection of poems, which both soothed and provoked her listeners.

However, Gian Luigi had already informed his wife that there would be no recitation of poetry after dinner. In fact, there would be no dinner, or any festivities. There would be no idle chitchat, no gambling, no games of chance, no dancing, and no music, not even a sweet song of love that so often would accompany holiday banquets. Gian Luigi had made up his mind. He would be the evening's sole protagonist.

The grand hall occupied nearly half of the villa's first floor.

There was nothing fancy about it. No fine paintings or intricate tapestries graced the limestone walls; the light orange-brown terra-cotta floor hardly managed a glimmer; and the fireplace, although massive, featured blocks of dull, colorless sandstone. Only the creamy white balustrade of Carrara marble that ran across the entire second floor overlooking the grand hall revealed a hint of ostentation. It was where everyone's eyes naturally shifted when in need of elegance and beauty, and it just so happened to be where Gian Luigi decided to present himself to his distinguished guests. He exited the family library, walked slowly and purposefully to the marble railing, and peered over it to the crowd below. His eyes seemed to hover inscrutably over the heads of everyone in the room, never focusing on one person in particular, like a man possessed.

He glanced to his right, where Eleonora stood at the far end of the second-story hall, her eyes welling with tears. She had tried desperately to stop him from what he was about to do, warning him of the dangers that lay ahead and begging him to listen to reason, but fate had taken over. There was nothing more she could say or do. His gaze lingered on her for a moment more before turning back to address his guests in the grand hall. He waited until everyone recognized his presence and for all the clamoring to finally cease. He had no intention of descending the stairs to join his guests, not yet, but rather made it clear he wasn't moving from that very spot. His body language displayed ultimate calm, and the level of gravitas he exuded surprised everyone who knew him.

"The time we have longed for is upon us, my friends," Gian Luigi began. "Welcome, welcome to you all."

Whispers circulated through the crowd and quickly died down.

"The future of our native city and all its territories is at hand," he continued. "Freedom is within reach. The tyranny of the Doria family will meet its end on this very night, and a true government of the people will finally be ours."

He paused to catch his breath. Only then did he realize how much pressure he'd been under during all those months of planning and subterfuge, all those sleepless nights, and all those many doubts that racked his soul. Without Gianbattista Verrina's encouragement and sheer faith in his abilities he would have turned back a thousand times. But he was alone on that balustrade now; no one to boost his self-confidence stood at his side, and there was no one to assure him he was right. All he had was the air that filled his lungs, literally breathing life into him and strengthening his resolve.

The room remained deadly silent. No one dared move. The die had been cast, and they could feel it. Something bigger than themselves was about to sweep them up and carry them either into the depths of despair or to the empyrean heights of glory. Gian Luigi could almost see their minds racing with alternating images of liberty and death. Those were the two choices they would soon be offered. After tonight, any pleas of ignorance or even innocence would fall on deaf ears should his plan go terribly wrong.

"We have been content for years with the crumbs from the Doria table, while Giannettino sits perched to take everything for himself," Gian Luigi continued. "We have for years acquiesced to the rule of the Doria family, asking permission to do what Giannettino and the rest can carry out with absolute abandon."

Gian Luigi took a step back while the more vocal in the crowd expressed their consensus with shouts of "Liberty!" and "Freedom for Genoa!" When the cries had sufficiently died down, he approached the railing once again, this time with more force and outrage in his voice.

"Have they forgotten that we Genoese are sons of warriors?"

The cries of "Liberty!" grew louder and spread like wildfire throughout the room. Gian Luigi had struck a nerve. He knew then that Verrina had cherry-picked his guests just right and that he could continue his harangue unobstructed.

"Our Prince has made Giannettino his second-in-command, and already he shows signs of cruelty and despotism. Can you imagine what forms of tyranny will befall us when the old man dies—which appears to be imminent, my friends. I have seen him this very day, with my own eyes!"

Slogans of "Liberty!" interrupted Gian Luigi once again.

"Are we all so naive as to believe he will be happy to simply fill his uncle's shoes? To carry on the old man's work? No, he will declare himself duke of our fair city, enjoy the protection of the Holy Roman Emperor, and rule over us all with an iron fist!"

Up until that point, nearly everyone was under the impression they were witnessing only the beginnings of a revolt, its initial stages, and that there would be time to clear a reasonable path toward deposing the man they viewed as the number one threat to their freedom: Giannettino Doria. But Gian Luigi quickly disabused them of that notion.

"It is my intention to assassinate that shamefully ambitious despot as well as the old man!" he cried out in anger. "This very night!"

As expected, the room fell silent.

"How is that possible?" shouted a prominent voice in the crowd.

"We are not ready!" cried another.

The grand hall went abuzz, a fraction calling for immediate revolt, others clamoring for more information, but most overwhelmingly skeptical that such a complex and dangerous endeavor could succeed on such short notice, and with virtually no planning. The count once again set the record straight.

"The city is in our power at this very moment!" he roared. "A large part of our government guards are with us. The keepers of our city's gates support our cause. More than three hundred of my finest soldiers stand ready to march. Hundreds of men of unrivaled skill and courage fill my galley in the harbor awaiting my signal to strike. Thousands from my lands along our Ligurian shores stand poised in the hills outside our gates, followed by dedicated soldiers from our loyal allies throughout the peninsula. All of them wish nothing more than to put Giannettino in his grave!"

No one said a word. *Could this be true?*, they inevitably thought to themselves. Several in the crowd whispered their doubts, but by now the overwhelming majority had been persuaded. Chants of "Long live Count Fieschi!" rose up, accompanied by slogans of "Liberty!" Nearly everyone came out and declared flatly that the time had indeed come to stop Giannettino in his tracks.

And for those few still unconvinced, Gian Luigi added these final words: "The night is peaceful and still, my fellow citizens. I ask you not to be participants in our righteous battle, but simply witnesses to a grand victory that has been in the planning for months. The Kingdom of France has championed our cause; the Republics of Florence and Venice will not intervene; and the Holy Father and his son, the Duke of Parma and Piacenza, support us both in word and in deed. There is no enemy at our door, my friends. The time could not be more auspicious for Genoa and the Republic, and victory!"

Count Gian Luigi Fieschi's "dinner" speech in Villa Vialata wrapped up at approximately the same time as Andrea and his family finished their evening meal. The tempers in the two households couldn't have differed more. Andrea kept the mood light and conversational around the table, as was his wont, despite Giovannandrea's hounding for more war stories, which Andrea adroitly skirted. Just as he was about to appease the boy with a promise that he would talk about Barbarossa at bedtime, Tonino entered the dining room with news that there was an inordinate amount of noise and confusion on the docks.

"Should I send someone to see what is going on, my Prince?" Tonino aksed.

Andrea straightened up in his seat, obviously concerned, but also notably irritated. "Noise? What do you mean, noise?"

Giannettino cut in before Tonino could reply. "It is nothing," he said. "I meant to tell you earlier. Gian Luigi plans to ship out in the morning, and—"

Andrea didn't give him a chance to finish. "Gian Luigi? Where in heaven's name is he going? Doesn't he see a storm is brewing?"

"He has high hopes, dear uncle, that is all I can tell you," said Giannettino with a smirk. "I think it is best we talk of this afterward, but I assure you, there is nothing here that requires our concern."

Andrea took Giannettino at his word and continued with his meal. Giovannandrea took advantage of the lull in the conversation to pick right up where they left off.

"If I go to bed right after dinner, will you tell me about Barbarossa then?"

Giovannandrea already knew a little about the pirate from his father, who began fighting alongside Andrea during that same period. Unlike Andrea, however, who refrained from overly boastful tales of his exploits at sea, Giannettino wore his adventures like a badge. He'd spoken to Giovannandrea so often about his forays with Barbarossa that the boy completely forgot that Andrea was his father's commanding officer at the time, hence his lapse earlier in the evening regarding Andrea's admiralship. Giovannandrea loved his father, and enjoyed eavesdropping on him when he crowed to his fellow officers of his exploits, but nothing compared to sitting on his mesiavo's knee hearing of days gone by. He was never so eager to go to bed in his life.

Giannettino enjoyed staying in the Palazzo del Principe during the holidays with Ginetta and the children, but Giovannandrea absolutely lived for it. The boy slept right down the corridor from Andrea. He shared a room with Placidia, who, despite her approaching ten years of age, preferred crawling into her parents' warm canopy when not in the security of her own bedroom. This, of course, would leave Giovannandrea all alone, just the way he liked it, and on special occasions like this one, he would have his dear mesiavo all to himself.

"You were going to tell me all about Suleiman?" Giovannandrea said the moment he hopped into bed.

The connection Andrea felt for Giovannandrea in that moment brought a tear to his eye. After spending a lifetime putting his feelings aside, such uncontrolled emotions always took him by surprise. His sentiments for the boy's father, young Giannettino, all those many years ago, were also quite strong, but what he was experiencing with Giovannandrea surpassed that by far. A sudden smile crossed his lips when he realized that he was probably enjoying this whole experience more than the boy.

"Suleiman the Magnificent was the grand monarch of the Ottomans," Andrea began. "He assumed control of the Empire immediately after the death of the grand sultan, Selim the Grim."

Giovannandrea pulled the covers tight under his chin, burrowing his head deeper into the feather pillow. He couldn't get much cozier, or much happier. Andrea brushed the boy's curls away from his eyes before continuing.

"Suleiman's navies raided our coasts and ran unchecked up and down the Mediterranean."

"What did he want?"

"Some say he wished to conquer our land and rob us of our faith, but I believe he only wanted our jewels, our money, and our respect. And he managed to get all three. His troops conquered much of the land we Genoese held as our own for so many years. They moved through the Greek islands with ease, and even sailed up the mighty Danube river to the walls of Vienna, home of the Holy Roman Empire, Suleiman's real target all along."

"Why didn't you stop him?" the boy asked innocently.

Andrea's smile was heartfelt. *Such simple questions for such tangled and confusing issues*, he thought to himself. Part of Andrea wanted to maintain the boy's sense of innocence for as long as possible, and part of him knew the time had come to enlighten him to the ways of the world. Giovannandrea had recently begun his education with Genoa's most prominent tutor. He studied Latin, and would soon be introduced to the disciplines of rhetoric and philosophy as was customary for young boys of certain privileged households. And of course, Genoa being a city built on commerce, rudimentary principles of arithmetic would find their way into the curriculum as well. But as far as Andrea was concerned, nothing could replace the practical instructions handed down from generation to generation. Learning about history through books was one thing, and learning it firsthand was yet another. The quality of knowledge between the two was intrinsically disparate. In the grand scheme of things, Giovannandrea was being handed a precious gift.

"Sometimes I stopped Suleiman, and other times he stopped me," Andrea quipped. "But in the end, I realized all I was doing was forcing him to find a suitable man to oppose me, which of course he did."

"Barbarossa?" said the boy in a near whisper as if invoking a ghost.

Andrea nodded in agreement. "He was already a notorious pirate off the Barbary coast of Africa when Suleiman made him commander of the Ottoman fleet."

"Was he from Africa?" the boy asked.

"Some say Barbarossa was born on Lesbos, a Greek island that once belonged to us."

Giovannandrea sat up straight in his bed. "You owned it?" he asked, his eyes beaming with excitement.

Andrea laughed. "No, not me," he quickly replied, "the city of Genoa."

The boy lay back down, somewhat deflated, but eager to hear more.

"Others say his father, Yacub, was an Andalusian Jew chased from the shores of Spain by King Ferdinand," Andrea went on to say. "I never got to ask him which, if any, of the two stories was true."

"You met him?"

"Yes, he came right here, to this palace."

"Does he really have a red beard?"

"A very long one," Andrea said.

"Longer than yours?"

"And curlier," said Andrea. "He came to pay the ransom for Dragut's freedom, the man your father captured. I found him to be a likable fellow."

Andrea stopped to think a moment, his mind harkening back to the pirate's momentous visit. He remembered feeling that perhaps if it were a different time, or a different place, they would have been the best of friends. And, of course, there were more than a few wagging tongues that accused the two men of being just that.

"Barbarossa is a funny name," said Giovannandrea.

"His real name is Hayreddin—or I should say, *was*," said Andrea.

"Did he change it?"

"No, he is no longer with us," Andrea said, his eyes registering a hint of sadness. "He died just last year."

"Did he ever defeat you in battle, Mesiavo?" asked the boy. "Poæ says you were the greatest fighter of all time."

Andrea let out a chuckle. "Now I've heard everything," he said. "Just like with Suleiman, sometimes I stopped him and sometimes I didn't."

Giovannandrea's brow furrowed. *How could this be?* he thought. *A pirate could defeat a grand admiral of the Genoese Republic?*

The boy looked up, his eyes meeting Andrea's square on: "Was it when you got that scar on your knee that he beat you?"

"Actually, I defeated him that time," said Andrea. "Nearly all his men were killed, and I sailed back to our port in Sicily victorious and with a galley full of booty."

"Then when did he beat you?"

"We always outnumbered him, but Barbarossa was brilliant. And his ships flew like eagles across the waters, powered by thousands of Christian slaves, while we sometimes had to depend on God's willingness to fill our sails."

"But your galleys must have had oarsmen, too."

"Yes, but pirates' barques were usually smaller, quicker vessels that could outmaneuver us. We often relied on our overwhelming strength, which served us well, but not always."

Andrea paused a moment, hesitant to jump right into his most notorious defeat against Barbarossa. They were harsh memories. It wasn't so much the battle that bothered him, but rather the criticism he received afterward. The manner in which he conducted himself during the conflict upset a good portion of his allies. Andrea was convinced, however, that he had made all the right moves, and he returned to Genoa with his fleet in excellent shape, without so much as a scratch, as proof of it.

"It seemed nothing could stop Barbarossa," Andrea said, his voice breaking into a more narrative stride. "Sardegna, Sicily, Marseille, the coast of Spain, Corfú, the Greek islands, and even our Ligurian shores fell victim to his raids. Cities were fortified, villages were abandoned, and thousands of our Christian brothers were carted off as slaves. The pontiff in Rome finally assembled a Holy League to subdue him. He called upon Spain, Venice, Charles V, the Papal States, the Knights of Malta, and our dear Republic to join forces. I was made admiral of the entire allied fleet."

Giovannandrea stared up at the frescoed ceiling, mesmerized by Andrea's words while at the same time drifting off to sleep. It was all he could do to keep his eyes open.

"In the summer of 1538, a year before you were born," Andrea continued, "the flotillas of each of our allied partners were scheduled to meet off the island of Corfú. The Venetians and the papal ships were the first to arrive, and were eager to engage with the enemy. The papal commander promptly dispatched a squadron of galleys to the Ottoman fortress in nearby Preveza on the coast of Greece."

"A surprise attack!" said Giovannandrea, coming back to life for a moment.

"Not quite," Andrea replied. "They were beaten back to Corfú and forced to wait for the entire fleet to arrive. Once assembled, we numbered one hundred and twelve galleys in all, fifty galleons, one hundred and forty barques, and more than sixty thousand armed warriors. Barbarossa's fleet was tiny by comparison: one hundred and twenty-two galleys and only about twelve thousand soldiers."

Andrea could see the boy's mind working, despite the fact that he could hardly stay awake.

"They had fewer ships and fewer soldiers, but they had a fortress on land," Giovannandrea said.

A smile creased Andrea's lips. "Very good. You understand the value of controlling the coast."

"So what did you do?"

"We sent another squadron of ships down to the fortress, but by then Barbarossa had entrenched his ship too well in the gulf. It was useless."

"Because the fortress had cannons to protect his fleet," said the boy.

"Exactly, my little admiral," Andrea replied proudly. "So, we sailed south. Our idea was to stage an attack on the Greek city of Lepanto, an Ottoman port. And why do you think we did that?"

"To force the pirate to come out in the open?"

"Excellent, my boy. But coordinating all those ships within a coalition of states that do not necessarily like or trust one another proved nearly impossible," said Andrea with a notable hint of anger in his voice. "Our immense size proved more a detriment than a benefit. We were left too spread out and vulnerable, and Barbarossa wisely took advantage of the poor winds, which he knew we depended on, to stage a daring strike against us. Our papal and Venetian ships, led by a huge flagship with the fire-power to frighten Satan himself, staved off the Ottoman attack well enough, so I steered the rest of our ships farther out to sea, hoping to lure the pirate into open waters and away from their fortified coast." Andrea paused a moment, then asked the boy directly: "And what do you think Barbarossa did then?"

"Attack?"

"A lesser commander would have. But Barbarossa's genius rose above that of all others, and of course, being the pirate that he was, he wanted to live to fight another day."

"Are you saying he retreated?" the boy whispered, his eyes folding shut. He was practically talking in his sleep at this point.

"Not exactly. He simply refused to take the bait."

"So you attacked him," said Giovannandrea, obviously expecting a simple "yes" or at least a nod.

Andrea looked his young nephew straight in the eye. "Suffice it to say, we both lived to fight another day."

Chapter Fifteen

THE FIESCHI INSURRECTION

Andrea went to bed a happy man that night. He had entertained two prominent guests, important men for Genoa's political health and well-being, and he had spent precious hours with his close family, which fed his soul. The wine went a long way toward heightening his spirits and the savory breads, sweets, and sumptuous dinner helped nourish his ailing body. All in all, a very successful day. *Perhaps by tomorrow my aching bones and swollen joints will have healed*, he thought to himself as he entered his bedchamber, *and my joy will be complete.* That was the last thought he had before drifting off to sleep.

By rights Andrea's dreams should have reflected the same calm and satisfaction that he felt all evening, and in a sense they did. The still waters of the Mediterranean, so icy blue and crisp, that filled his subconscious almost immediately upon falling asleep certainly evoked a sobering peace. But just as in his most unbearable dreams, the sky seemed to go on forever, no clouds dotting its infinite space; not a single figure, alive or dead, darkened the tranquil waters; no ships in the distance; no sun or moon on the horizon; and no iconic pods of dolphins propelling themselves joyously into the air. Most of the ingredients that made up his recurring nightmare were there, especially the stillness and quiet of it all. What was missing for this pleasant dream to cross the line into the realm of his most menacing nightmare, however, was the rising tide of blood-red waters and the eerie void that always accompanied it. It was a deep, disturbing emptiness that drained a person's soul and filled it with desperation, fear, and loneliness—a loneliness he'd felt his whole life, one that both repulsed and defined him.

The otherworldly calm that ordinarily inhabited these dreams and so often awakened Andrea never fully materialized this time. This was to be a pleasurable experience, a restful sleep. And, paradoxically, the clamor of hundreds of far-off voices that began to filter into his consciousness, breaking the eerie silence, served to lull Andrea even deeper into slumber. Unfortunately, the chattering in the distance was not part of his dream, but the sound of seamen busy at work in the harbor readying Gian Luigi's galley for the evening's hostilities. Under the cloak of night, phase one of the rebellion was underway.

Meanwhile, all the main actors in the planned revolt were meeting in the cavernous depths of Villa Vialata's wine cellar. Gian Luigi showed up in full body armor: helmet, breastplate, and shoulder pauldrons of high-carbon steel; full leg armor; and finely polished gauntlets. His three brothers—Ottobuono, Gerolamo, and Cornelio—also came fully suited.

Gian Luigi's principal co-conspirators—Gianbattista Verrina, Vincenzo Calcagno, and Raffaele Sacco—arrived as well, each armed to the teeth.

Gian Luigi took command instantly. He barked his first order to Verrina. "Gianbattista, you take the galley to the mouth of the basin! No ships are to come in or out!" His hand then rested on Cornelio's shoulder. "And you take fifty men with you and secure Porta dell'Arco. We must have free access to that gate throughout the night, do you understand?"

Cornelio acceded to the order with a nod.

"And dispatch a courier to me the moment it is done," Gian Luigi added. He turned to face his younger brother. "Otto-buono, go to Porta San Tommaso and Porta Sant'Antonio, and take sixty men with you. Maintain control over them until I say otherwise. And take Vincenzo with you," he said, pointing to Calcagno.

"As for me, I shall wait at the dock until our galley gives the signal," Gian Luigi said to the whole group. "A lone cannon shot off the galley's starboard side will assure us that it has assumed its proper position. Only then do we board Andrea Doria's ships to liberate his slaves."

"Gerolamo, you shall have the most dangerous job of all," said Gian Luigi, his voice now rising with emotion. "Infiltrate the arsenal through the front gate. But remember to wait until you hear the cannon blast before starting your assault. And be careful."

He parsed his words very carefully when describing this

segment of the operation. It required exact timing and precision. The soldiers charged with protecting the arsenal were particularly well armed because of their twin duties of safeguarding the port and supervising the enslaved oarsmen on all the ships. Soldiers that Gian Luigi had recruited from his castles up and down the coast were waiting on the outskirts of the city for that same cannon blast. Their instructions were to enter the city en masse upon hearing it and, at the same time, dispatch several boatloads of men into the harbor to penetrate the arsenal by sea.

As the Fieschi brothers filtered into Genoa's narrow streets to carry out their various missions, Gian Luigi split off with a small squadron to take his position on the dock. He marched through the gate of St. Andrew, then onto the Prione, past the church of San Donato in the Molo district to Vico Salvaghi, and finally to the marina, a stone's throw from the Cattanei Bridge. Not long after arriving, he received word that both Porta dell'Arco and Porta San Tommaso had encountered some resistance, but were finally secured with only minor casualties. News that Porta Sant'Antonio was also under his command emerged just a few minutes later. Rebel losses there were also minimal. Everything was going according to plan.

It won't be long now, Gian Luigi thought to himself. *And the city shall be mine.* Caught up in his own enthusiasm, he gave the order to fan out through the city and shout "Fieschi and freedom!" and "Liberty to the people!" hoping to stir up support among the citizenry.

"The people of Genoa must share in our glory!" he exclaimed.

"Once the Doria see that the city has risen up against them, they will have no choice but to surrender their power!"

The general pandemonium and deafening appeals for liberty reached such a disturbing level that even some of those residing outside the walls of the city were rudely awakened.

These cries for freedom were, in fact, the very sounds that crept into Andrea's otherwise tranquil dream and that, ironically, lulled him even deeper into unconsciousness. The same was not true for Peretta, however, who, being a mother of three, had learned quite early in life to sleep lightly. She jumped up and ran into the corridor to better discern what was happening. Quickly realizing something was afoot, she hurried to Giannettino's chamber door. Rather than knock, she quietly let herself in so as to not rouse Ginetta, or little Placidia, who had inevitably fallen asleep in their bed. Ginetta, of course, woke up the second she entered.

"What is it?" she asked.

"There are worrisome noises coming from the port," Peretta whispered.

By this time Ginetta could hear the chaos herself. "What in God's name could it be?"

"I don't know," Peretta replied, "but perhaps Giannettino could tend to it without having to bother Andrea."

"Of course," said Ginetta. Then, careful not to awaken Placidia, she reached over and tapped her husband lightly on the shoulder.

Peretta rounded the canopy to Giannettino's side of the bed as he emerged from a profound sleep.

"Good Lord, woman, what is it now?" he growled, still half asleep, then pulled the covers up around his neck and nestled deep into the pillow in protest.

"Giannettino, you must wake up," Peretta uttered in a loud whisper. "Something is amiss in the harbor."

Upon hearing those words Giannettino's eyes bolted open. But in that same moment, he remembered what Gian Luigi had told him.

"It's nothing," Giannettino replied. "It's only Gian Luigi's men. Now, if you don't mind, I'd like to go back to—"

He stopped himself, interrupted by the loud cries emanating from the harbor. They were hardly the usual sounds of men preparing for a long sea voyage. He immediately turned his attention to Peretta.

"Advise the guards that I shall need their assistance."

As Peretta raced out the door, Ginetta rose to help her husband. "Peretta has asked to keep your uncle out of this," she said.

"I'm sure it's nothing," Giannettino said. "I shall be back within the hour."

At the same time, down on the docks, the freezing winds were making it increasingly difficult for Gian Luigi to remain calm while waiting for some form of communication from his galley. The cannon blast was long overdue. He'd nearly exhausted his patience when a young soldier finally came running with a missive in his hand. Gian Luigi snapped it from him and read it.

Count Fieschi, the galley has run aground just off the Cattanei Bridge. It cannot be moved.

Gian Luigi stared at the letter long and hard in disbelief before crumpling it in his angry fist. Something had to be done, and fast. The proper positioning of the galley at the mouth of the basin was of vital importance to the success of the operation, since it would block any attempt by members of the Doria family to escape by sea, but more importantly, it inhibited incoming aid to the city's defense.

Gian Luigi called out to his guards, "To the Cattanei Bridge!"

Then, as if the beached galley weren't discouraging enough, another courier came racing to his side with the news that Genoa's citizens were showing reluctance to support the revolt. There seemed to be no mandate for a change in leadership, at least at this early stage. Gian Luigi's rage and frustration grew so intense he nearly strangled the courier on the spot.

"Never mind the Cattanei Bridge. To the *Capitana*, now!" Gian Luigi bellowed. "Once the people see that the Doria have lost control of their ships, they shall join our ranks. Of this I am certain." Then, turning to one of the guards, he shouted: "Tell Gerolamo to overtake the arsenal immediately! There will be no cannon blast!"

The guard ran off, and within seconds Gian Luigi and his squad were on their way to free the *Capitana* of all its enslaved oarsmen.

By some miraculous stroke of fortune, Giannettino did not encounter Gian Luigi and his men as he stormed the port. Nor did he witness any Fieschi soldiers, or citizens chanting slogans, on his way down the hill from the Palazzo del Principe. He was determined, however, to find out what the ruckus in the arsenal was all about.

On the other side of the harbor, Gian Luigi boarded the *Capitana* like a hero in all his glory. Row by row he hacked the chains that tethered the slaves to their posts, and one by one they ran off free men. Their squeals of joy filled Gian Luigi with renewed hope.

"Go out there. Run through the streets. Proclaim your support for the Fieschi!" he cried. "Long live the Fieschi!"

Having liberated the *Capitana*, he hopped aboard a second galley, carrying with him the same message of rebellion and receiving the same euphoric response from the enslaved oarsmen. At the same time, his soldiers filtered into the city from the outlying hills. Despite the previous setbacks, victory appeared close at hand.

Meanwhile, the situation at the arsenal had gone through a radical change in the last few minutes. By the time Giannettino marched to the heavily fortified front entrance, chaos had transformed into a deafening silence, which raised his suspicions even more. His men pounded on the massive oak gate fortified with tons of wrought iron and steel.

"Open this gate!" cried Giannettino. His demand was met with more silence. *Could it be there is nobody minding the gate?* he thought to himself. "I want to speak with the captain! I demand that you open this gate!"

After another round of pounding, Giannettino could make

out a faint murmur on the other side, which prompted him to rap on the door even harder with the hilt of his sword. "Is everything all right?"

Everything inside the arsenal was far from all right, however. The captain lay dead on the ground at the foot of the gate, his throat slit. The signs of a fierce battle were manifest everywhere. Gerolamo Fieschi stood with his ear to the oak door, his sword gripped tightly in his fist.

"Captain!" Giannettino cried out once again.

At that point, a Fieschi soldier, who had a clear sight of Giannettino and his men through an arrow loop in the arsenal's wall, crept over to Gerolamo and whispered to him.

"It is Giannettino Doria," the soldier hissed.

"How many are with him?" Gerolamo asked.

"I saw no more than five," the soldier replied.

Gerolamo's reaction was instant. "Open the gate," he ordered. "Let him in."

Giannettino's suspicions had reached such a level that he instructed his guards to prepare for the worst. He was just about to give the door another rap when he heard the deadbolts unlatch.

"I see you have finally woken up," Giannettino quipped, certain that the captain's face would be the first one he saw. However, when the gate opened enough to catch a glimpse of the battle scene inside, Giannettino's instincts took over: He called on his men to rush the gate.

Without hesitation they slipped through the widening crack in the door with Giannettino in the lead, and stormed the courtyard. Once inside, his men immediately realized they were greatly outnumbered, but there was no turning back. They dove headlong into battle.

Gerolamo Fieschi singled out Giannettino and went for him with a vengeance, his sword outstretched. Giannettino managed to turn the tables on Gerolamo's lunge with a skillful parry and an aggressive riposte that sent Gerolamo backing up against a wall. As Giannettino went in for what seemed to be a fatal blow, a shot rang out from a rebel's arquebus.

The lead ball caught Giannettino in the throat, barely a centimeter from his protective breastplate. After a moment's shock at having been hit, he watched as blood gushed from his jugular like rushing water from a fountain. His knees weakened, his body went limp, and he dropped onto the cold gravel, where he slowly bled to death.

At that moment, as if he had felt the sting of that fatal bullet himself, Andrea bolted from a dead sleep. He sat up in his bed still half conscious, experiencing a profound sense of disquiet and confusion.

"Peretta!" he cried out. Something had gone horribly wrong; he could feel it. "Peretta!" he shouted into the darkness.

Within seconds his dear wife burst into the room, holding an oil lamp to light her way. Peretta had been awake for the past hour waiting patiently with Ginetta for Giannettino's return. As inured as Peretta was to these sudden alarms, and Andrea's long, arduous crusades to the coast of Africa and the Levant, she couldn't ignore Ginetta's genuine fear and anxiety. Giannettino's poor wife hadn't yet grown accustomed to his life as a man of war.

"Is something wrong?" Peretta asked.

"I'm not sure," Andrea replied, still trying to get his bearings.

"Was it that nightmare again?"

"No. There's something in the air. I can feel it."

Peretta thought for a moment whether she should tell him about Giannettino checking on the commotion in the harbor, but decided against it. *Why get him involved?* she reckoned. *Giannettino is perfectly capable of dealing with whatever is going on.*

"And how did you get here so quickly after I called for you?" he asked, clearly coming to his senses. "You weren't sleeping. What is wrong?" His tone resembled that of a commanding officer rather than that of a loving husband.

"There were some sounds coming from the harbor that concerned Giannettino," she finally said. "He is down there now sorting things out."

Andrea's own anxiety regarding the whole affair suddenly rushed to the surface. "But he assured me it would be no problem," he said, crawling out of bed. "What sounds could have possibly provoked him to go down there?"

"Where do you think you are going?" Peretta howled. "You are going absolutely nowhere in your condition."

"I shall get to the bottom of this," he shot back. Then, as he struggled to his feet, a sudden knock at the chamber door caused him to plop back down again. "What is it now?" he screamed. "Come in!"

One of the house guards hurried into the room. It took a

couple of seconds for him to catch his breath before uttering a word. He'd evidently sprinted all the way from his post at the front gate.

"A messenger has sent word that rebel soldiers have taken control of the Porta dell'Arco and Sant'Antonio," the guard exclaimed. "San Tommaso has also just fallen to the rebels. All with considerable casualties. I fear they are coming to the palazzo as well, my Prince. You and your family are not safe here."

Ginetta came running into the bedchamber just in time to hear that last statement. She let out a scream. "What about the port? Is there any word from the port?"

Both Andrea and Peretta leapt to her side.

"Ginetta, you must calm yourself," Peretta whispered as they embraced.

Without missing a beat, Andrea turned to the guard. "Well, you heard her!" he bellowed. "What is the situation on the port?"

"Nothing yet, my Prince."

"Call all the palace guards here at once!" Andrea barked.

"That is impossible, my Prince," the guard said meekly. "Everyone else accompanied the admiral to the port."

"You mean to tell me you are here *alone*?" Andrea roared.

"I'm afraid so, my Prince," said the guard. "And there is every indication the rebels are coming here next."

"How can this be?" Andrea mumbled to himself. "Are the Fieschi behind this?" he asked the guard, unfortunately already knowing the answer.

"The rebels have swept the streets of the city chanting

'Fieschi and freedom' and 'Long live Count Fieschi,' my Prince. I fear it is, indeed, their doing."

"Gian Luigi's doing," Andrea reiterated with a scowl.

There could have been no greater disappointment in Andrea's eyes than if Giannettino himself had betrayed him. *Eighty-one years I have lived on this earth*, he said to himself, *and I have learned nothing of human nature and the cruelty of man.* He placed the blame entirely on his own shoulders for this whole debacle. Within moments he and his loved ones would have to flee to safer ground because of his blind trust in a young man whose motives for revenge Andrea chose to entirely ignore. Why did he so heedlessly dismiss Gian Luigi's purported disloyalties? After all, it was no secret that Fieschi and Doria family interests clashed more often than not over the years. And given the man's proud noble upbringing, his humiliation over his cancelled marriage with Ginetta, and rumors of a romantic tryst between his own wife, Eleonora, and Giannettino, it was no wonder Gian Luigi wanted to lash out. His thirst for revenge should have been expected, or at least suspected.

But the one thing Andrea knew for certain was that, given the toxic political climate on the continent, Gian Luigi could not have done this alone—and it surely wasn't cooked up overnight.

Chapter Sixteen

GENOA, LIBERTY, AND DEATH

Andrea knew Maria della Rovere, Gian Luigi's mother, quite well. Like the Fieschi, the della Rovere family produced a multitude of bishops, cardinals, and popes. Pope Sixtus IV was her uncle and a loyal friend of the Doria clan. Maria's spirit and pride in her della Rovere roots defined her strong and domineering character, a trait she instilled in all her children. To disrespect their honor or diminish their virility, therefore, qualified as a capital offense. Gian Luigi had already suffered a major indignity and embarrassment at the hands of Adamo Centurione, Andrea's dearest friend, as well as by Andrea himself over his cancelled betrothal to Ginetta, but the real blow to his integrity came just a few years later, and lay at the emotional heart of his hatred for Giannettino and the Doria family. Ever since Ginetta's marriage to Giannettino, Gian Luigi's wife, Eleonora, never once bothered to accompany him during his visits to Andrea's palazzo, and apparently for good reason. True or not, the rumor that Giannettino had taken advantage of Eleonora when she was a young and innocent newlywed circulated throughout the city and hovered like a dark cloud over her marriage to Gian Luigi for years. It proved simply too much for Gian Luigi to take sitting down.

In Andrea's mind, infidelity and dishonor could no doubt provide a strong emotional underpinning for bold acts of revenge like this one, but to find the true motives behind such dangerous undertakings, one had to delve considerably deeper. *How in heaven's name did Gian Luigi coordinate all this?* Andrea kept thinking to himself. *Surely he is being manipulated by powers both within and outside of Genoa's city walls. Who could they be? And why?* These questions haunted Andrea, a man who, up until a short time ago, could anticipate a threat well before anyone else. *Is it my age?* he thought. *Have my sentiments blinded me?*

In the end, he conceded that his eighty-one years had slowed him down a bit, and that perhaps he let his emotions muddle his assessment of a person he had always held dear—but when it came to unearthing the political, military, or economic rationale behind a conspiracy, Andrea was still at the top of his game. While the entire house was preparing for a covert escape into the mountains, Andrea spent the time piecing together rumors, innuendos, and known facts on Gian Luigi and the Fieschi. What he eventually deduced from his expeditious analysis only depressed him more.

The repercussions from the reforms of 1528, which favored many of the newer, merchant-based families, still lingered in the minds of many of the nobles, the Fieschi in particular. Andrea knew this, and accepted it as a necessary compromise at the time, but what he hadn't figured on was the dissatisfaction of some of the newer families whose businesses hadn't flourished as much as expected, or who weren't part of Andrea's inner circle. And, of course, the hardcore idealists constituted a good portion of the remaining conspirators; they envisioned a pure and fully representative republic instead of the two-tiered system of alberghi and common people that was ultimately installed. *Such dreamers will always exist*, Andrea reasoned, *but their ideals will get them nowhere without powerful friends.* The next part of the puzzle for Andrea was finding out exactly who those friends were.

Mulling over the usual suspects of Italian city-states who wished Genoa harm, Andrea immediately thought of the Vatican. Pope Paul III, who took office shortly after the Sack of Rome, was no friend of Emperor Charles V and Spain. In fact, there was no love lost between Paul III and Andrea either. A few years back, in a vicious round of tit for tat, Andrea sent a very young Giannettino to Civitavecchia to abscond with four papal galleys after the pope confiscated a large tract of land from Andrea to boost his coffers. From that time forward, Giannettino and the entire Doria clan were viewed with a jaundiced eye in Rome. Using the Fieschi to oust Andrea, therefore, fit perfectly into Paul III's grand scheme of empowering his son, the duke of Parma, whose territory sat conveniently between the Genoese Republic and the Duchy of Milan, which the Holy Father desperately wanted under his control. When Gian Luigi visited the pope in Rome after purchasing four galleys from his son in Parma, Paul III offered Gian Luigi the world on a silver platter: With the support of a key representative of the Kingdom of France, the pope promised Gian Luigi all the money he needed to arm his galleys, plus two hundred soldiers and the title of captain of the papal ships. A payment of twelve thousand gold *scudi* was added to sweeten the deal. Whether Gian Luigi realized it or not, he was being pulled into a conspiratorial web of his own making.

Gian Luigi could easily recruit men from his feudal lands, Andrea thought to himself. *It would also be reasonable to assume that armed militia from neighboring Piacenza would lend support by land, and that the pesky French may even attack by sea,* he concluded. *And corrupting some of Genoa's merchants would not be too difficult either!* Andrea's mind continued to race. Of course, he was correct in assuming that Gian Luigi could have employed hundreds of men from his castles to fight for him, and that the fear of an imminent Giannettino regime would sway more than a few influential merchants to rally around his cause. But as it turned out, Gianbattista Verrina, a staunch republican, managed to dissuade Gian Luigi from relying on France for any military support. It seemed Verrina was able to tap into a part of the young count's conscience that longed for a pure and fully representative Republic.

While Andrea pondered the various factors that might have gone into the rebellion, Peretta was busy organizing the logistics of their escape. She had already summoned several maidservants into her chamber to gather her valuables into leather sacks and mount them on mules. She ordered that the same be done in Andrea's room.

"When I give the word," she said to the servants, "we shall all ride to the convent at San Teodoro." She then consoled a distraught Ginetta, who had scurried into the room. Ginetta hadn't heard anything yet regarding her husband's well-being, and was naturally upset.

"Please do not worry, my dear. I shall send a message for Giannettino to join us at the convent," Peretta said. "Do not awaken the children until we are ready to depart."

By the time Peretta came rushing into Andrea's room, the servants had already emptied his armoire and cedar chest of all its gems, gold, and awards, including his medal of the Ordine del Toson d'Oro given to him by Charles V.

"Everyone and everything is ready to go," she informed Andrea.

"We must leave word for Giannettino to join us," Andrea said as he draped his woolen cape around him and donned his warmest fur beret.

Peretta didn't let on that she had already taken care of that. "I shall have a servant seek him out and tell him to meet Ginetta at the convent," she said. Then, as she helped Andrea fasten the strings of his cape, she whispered, "The horses are ready for your journey. Your cousins Filippino and Agostino will meet you in the stables."

"From there I shall prevail on my friendship with the Spinola family in the hills outside of the city," Andrea added. "Filippino, Agostino, and I should be quite safe there."

"Be careful, my dear Prince," she said, wrapping her arms around him. "The ride is long, and you mustn't allow your fever to return."

"I should hardly notice something as trivial as a fever," he said, trying to find some levity in the situation. "The aching in my bones will drive me to distraction."

Peretta stood on her tippy-toes to give Andrea a kiss. He, in turn, bent down just enough for their lips to meet. Their hug went on a bit longer than usual, each secretly fearing they may never see each other again.

"On second thought, have Giannettino join us in Masone," said Andrea, alluding to a small town in the foothills. "I don't want his presence in the convent with you and the children to attract any more hostility than necessary."

Peretta was touched by the thought, and was about to give him another kiss when one of the guards that had accompanied Giannettino to the arsenal bolted into the room. Blood oozed from his left shoulder, completely saturating his shirt and doublet. He stumbled up to them, appearing as if he was about to collapse, but was intent on delivering his message.

"My Prince," the guard blurted out, "the arsenal has been taken."

"Giannettino! How is Giannettino?" Peretta cried.

The guard took a moment before finding the courage to respond. "The admiral is dead, my lady."

Peretta's eyes widened in shock. She tumbled back onto the canopy bed, paralyzed and unable to speak.

In that same instant, the guard turned to lock eyes with Andrea. "The admiral has been shot, my Prince," he said solemnly. "Our dear Giannettino is dead."

Only then did Peretta find enough wind in her lungs to

cry out in despair. Andrea stood frozen for a moment before hurrying over to comfort his wife.

"Please, Peretta, do not wake the children," Andrea said, holding her in his arms. "We must leave it to Ginetta to tell them of their father."

Realizing the wisdom of his words, Peretta could do nothing but fall back onto the bed once again and weep.

Seeing that the guard no longer had the stamina to remain standing, Andrea spun around and rushed to his aid. He caught the guard just as he was about to drop.

"Here, take a seat, man," Andrea said. "You have lost much blood." As he helped the man into a chair, Andrea asked him once again about Giannettino just to be certain: "Are you sure of what you have said?"

"I was there, my Prince," the guard said, coughing up blood. "He died fighting for the Republic."

On the heel of the guard's words, Ginetta bolted into the room, her arms flailing like a madwoman. Her scream cancelled out every other sound. Andrea left the guard's side to grab hold of her; Peretta leapt off the bed to join them. There seemed to be no end to Ginetta's tears and nothing anyone could say to calm her down.

"Is it true?" she shouted. "Is it true what the servants are saying? Is it?"

Peretta took her in her arms. "Please, Ginetta, my dear, please try not to wake Giovannandrea and your dear little Placidia."

Ginetta buried her face in Peretta's shoulder to muffle her

cries. "Is it true?" she asked again, finally managing a semblance of calm. "Have they killed my Giannettino?"

Peretta breathed deeply. Finally, after a few moments of peering soulfully into Ginetta's eyes, all Peretta could muster was a slow, deliberate nod. Ginetta's knees gave way. Peretta held on to her tightly, stopping her from crumpling to the floor. Andrea leaned over and, swallowing every ounce of pain running through his old and arthritic body, swept her up and lay her down on the canopy.

"My sweet Ginetta," Andrea whispered, "we must be strong now. For the sake of your beautiful children, and the future of our Doria name, we must leave before we all suffer your brave husband's awful fate."

As all the lights went out in the Palazzo del Principe and everyone met in the stables for their flight to safety, rebel activities continued to gather momentum down on the port. Gian Luigi had already freed the first and second of Andrea's galleys of its enslaved oarsmen, and was about to head to the third, but the pandemonium created by the liberated slaves began to concern him. Rather than filter into the city, or parade through the port in celebration of their newfound freedom as expected, the slaves boarded several of Andrea's remaining ships. It quickly became apparent that unshackling their fellow slaves accounted for only part of their overall goal. Sailing the Mediterranean as free men on heavily armed Genoese galleys was becoming their dream come true. Gian Luigi's role as liberator was quickly redefined as enforcer of the peace in the blink of an eye.

Seeing the level of disorder spread like a virus across the

harbor, Gian Luigi assembled his men on the bridge of the *Capitana*.

"The havoc is too great," he grumbled. "We must put an end to this folly before declaring victory. A city with thousands of enraged slaves on the loose does not bode well for our new republic."

He ordered his men to accompany him onto the next ship, swords drawn and arquebuses loaded, to quell the turmoil. One by one, they descended the plank onto the wharf and quickly boarded the neighboring vessel. Being unarmed, many of the slaves fought back with whatever blunt instrument they could find, but the superiority of sharpened blades and lead bullets over simple broom handles and tin buckets became evident all too soon. The rebellion within the rebellion was duly tranquilized. The incorrigible among the slaves were dealt with severely, and the rest fell in line after being promised amnesty in the new republic.

"It is time to go into the city, my fellow patriots!" Gian Luigi cried out. "Our comrades at Porta dell'Arco, San Tommaso, and Sant'Antonio shall join us there, as will our friends in the arsenal. The senate and the good people of Genoa cannot deny us our victory now. They will rally around us, I am sure of it, and we shall be proclaimed their liberators."

The count had not only managed to whip his men into a frenzy, but himself as well. He held his chin high and puffed out his chest with all the pomp and arrogance of a second-rate tyrant. He was determined to exploit this moment of self-aggrandizement for all it was worth. He needed a release, something to unruffle his tattered nerves, to bolster his sense of self-worth and help him carry on. There was still much he needed to do and still too much weakness in his character to proceed without the obligatory boost to his ego.

Gian Luigi's men heeded his call to join the rest of the rebellion in the streets of Genoa. They tramped down the gangplank and ran off down into the marina.

Gian Luigi waited until the last man had disembarked before descending the plank. For all his bravado and swagger throughout the evening, he had actually engaged in precious little combat, and despite all his dreams of commanding a fleet of his own, his skills as a seaman were negligible. In the end, his own worst fears of inadequacy and ineptitude proved to be true. His experiences aboard floating vessels of any kind being next to none, except for the occasional recreational sailing trip with friends and family, he didn't account for any sudden movements in the boat's position caused by inclement weather or changing tides. He stepped onto the plank during one of those minor shifts without considering the possible consequences. Certain realities simply escaped him. He thought only of his well-deserved glory and could see only accolades and adulation in his future.

The vessel's sudden pitch starboard, pulling the gangplank away from the secured position on the dock, caused Gian Luigi to fall headlong into the water. Under normal circumstances such an accident could be easily overcome by simply swimming several feet to the dock, but the weight of Gian Luigi's armor plunged him deep into the water's murky depths. No matter how much he tried, there was no coming back up. His fellow soldiers remained oblivious to it all. And even upon discovering that Gian Luigi was not behind them, they had no idea of his whereabouts.

Gian Luigi died a slow, silent death. The cheers of the adoring crowds, the respect of his peers, the love of the common people, and all his many dreams of power perished with him in that instant. But, most significantly, the rebellion had breathed its final breath.

After hours of confusion, with Gian Luigi's brothers and fellow conspirators wondering what could have possibly become of him, his body was finally discovered when the morning sun brightened the limpid waters of the Genoa basin. The silvery sparkle of his armor was impossible to miss. By then, the fervor that had energized all of his loyal soldiers had faded, and the Genoese people remained locked up in their homes awaiting some form of clarity. They had been left without a leader, which dampened their spirits, and which, conversely, emboldened the senate to stage a credible resistance. Members of the government trumpeted the death of Gian Luigi throughout the city, and demanded that nobles arm their dependents and have them join the Genoese troops. The result was instantaneous; scores of rebel troops abandoned the cause, and all those who might have earlier been inclined to support the new regime found themselves vulnerable to government retribution. Not wanting to inflict any further pain and bloodshed upon the city, the senate agreed to a truce. They pardoned all the Fieschi brothers and their co-conspirators under the condition that they leave the city forever. Peace had been restored.

As for Andrea, by early morning he had reached Masone. He remained in constant contact by courier with the goings-on in his native city throughout the night, but word of the rebellion's failure had yet to arrive. Just like his many experiences at sea, and his battles with Turks and pirates alike, all he could do was wait. But rather than fixate on the events that precipitated his grand escape, he thought back on his journey to the convent of San Teodoro with his family and servants. Since Ginetta had decided not to inform Giovannandrea and Placidia of their father's death until they were safely inside the walls of the church, Andrea found it nearly impossible to leave them for Masone without somehow lending his moral support.

When Giovannandrea discovered that Andrea wasn't staying at the convent, he begged his mother to let him ride with his dear mesiavo. Her refusal drove the boy to tears. Ginetta, too, couldn't hold back her misery, weeping continually as she tried to restrain her son from climbing atop Andrea's horse with him.

Seeing that Ginetta was in no condition to remedy the situation, Andrea took it upon himself to utter the first word.

"Giovannandrea, please, I must tell you something," he said to the boy.

Andrea glanced over at Ginetta, who stood staring right at him, not sure what to say or do. He couldn't discern her mood at first, but her expression suddenly loosened. Something had taken hold of her. She gave Andrea an affirmative nod, then reached over and took Placidia in her arms, cuddling her like a newborn child.

"And I have something to say to you, my dear Placidia,"

Ginetta whispered to her. She then turned to Giovannandrea and told him in no uncertain terms: "Your mesiavo will take you for a short ride, then you will come back with us and let him continue his journey to safety. Do you understand me, my son? Your father is not with us now, and you must be a man."

Ginetta led Placidia into the convent, followed by Peretta and all the servants. Andrea lifted Giovannandrea onto his horse and trotted off down the path.

"Why is Moæ crying so much?" the boy asked.

Andrea reduced the horse's trot to a slow walk. He held the boy in the saddle in front of him, hemming him in with his outstretched arms as he gripped the reins. Andrea found it nearly impossible to find the right words, but as he harkened back to that particularly warm morning in November when his father died, he rediscovered the long-lost feelings of that awful day. Despite his eyes welling with tears, and his voice cracking as he spoke, he told the boy the tragic event of earlier that night, and cried with him as if they were both mourning their loving father. When Andrea finally brought Giovannandrea back to his mother at the convent, the boy hugged her with all the love he could muster.

"I shall miss my dear poæ," the boy said.

Then, taking command of the situation, he reached for his mother's hand and walked with her to the convent door. Before entering, he turned to his mesiavo, gave him a goodbye nod, and walked inside.

Andrea knew right there and then who would succeed him as admiral of the Genoese fleet.

Chapter Seventeen

THE DORIA LEGACY

Andrea Doria outlived them all. His French nemesis, Francis I, died just two months after the Fieschi conspiracy. He was succeeded by Henry II, who also passed away before Andrea. Charles V retired to a monastery in 1556 after a long illness, and died two years later, leaving much of his empire to his son, Phillip. And Andrea's dear Peretta eased gently into her last days of life while Andrea was rushing back to Genoa from a protracted battle off the coast of Tunisia with his perennial adversary, Dragut. He managed to return home just in time to assist her during her final moments. She was seventy-two. Peretta was surrounded by the entire Usodimare family, as well as the multitudes that made up the Doria clan, when she died.

It wasn't until Andrea reached the ripe old age of ninety-three did his body completely give out on him. But up to that point he fought with much of the vigor and cunning as he did in his early years. The death of Giannettino had, in its own convoluted way, given him reason to go on living. Without a courageous and gifted successor to safeguard the Genoese Republic, he could not forsake his obligations. He had to wait until Giovannandrea was of age.

The French, as always, gave Andrea plenty to do. They reverted back to their old tricks in 1554 by stirring up deep-seated separatist feelings on the island of Corsica, which once again forced Andrea to dispatch his fleet in defense of the Bank of San Giorgio. By early the following year, the Genoese had gained control of the island, but the French waged an effective counteroffensive in the ports of Bastia, Corte, and San Fiorenzo that prompted Andrea to assign the sixteen-year-old Giovan-nandrea to his first mission. The boy's physical, mental, and emotional makeup resembled that of his father's almost to a T, traits that immediately led him to gain the respect of his allies and enemies alike.

A few years later, despite the Peace of Cateau Cambrésis between France and Spain, which essentially ceded Corsica to the Genoese Republic, Andrea was compelled to intercede again when the French refused to leave the capital of Bonifacio. He dispatched Giovannandrea to kick off another round of fighting. By now, at the age of nineteen, Giovannandrea had assumed full control of the Genoese fleet. With his youth, and Andrea as his mentor and chief advisor, Giovannandrea seemed unbeat-able. While he sailed the Mediterranean in the service of the Spanish and his beloved city, Andrea retired to the Palazzo del Principe full-time, where he received friends, ambassadors, and kings, like a sovereign of a powerful and influential state, which Genoa appeared to be slowly becoming. The problems of the world that Andrea strove to fix involved many of the same issues that kept him busy in his youth, only now Genoa assumed more of a leading role in shaping events.

The Barbary pirates also never ceased to be a thorn in Europe's side. Eager to end the threat the pirates posed on the continent's security once and for all, Andrea counseled Spain to stage a massive attack on Tripoli, a major corsair stronghold on the Barbary coast. In the winter of 1559, after months of preparation, Giovannandrea sailed to Sicily with thirteen galleys to initiate the first phase of the operation. Inclement weather, however, obliged him to hold off until September of that year, when, once again, he had to postpone the mission due to storms and unusually high seas. The Genoese fleet docked on the island of Malta until February of the following year, then sailed to Tripoli in hopes of staging a surprise attack. Dragut was nowhere to be found, however, and the city was empty. Obviously, the well-connected pirate had learned of the planned assault and departed for Constantinople to seek help from the Turks. In the meantime, Giovannandrea was joined by Spanish and papal ships, bringing the total number of Christian vessels to one hundred and twenty-two. Shortly thereafter, they took possession of the island of Djerba off the coast of Tunisia. But Giovannandrea didn't know at the time that Dragut was heading his way with one hundred and twenty Turkish ships and enough firepower to seriously threaten the Christian fleet.

Giovannandrea caught wind of the proposed attack in time to prepare for the enemy assault, but unlike his mesiavo, his physical constitution was weak. He fell ill several days before the Turkish fleet's estimated arrival, which severely affected his stamina. In early May of 1560, the Turks struck at the heart of the Christian fleet with all the fury of a late summer hurricane. Their defeat was unequivocal. Eighteen Spanish ships were lost and four thousand soldiers perished. Many who survived found themselves chained to an oar in the underbelly of a pirate's galley. In the melee, thousands more went missing. Admiral Giovannandrea Doria was one of them.

When Andrea received a letter regarding Giovannandrea's unknown status in late May, several weeks after the Battle of Djerba, he was sitting on the long terra-cotta loggia of his palazzo, overlooking the Genoa basin. Waiting there in his X-shaped chair for signs of his dear nephew to miraculously appear had become his daily routine ever since. As the mornings grew chillier, he had Tonino fetch him the woolen blanket off his bed to keep his aching knees from stiffening, and Tonino always made sure to bring him a cup of hot China tea fresh off the trade ships coming from the East. Andrea learned to enjoy that particular brew and often joked that he couldn't survive the harsh Genoese winters without it. Five months had gone by without a single word regarding Giovannandrea. Many had figured him for dead, but Andrea refused to give up hope and, more importantly, he refused to die until he was certain of his nephew's condition one way or another.

As Andrea reached for his cup of tea on one uncommonly warm day in November, he noticed a ship on the horizon. Although the rest of his aging frame was falling apart, he still possessed the eyes of a falcon. There was something about this galley that filled him with a sense of optimism he hadn't felt in a long time. It freed his spirit. He called for Tonino in that instant. His trusty servant came running.

"When Giovannandrea arrives this afternoon—" Andrea began.

Tonino boldly interrupted him. "My Prince, there still is no word from—"

"There are two things to which Giovannandrea must swear. The first is that he must never, under any circumstances, abandon our alliance with the Spanish throne. And second—and this is of vital importance, Tonino, you must not forget to tell him," Andrea insisted. "Every political decision he makes must ensure the autonomy of the Genoese state. Is that clear?"

"Yes, my Prince, but—"

"There are no 'buts,' do you hear me!" Andrea roared, scaring Tonino half to death. "And that is not all. I want to be buried with the chain of the Ordine del Toson d'Oro around my neck."

"Yes, sir," Tonino replied. "Will that be all?"

"No, that will not be all, my dear Tonino. I demand that you stay in the service of the Doria household to take care of Giovannandrea," Andrea said with a smile.

"It would be my honor, my Prince," Tonino said, smiling right back.

"And for the love of God, call a priest, will you?" he said, stifling a cough. "Don't you see I am in desperate need of receiving my last rites?"

Tonino stood there, confused. "But—"

"What are you waiting for? Go!" Andrea cried, his voice losing a bit of its thrust.

"Yes, my Prince," Tonino said sadly. He took a few steps back, turned, and hurried off.

Andrea never took his eyes off that galley as it neared the harbor. He could feel a smile forming on his face and a certain lightness that warmed his heart. The shooting pains in his joints left him, and the aching bones to which he'd grown so accustomed seemed to disappear. He decided it was time to close his eyes for good, which he did without hesitation. He died moments later. It was the twenty-fifth of November, 1560, just five days before his ninety-fourth birthday.

Epilogue

Andrea Doria was buried without pomp and circumstance in the crypt beneath the high altar in the church of San Matteo, where, to this very day, thousands of visitors each year pay homage to him as Genoa's beloved pater patriae. Although he no doubt possessed many of the imperfections associated with powerful men of the period, his fearlessness in battle, cunning as a military officer, and relentless pursuit of liberty catapulted him well above the rest. His achievements on land and on sea served his native Genoa well, and kept Italy, as well as the entire European continent, safe from its mortal enemies on the eastern shores of the Mediterranean. Thanks to the firm republican foundation he established with his reforms of 1528, Genoa managed to secure its freedom from foreign occupation for a good part of the next three hundred years. In 1814, the Republic was absorbed into the Kingdom of Sardinia under the royal House of Savoy, who then helped bring about Italy's unification and long sought-after independence as a sovereign nation in 1861.

Admiral Andrea Doria is remembered today as a patriot, an ardent fighter for self-rule, and one of Italy's last great condottieri.

About the Author

Maurizio is an award-winning screenwriter, documentary filmmaker, and educator. Holding both American and Italian citizenship, Maurizio has lived and worked in Italy for the past twenty-three years where as an associate professor at a small liberal arts college in Rome he specialized in Italian theater and film while also teaching courses in scriptwriting and adapting literature to the screen. He started out writing plays immediately upon receiving his M.A. in Italian Studies from Middlebury College. His two full-length Italianate farces, *The Abductors* and *Big Deals*, were produced in Santa Cruz, California, and his one-act play, *Joyride*, found success in San Francisco and New York City. As a screenwriter, five of his feature-length scripts have been optioned, three of which were either winners or finalists in prominent screenwriting contests. His crime drama, *Ferryman's Grotto*, set in the hills of central Italy, and his musical drama, *One Night in Asbury Park*, were also honored as quarter-finalists and semifinalists, respectively, in the prestigious Nicholl Fellowship in Screenwriting competition. In addition, Maurizio has co-produced two award winning, short documentaries: *Uno degli Ultimi* and *Beneath the Underdog*. He is the author of *The Making of a Prince: A Novel Based on the Life of Niccolò Machiavelli*.

Maurizio now lives in a quaint hilltop village in northern Lazio, just a stone's throw from the Tuscan and Umbrian borders, with his wife of many years. He has finally abandoned academia to live the good life writing screenplays and novels full time.

ALSO FROM THE MENTORIS PROJECT

America's Forgotten Founding Father
A Novel Based on the Life of Filippo Mazzei
by Rosanne Welch, PhD

A. P. Giannini—Il Banchiere di Tutti
di Francesca Valente

A. P. Giannini—The People's Banker
by Francesca Valente

The Architect Who Changed Our World
A Novel Based on the Life of Andrea Palladio
by Pamela Winfrey

At Last
A Novel Based on the Life of Harry Warren
by Stacia Raymond

A Boxing Trainer's Journey
A Novel Based on the Life of Angelo Dundee
by Jonathan Brown

Breaking Barriers
A Novel Based on the Life of Laura Bassi
by Jule Selbo

Relentless Visionary: Alessandro Volta
by Michael Berick

Retire and Refire
Financial Strategies for People of All Ages to
Navigate Their Golden Years with Ease
by Robert Barbera

Ride Into the Sun
A Novel Based on the Life of Scipio Africanus
by Patric Verrone

Rita Levi-Montalcini
Pioneer & Ambassador of Science
by Francesca Valente

Saving the Republic
A Novel Based on the Life of Marcus Cicero
by Eric D. Martin

The Seven Senses of Italy
by Nicole Gregory

Sinner, Servant, Saint
A Novel Based on the Life of St. Francis of Assisi
by Margaret O'Reilly

Soldier, Diplomat, Archaeologist
A Novel Based on the Bold Life of Louis Palma di Cesnola
by Peg A. Lamphier, PhD

The Soul of a Child
A Novel Based on the Life of Maria Montessori
by Kate Fuglei

What a Woman Can Do
A Novel Based on the Life of Artemisia Gentileschi
by Peg A. Lamphier, PhD

The Witch of Agnesi
A Novel Based on the Life of Maria Agnesi
by Eric D. Martin

For more information on these titles and
the Mentoris Project, please visit
www.mentorisproject.org

Made in the USA
Monee, IL
16 July 2022